IN THE LAND OF DEAD HORSES

—A NOVEL—

IN THE LAND OF DEAD HORSES

—A NOVEL—

BRUCE McCANDLESS III

GREENLEAF
BOOK GROUP PRESS

Published by Greenleaf Book Group Press
Austin, Texas
www.gbgpress.com

Copyright © 2021 Bruce McCandless III

Distributed by Greenleaf Book Group

For ordering information or special discounts for bulk purchases, please contact Greenleaf Book Group at PO Box 91869, Austin, TX 78709, 512.891.6100.

Design and composition by Greenleaf Book Group and Erica Smith
Cover design by Greenleaf Book Group and Shaun Venish
Photo illustration by Shaun Venish, based on original photo by Kyle Glenn via Unsplash.com
Author photography by Patrick J. Cosgrove

Publisher's Cataloging-in-Publication data is available.

Print ISBN: 978-1-62634-863-9

eBook ISBN: 978-1-62634-864-6

Part of the Tree Neutral® program, which offsets the number of trees consumed in the production and printing of this book by taking proactive steps, such as planting trees in direct proportion to the number of trees used: www.treeneutral.com

Printed in the United States of America on acid-free paper

21 22 23 24 25 26   10 9 8 7 6 5 4 3 2 1

First Edition

For Emma and Carson

TEXAS

1908

1. The Mine

Coulter County, September 29

K elso allowed himself half a slice of optimism. It was working. They had dislodged the rock. Ramon's mules hadn't been
strong enough to budge it—not even with Paco and Norberto
grunting and cursing alongside them. So Kelso had reluctantly
reached into his wallet and sent two of the men off to buy a horse
in San Luis, six miles to the west. The purchase cost him thirteen dollars and most of the day. The horse was an ill-tempered
gelding, gone in the teeth but big and still plenty stout. And
now, with the horse, two mules, and four men pulling—four
men, because Kelso himself grabbed one of the ropes and heaved
against the great weight—the stone was moving. It was a massive
slab of limestone, cleverly wedged into a four-by-four-foot aper-
ture in the earth.

A ton of dead weight. Maybe two.

Gravel and dirt showered down around the excavation.

The mules stamped and danced, and Ramon's quirt snaked
out to pop the flesh of the nearest animal. Ramon, tall and sullen, had a habit of whipping the animals. Sometimes it irritated
Kelso, who had a soft spot for beasts, particularly horses. Now,
though, it seemed appropriate.

"Pull!" said Kelso. "*Halar*, goddammit!"

Paco grimaced as he strained at the rope. He was easily the strongest man Kelso had ever employed, and his fleshy shoulders shook with the intensity of his effort. Slowly, ever so slowly, the megalith shifted. It slid down the slope toward them like an unwilling infant being pulled from its mother. An inch, maybe. Now two. And coming faster. Just as it seemed as if their task was done, the lower lip of the rock caught on the uneven surface of the canyon floor and stuck fast. Kelso and Ramon clambered up on top of it. They hammered pins into the back end of the stone and attached the lines, then set the team to heaving again. The rock heeled over, nose first, and fell toward them in a cloud of dust. The sound was a god's footstep, a distant thunderclap. The entrance to the little cave stood like a black eye in the canyon wall.

The men paused to consider their work. They'd spent three days searching for the rock. They'd spent another two digging and hacking at the native brush to get to it, several hours hammering a first set of steel pins into the boulder, and most of today attempting to pry and pull it from its resting place. It was clearly the right stone. The glyph was unmistakable, and it matched the map. But it couldn't have been any harder to move if it had been cemented in place. Kelso had seriously weighed the possibility of blasting it out, but he'd ultimately dismissed this idea for fear of what the dynamite might do to the cave and its contents, if there were any. Now they'd done it, and without any blasting. The entrance was open. Unfortunately, the Irishman had been focused so intently on the task at hand that he had no clear plan for what to do next. Other than the obvious, of course—go in.

Paco and Norberto exchanged glances. Normally sedate, the men now seemed fully alert. Funny how the prospect of sudden wealth could boost a man's faculties, thought Kelso. He blotted the sweat from his forehead and ran a hand through his greasy white hair. He wanted to say something enthusiastic and stirring, but the words eluded him. He was too damn tired. And too damn sober.

"Take the traces off," he grunted, between gulps of warm water. The rosary beads he wore traveled down his wrist as he lowered his canteen.

"*Ahora?*" answered Norberto. The scrawniest of the crew, further distinguishable by his ruined teeth and the wispy moustache that clung to his upper lip, Norberto was also the hardest to tolerate. He seemed unable to follow a direct order and echoed every one of Kelso's directives with a question. He was a skulker. An ingrate. A cutter of corners. When he couldn't find insects or lizards to torture with his penknife, he liked to cut himself and let the bright blood make ribbons down his forearms. Kelso was going to be glad to be rid of Norberto when they found what they'd come for.

"*Sí*. Now. Let the animals rest."

"What about the wagon?"

"Leave the wagon. It's hidden. Let's see what's in our cave."

They sat for a while in the dust, contemplating the toes of their boots and waiting for their hearts to slow as Norberto ran his errand. The sun had set below the western rim of the canyon, and the arid earth around them, choked with achiote and mesquite trees, was shading from purple to blue. In a few minutes the sweat in their shirts would cool as the evening grew chilly. Kelso wasn't going to wait for that. He'd never been able to sit still. Since the age of sixteen, he'd spent his life on the move, frequently searching, sometimes fleeing, both perpetrator and victim of a seemingly endless series of small scams and disappointments, from the frozen fields of the Klondike south through the teeming foothills of the Comstock in Nevada and now down into the harsh brown badlands of the Chihuahuan Desert. Though he wasn't always as honest as he might have been with his partners

and investors, he nevertheless believed in his soul that treasures
rested beneath the earth, just waiting for a man with sufficient
energy, intelligence, and good fortune to find them. Most of
the time, that man wasn't him. But maybe his luck was changing. He was nearly destitute, deep in the middle of nowhere,
sweltering in the autumn sun of West Texas and surrounded by
the gloomiest sons of whores he'd ever had the displeasure of
working with. The men he traveled with didn't even drink, for
Christ's sake. He'd never known a hired hand to refuse a tipple.
And yet faith strengthened him still. He was John Patrick Kelso
from County Clare, by way of the Bowery and a dozen more
sordid neighborhoods to boot. But on the way up. Watched over
by saints. Treasure Hunter, his business card said. Impresario of
the Underworld. Miner of the World's Lost Wonders. He had
a well-heeled client waiting for news back in Austin—a client
who'd shown no qualms in funding his dig in the first place.
Incredibly, the cave was right where Ramon's battered old map
had said it would be. And now it was open. So maybe it was
his turn at last. Fortune and glory. Champagne and chocolates.
Women stroking the soft skin at the base of his neck. The entrance
to the cave loomed like an invitation. Or a challenge. Was it one
more rathole in a long line of ruined prospects? Or was it finally,
after so many disappointments, the dark portal to prosperity?

There was only one way to find out.

"*Listo?*" he said. He stood and swatted the dirt from the seat
of his pants.

"*Sí*," said Ramon. "But I enter first. *Primero.*"

Kelso shook his head at the absurdity of the suggestion. In
truth, though, he might have guessed a challenge was coming. By
some invisible but unquestioned authority, Ramon's word, on the
rare occasions he spoke, was law among the Mexicans. Only they
weren't Mexicans, as Kelso had been pointedly reminded on more

than one occasion. They were Mayans, Ramon had said. A different people. A better people. They'd been fighting the Spanish and then the Mexican government for generations, and until recently they'd been able to boast a nation of their own in the sweating jungles of the Yucatan. No matter. If you don't want to be called Mexican, Kelso ruminated, don't live in Mexico. Whatever he was, Ramon claimed pride of place. Paco and Norberto made sure he ate first. They carried his personal effects—two leather satchels and a duffel bag, the contents of which Kelso had never managed to see. Ramon had deferred to Kelso's directives all during the expedition, but he'd clearly had to think about it on several occasions. Now he was thinking again. The Irishman knew he had to respond decisively.

"Not a chance. I'm first."

"*Nuestra carta, señor.*" Ramon said this as if it settled the question. "Our map."

"Your map. *Mi plata.*"

"Yours?"

"As far as you're concerned, yes. I obtained the funds. I paid for the provisions. Therefore, it's my expedition. I go first."

Ramon glanced at his companions before he gave a small shrug. "As you say."

"You're damn right, as I say. What about you, Paco? You ready?"

Paco remained impassive. In the twilight the big man's mouth looked like a gash across his face. Kelso recognized this as his time-to-do-business demeanor. In less focused moments he smiled easily, the better to show off the gold caps on his two front teeth.

Kelso wrinkled his nose and spat.

"Saints preserve us. I've had livelier company in a graveyard, so I have. There's something dead in there, if you haven't noticed. Smells like Satan's arse. Light the torches, amigos."

The sound was unmistakable. It was the deep drumming of hooves. The pack animals were running. Leaving.

"They weren't hobbled?"

"Just tied, *jefe*," said Norberto. "But they don't go far, I think."

"You'd better hope not. We're gonna need 'em to haul off whatever we find in there. Let's take a look."

Kelso picked up a leather satchel and slung it over his shoulder. He grabbed one of the torches and took a knee just outside the hole in the earth, glancing back to make sure his companions were following. The entrance to the cave was so small that he had to crawl for several yards, but it led to a narrow passage that was almost five feet tall. The passage proceeded gradually downward. Even holding his torch directly in front of him, Kelso couldn't see more than a few feet ahead. He heard the commotion before he could spot it and was therefore prepared when a swarm of bats came churning past him, all frenzy and confusion. He ducked and pulled his chin to his chest. The skinny man at the rear of the file dropped flat on his stomach. Kelso looked back and couldn't help but laugh.

"Need to change your *pantalones*, Norberto?"

His companions either didn't get the joke or didn't think it was funny. Perhaps they were too busy surveying the cave. Just a few yards farther in, the passage opened up into a rectangular chamber, roughly the size of a rich man's library and at least thirty feet from floor to ceiling. Variations in the darkness indicated there were gaps in the rock that formed the roof of the cave. Against the near wall of the chamber stood two piles of bones, many of them broken. Two wooden helmets lay nearby, badly decomposed, alongside a jumble of ancient spears.

Silence hung like a shroud from the distant ceiling of the cavern. The smell of bats and bat shit and foul water weighted the air. And beneath it, like the piers of a crumbling house, lay the stench of death.

"Mother of Mercy," Kelso murmured. "It's real."

Near the far end of the chamber stood what looked, at first glance, like a rowboat hewn from an outcropping of the native rock. Kelso moved toward it, stumbling over the remnants of a wooden shield as he did so. Squinting in the gloom, he used the torch to inspect the images carved into the stone of the boat-like edifice. Once he'd focused, he recoiled involuntarily from the bizarre iconography. Strutting demons waved daggers as they drove tiny human figures in chains before them. A snake coiled around the legs of a naked woman, its monstrous head looming directly above her, its mouth open wide as if to swallow her whole. A creature with the body of a man and the features of a bat held a severed human head as if to display it as a warning to any viewer who should happen upon the scene in the long centuries to come. The Irishman's Catholicism had been beaten into him by a grandmother who was fond of lashing him with a leather strap as she recited the names of the saints. It was her voice he heard now, screaming at him to look away, to hide his eyes. "The dark doings of pagans," she shrieked. "Abominations in the eyes of the Lord!" But something about the pictures held Kelso in place. Lurid and unsettling as they were, it was several minutes before he could break away from the stares of the figures that gazed out at him from the carvings, cold and implacable, amused at his horror, frozen forever in their acts of carnage.

It was the odor that brought him back: the smell of mortality, rank and cloying, like an invisible visitor crouching in the chamber. A voice in the back of his brain hissed that he should get back to business and out of this temple of shadows as quickly as possible.

Kelso's vertebrae crackled as he straightened to examine the wall of the cavern in front of him. Unlike the other walls, which were rough and unfinished, this one had been planed to geometrical perfection and elaborately sculpted to mimic the façade of a massive palace, with columns and doors, a symmetrical roofline, and a giant throne carved into the rock. A stack of spears and staffs stood to the right of the throne. A mound of skulls rose at its foot. The wall receded into darkness where it joined with the cavern ceiling, but every foot of it seemed to have been decorated with the intricate carvings. Kelso realized that he was gaping. A scrap of burlap drifted away from his torch, and the Irishman followed its path to the floor. This brought him back to the contents of the little boat. But it wasn't a boat, he realized. It was a sarcophagus, fashioned so the halves of each end curved to meet the other like the bow and stern of a canoe. In the dirt beside each side of the sarcophagus lay two human skeletons. Two of the four skeletons held spears. The two others gripped black wooden clubs with teeth of glass around the edges. The bony figures were arrayed to suggest a set of sentinels left to guard the tomb. But to guard against what? The lid of the sarcophagus, also stone, lay broken in pieces on the far side of the vessel. Looting bastards. Someone had been here before him. Such was the case in Egypt. Kelso had read that after centuries of theft and plunder, there was precious little left in the tombs of the pharaohs to be carried off.

The Irishman took a step forward and gazed down into the sarcophagus at the remains of a man—or what might have been a man at some point in the past.

"Jesus, Mary, and Joseph," he whispered, and crossed himself. He felt for a moment as if he was going to be sick.

The thing that lay in front of him was naked except for fragments of a stained loincloth around its midsection and a crown of beaten gold on its head. Affixed around each of the figure's wrists and ankles was a silver manacle, much larger than necessary to encircle the withered flesh of the limbs, that was bolted onto the stone of the crypt. Between the upper extremities and the torso lay some sort of scrim or thin sheet, though it looked almost as if the material was flesh and attached to the thing's inner arms. The head alone lay undiminished by the elements. The skull was massive and seemed about to burst out of the layer of cracked skin that encased it. Age and decay had eaten away at the corpse's features, leaving its face looking grotesquely angular and vaguely threatening, with pronounced cheekbones and enlarged nasal sockets. Through some peculiarity of the arid environment here on the eastern outskirts of the desert, the eyes were intact and open, though yellowed and sunk deep in their sockets. The over-sized jaws were open wide, displaying two rows of discolored but still-sharp teeth. The scene was like a glimpse of some nether region never meant to be seen by the living, a hellish bier for the ruler of a kingdom of suffering and sin, and Kelso eventually looked away. *Ignore the beast's eyes*, he told himself. *You've come for the crown.* The crown was spangled with bullet-sized rubies. These he would take. The gems and the crown and the thick silver manacles. Everything else he would leave and try to forget. The stench of the place. The black claws on the corpse's fingers and toes. The pile of tiny skulls—children's skulls, he realized—at the foot of the sarcophagus. Most of all what he hoped to leave behind was the rictus of death on the misshapen creature's face, like a grin aimed squarely at the sanity of any rational man who beheld it.

Enough with all the bloody drama. He'd found it. He'd won. Finally.

He was two feet away from a fortune. After all these years of dirt and doubt and dismay, it was suddenly here in front of him. Kelso's heart was pounding, and he felt tears start in his eyes. He reached for the crown without quite realizing what he was doing. Just before he could touch it, though, his arm was seized by a brown hand.

Paco.

The Irishman chuckled. He'd jumped a foot at the unexpected contact. But the big man's grip was powerful, and the next thing Kelso felt was a surge of anger.

"You daft brute. What are you—?"

He raised the torch with his other hand and glanced at the men around him. They were contemplating the figure in the sarcophagus with rapt attention.

Almost devotion.

"Who gives you leave," said Ramon, "to steal from a god?" It wasn't the shock of hearing Ramon speak his suddenly unaccented English that raised the flesh on Kelso's forearms. It wasn't even the words he spoke, which made little sense to the Irishman. It was the realization that the three men who were his only company in this underground chamber were standing very close, their dark eyes glittering in the flickering torchlight. It was the sense that maybe he'd misjudged his companions, and that this error was going to be difficult to remedy.

"Fuck me," said Kelso. "And what manner of mischief is this?"

The men around him were silent.

"Let's not louse this up, boys. *Hermanos*. We've come too far. You want a bigger share of the take? It can be arranged. Sure, and these items"—Kelso gestured at the weapons and stone carvings around them—"will bring a fortune back east. They're five hundred years old, at the least. My client has already offered—"

Ramon's voice was as flat as a farm field horizon. "We don't give a damn about your client."

Kelso tried to work up a companionable chuckle. He'd been in tight spots before, and he knew the drill. First of all, he had to keep talking. Nothing too awful could happen as long as you kept your mouth moving. Promise. Embellish. Flatter. Cajole. "Aw, hell. Neither do I, if you want the truth of it. He's got the soul of a bookkeeper, that one. An arsehole as tight as a nun's in a rowboat. So let's forget him and get down to brass tacks, as they say. Is it the gold you'll be wanting? You fancy the crown?"

Ramon shook his head.

"There is only one thing we want from you, *Señor* Kelso." Paco placed one of his huge hands on Kelso's shoulder. "It is a great honor," he said, his voice a low rumble. Norberto chuckled. He was so close that Kelso could feel the little man's breath on the back of his neck, sticky and warm, like an unwanted kiss.

"But maybe," Paco whispered, "you won't like it so much."

Kelso wondered for a moment if he was dreaming. Not a good dream, but a dream. He persevered.

"I'm not opposed," he insisted, "to any reasonable offer." To this statement he added a wink.

Ramon contemplated the Irishman's words for only a moment. He reached into his woven bag and brought out a thin knife. It was a weapon unlike any J. P. Kelso had seen before. The handle was fashioned of wood and elaborately curved, like a question mark, and the blade was hewn from jagged dark stone. The Mexican— no, not Mexican—the *Mayan* held it in his open palm.

"Here's my offer," he said.

And then, oddly, he started to laugh.

Say what you will about the Irish. Centuries of madness, mud, and starvation have toughened them up. They don't die easy.

Paco stood six foot four and weighed two hundred and forty pounds. Despite his great bulk, he and Norberto had trouble pinning Kelso's arms to his sides. When they finally did, the Irishman flailed so violently that he extinguished one of the torches. His screams were an assault all their own, piercing and pathetic and somehow infuriating as well. Finally, though, the men managed to spread the treasure hunter out on a large, flat rock just a few feet from the sarcophagus. Norberto shattered his kneecaps with a chunk of limestone, which ended the kicking, though it did nothing for the noise. Paco finally shoved a wad of burlap into his mouth, which lowered the volume considerably. The Irishman fought even harder when Ramon ripped open his waistcoat and shirt, and he shrieked and sobbed through whatever invocation Ramon spoke to the skies that couldn't see them, the heavens beyond the roof of rock that hid them from the world.

Ramon, Kelso thought—insofar as he was still capable of thought. Of course. He'd been the leader since they met in Veracruz. The man with the mysteriously acquired map. The man with the silent comrades, the muscle, willing—at Ramon's bidding—to do as the gringo commanded. He'd been patient, Kelso recalled. As patient as a spider. But no more. Now Ramon's face was flushed with victory and anticipation. He nodded at the Irishman as if they were partners in an enterprise of secret and ter-rible significance, and this was when Kelso realized his brief run of good luck had expired. He started singing then, an old song, as Irish as the streams of Bunclody. Of course, it didn't sound like a song. Beneath the burlap stuffed in his mouth, Kelso's ballad sounded more like the cries of an angry baby. Ramon paused, momentarily puzzled. He exchanged glances with his compan-ions. Then he reared back and raised the stone-bladed dagger over his head. The gag popped out of the Irishman's mouth at almost the same moment, and the cavern filled with the ancient music of fear and misfortune. Overhead, in the darkness, a storm of bats filled the air with the voiceless panic of their sudden flight.

"May the god awaken," said Ramon.

He brought the knife down hard. He had much to do, and he was just getting started.

2. Bushwhacked

Piedras Blancas, October 7

For Jewel Lightfoot, it was a familiar feeling. The dizziness. The sense that the world was spinning rapidly around him and that looking at any passing piece of it meant another piece was slipping away, sliding down into some dark corner of his mind where he couldn't quite reach it. The lights were too bright for his head. The voices around him had become a vague, annoying tangle of sound. It was the same problem. Listen to any one of them, and he lost the sense of the others. It was like trying to shoot a single bird in a covey of doves, or chasing a leaf as it blew through the woods. It was like . . . Hell, he didn't care what it was like. Sergeant Jewel Lightfoot was staggering drunk again, and mostly what he wanted was a bed.

Of course there were words about the folly of drunkenness, fine sentences written by wise men that made considerable sense when you were sober. He'd read them. He even believed them. He wasn't proud of himself when he had to stumble out of a dirt-floored piss pot like the Prairie Star and make his way through the won't-it-ever-quit heat of a South Texas evening, staring at the ground as if it wished to do him ill. But he didn't need to look up anyway. Piedras Blancas only had four blocks, and he knew by heart the way to the adobe casita where he was lodging. Through the alley, left at what passed for a street in these parts, a right just past Lupe Gamez's millinery shop, then back behind the stable and corral to the Barrera place. It was shady there. Cooler. If it was too hot inside, he could stretch out in the grass beneath the little grove of pin oaks and sleep until the world stopped spinning. He'd be there in ten minutes. He was doing fine—slow, but fine—till he saw the boots blocking his path.

Standing around him were three men. Or possibly boys. They were big enough to be men, but still beardless and soft-eyed.

The silence of the evening settled over them like a net. "Evenin', fellas," the ranger finally said. "Out for a stroll?"

"You're Jewel Lightfoot," one of them said.

"I am. What can I do for you boys?"

"Ranger."

"I'm a ranger. That's right. You need rangerin'?"

"You ain't as big as I thought."

Lightfoot squinted up at the sky. There wasn't a cloud to be seen. Another two hours of daylight, most like. Afternoons in South Texas lasted all evening. He knew where this was heading.

"I never am," he said.

"Unfasten the gun belt, smart-ass."

The ranger looked from one face to the next, his storm-cloud gray eyes taking a quick inventory of his opponents. The kid doing the talking, Leader, was a little older than the rest—in his early twenties, maybe. Hell, that wasn't so young. They all looked young these days. He was carrying what looked like a double-action Colt revolver in a side rig low on his right hip. To Lightfoot's right stood a heavyset fellow in overalls and faded long johns. This one hadn't missed many meals. He was two hundred pounds, easy, and thick through the chest and shoulders. Blue eyes. Bowl-cut bangs. Farm boy, no doubt.

Call him Haystack.

To Lightfoot's left stood the youngest of the bunch, a good-looking kid with long dark hair and a blue bandana tied around his neck. Pretty Boy was holding an antique service revolver, with the hammer cocked. He was dressed for the part— dashing desperado, by way of a dozen dime novels—but he didn't seem to be enjoying this encounter. His lips were pinched tight, and he declined to meet the ranger's gaze. Still, he wasn't as nervous as Haystack. The rube was sweating profusely, and the hands holding the shotgun were trembling. The ranger was partial to shotguns, though he had some reservations about this one. It was a beat-up Remington side-by-side, an old-time fire belcher for sure, and it was staring at his belly.

"Funny," said the ranger. "I was fixin' to do just that."

Lightfoot doffed his hat and wiped his brow with his sleeve. He was a slender man, lean and jut-jawed, slightly shorter than the average. He had close-cropped silver hair and eyes that almost matched. Now they were searching for some hint of salvation, but Lord, the sky was a torment. The ranger knew he needed to sober up quick. Twenty minutes ago would have been ideal. He scanned the dirt road. Two little girls stood watching from fifty feet away. Farther along was a mule cart raising dust as it entered town, an entire family riding in the rickety vehicle as the animal in front of it struggled with the load. Life. It was too damn something or other.

"And no gunslinger tricks, neither," said Leader.

"I entertained no such notions. You want to tell me what this is about?"

"Drop the belt, goddammit, or I'm gonna plug you where you stand."

So Leader was drunk too. Something about the formulaic nature of the threat told the ranger all he needed to know about the kid's mental state. He'd handled hundreds of drunks. Drunks weren't good shots. But then again, Leader didn't need to be especially accurate at this range. And the liquor made him unpredictable. Lightfoot let his gun belt slide to the ground. The kid was quick. Lightfoot had to give him that much. He hit Lightfoot square in the face before the ranger could even look up. A bright white star exploded in Jewel Lightfoot's brain. When it faded, he blinked. He could see clearly again. Funny how pain could help a man concentrate.

"This is about my cousin, you sawed-off piece of dog shit."

Lightfoot made a cup of his hands to catch the blood streaming from his nose. "Whoa, now. Let's not get worked up. What about your cousin? Do I know the man?"

"He ain't around to know or not know, seein' as how you killed him."

Lightfoot tried to pinch his nostrils shut. "Who told you that?"

The left hand now. Straight to the side of his head. It wasn't quite as bad as the first punch, and it had to have hurt to land. The ranger had an exceptionally thick skull. Still, he felt the earth tilt all over again. It was an act of will just to stay on his feet. He knew enough not to go down. Nothing good happened on the ground. Too many boots.

"Half a town told me that."

"Son," said the ranger, "we don't have to do this." Another right hand. To the temple this time.

"We sure as hell do. I thought you were a bigshot. I reckoned you was eight feet tall, from what people say. And here you are, drunk as a monkey. Grease stains on your pants. Smelling like a goddamn outhouse."

Lightfoot looked down at his pants. Sure enough, there was a greasy splotch in the shape of a potato on the right leg of his trousers. Where had that come from? He shook his head. "Was this the kid in Laredo, tried to take down the bank?"

"The—what? No, he wasn't down in Laredo."

"That harelip in Nogales? Wanted to sell me a stolen horse?"

"He was right here in Robertson County, goddammit. Liberty Rosario. You get that name in your head, you murderin' sonofabitch. Remember his name!"

The ranger straightened up. He stared at Leader with the one eye he could still see out of as Leader reared back to throw another punch. It was coming from somewhere around last Thursday, and it was going to do some damage. Stunned by the cheap tequila in his system and the blows he'd absorbed already, Lightfoot nevertheless realized he was falling. His right hand went out reflexively and brushed the two barrels of the big kid's shotgun, nudging them just a few inches to one side. It wasn't much, but it was enough. Haystack jerked back on the weapon. A load of steel shot roared past Lightfoot's cheek and caught Pretty Boy—the young one—belt-buckle high, tearing him almost in half. He was dead before he hit the ground. He just didn't know it yet. Haystack gaped in horror at what he'd done, and it was all the opportunity the ranger needed. From his knees, Lightfoot drove his left fist into the farm boy's groin. The kid collapsed like a burning building.

Leader saw what was happening and went for his gun, a sensible move but not quite quick enough. Lightfoot dove for his own. He came up with the Colt and fired before Leader could draw his weapon from its holster. The round tore away most of the man's left ear. Leader pressed both hands against his wound. He sank to his knees, screaming, his hands rapidly filling with blood.

The ranger snapped open the cylinder of his sidearm. Just as he'd thought. Five rounds left. He flicked the cylinder back in and trained the weapon on Leader. The one who'd started all this. They were both on their knees, a few feet apart. It would be a simple matter to put a bullet through the young man's forehead.

Tempting, too. He raised the weapon and sighted down its barrel. Why not? He tried to calm his pounding heart, to slow his
panting. Pretty Boy was lying on his side, breathing in short,
shallow gasps, holding his guts in both hands. His dark blood
pooled in the dirt. Leader was cussing, and Jewel Lightfoot was
starting to sober up. He knew because he could feel himself getting angry. And that, as those who knew the ranger could attest,
was going to be bad news for anyone in the immediate vicinity.

"You know," said Lightfoot, spitting a thin stream of blood
through his teeth, "I think I do remember your cousin. And if he
was here now, I'd shoot that sonofabitch all over again."

He stood. He plucked the pistol from Leader's holster and
tossed it as far as he could. Then he picked up the spent shotgun
where it lay in the dust. Holding it in one hand, he walked over
and brought the stock down on the back of Haystack's skull.

A crowd was forming. Two dogs. A little boy. An old man
leading a steer with a rope.

Lightfoot bent over and threw up his lunch, mostly beans
and tortillas, along with a fair amount of yellowish bile. This too
was observed with no comment by the townspeople. The sun was
invading his eyes. The vomit smelled of bad beer and resentment.
Dinner for the dogs. Another day in South Texas.

The ranger chose this moment to address the onlookers.

"One of y'all get over to the Prairie Star and fetch the doctor,"
he said. "*El medico*. And tell him he was right. I *am* bad luck."

3. The Farmhouse

Coulter County, October 10

T he farmhouse was hard to spot in the darkness.

In truth it was less a house than a hovel, a ramshackle structure dug into the side of a hill and extended outward by beams of rough-hewn oak. Mud and straw served as mortar, and the gently pitched roof consisted of cedar shakes and sod. And yet Nils Peterson, patriarch of this unimpressive abode and the family that occupied it, had reason to feel content with his prospects. His wife, Ilsa, had grown accustomed to the long days and hard work required to keep body and soul together here in Texas. His children had stopped pining for their former home, and his boys indeed were beginning to help with the chores. And there were lots of chores. Wheat, it turned out, was impossible. Even here, near the shallow creek the family called the Little Klaralven, the land was too rocky to permit cultivation on the scale needed to make wheat pay. But wool prices were steady, sheep seemed to thrive in the arid terrain, and Nils had needed only a little hired help to put together and care for a flock of almost a hundred animals. Assuming he could keep them alive through the winter—and winters were mild here, nothing like Gotland, his homeland, with its eight months of ice—he'd turn a healthy profit come shearing time. In the meantime he still had a fair amount of the cash he'd come to the New World with, and a decent stock of flour and honey and ham to last through the thin months. Things were going to be tight for some time yet. But no matter. Nils Peterson was healthy and the land was his, and so far the terrible sun hadn't done anything more than turn him a shade of brown his friends back home would have been amazed—and amused—to see. Swedish immigrants called their first year in America the *hundejahr*, or "dog year"—that period of time it took for a man to figure the lay of the land and start earning a living. Nils Peterson had reason to believe his *hundejahr* was almost over.

The chores of the day completed—twenty-four jars of okra pickled and put by, two cords of firewood cut and stacked, the milk cow settled in a barn somewhat bigger than the house—the Peterson family had gone to bed not long after nine, accompanied by Ilsa Peterson's nightly rendition of "Glädjens Blomster," a traditional hymn to the summer flowers of their homeland. Nils had his enthusiasms. He spoke often of plans and ambitions, dollars and acres. This was all well and good. But Ilsa Peterson, fair and flat-chested, with bright blue eyes and slender hands, was determined to keep some portion of Sweden alive in her children, even as her husband chided them for their difficulties with English and urged them to do better.

A gibbous moon hove into sight. Coyotes chattered in the cedar brakes to the south, reciting the many injustices done to their kind, and a horned owl passed over the yard as silently as a spirit departing this world for the next. Just before midnight, three men appeared out of the hills and advanced toward the farmhouse. One of the men was slender and tall, with black hair that hung to his shoulders. He gestured to his companions—one slight and skulking, the other massively built—and the trio took up positions around the dugout. The Petersons had no dogs to sound an alarm, as Nils had been relying on his herder's mutts to move the sheep as needed.

Paco, the largest of the three intruders, whispered a prayer of thanksgiving. He hated dogs. They were hard to shut up, for starters. More importantly, they bit. Paco was afraid of very few things, but dogs were a source of anxiety and embarrassment for him, and he was glad not to have to face one tonight. He felt a bead of sweat roll down his back. It was hard for a large man to be quiet. Finally in place, he paused to exhale.

He glanced down at the weapon he carried. It felt pleasantly heavy in his hand. Almost three feet long, it was a wooden club shaped something like a canoe paddle. Embedded in the wood around the perimeter were twenty jagged teeth of volcanic glass—obsidian, Ramon had explained. The club was called a *macahuitl*. Paco had taken it from the skeletal hand of one of the sentinels in the cave. Now he said the name of the weapon to himself as if it was a prayer.

Ramon used lantern oil to ignite the barn, and Nils Peterson stumbled out of his house a few minutes later to investigate why his milk cow was making such a commotion. The Swede, thirty-four years old, lanky and almost bald, was still shrugging himself into the sleeves of his long johns when Paco's club sliced through the flesh of his right shoulder, shattering his clavicle and digging deep into his thoracic cavity. Nils Peterson barely had time to emit a soft gasp before he hit the ground, his eyes open wide in surprise. Paco knew not to think. Ramon had warned him. Thinking made a man slow. He lifted the macahuitl again and brought it down on the right side of the farmer's head, crushing his skull.

Ilsa Peterson was next out of the house. Now wearing J. P. Kelso's sweat-stained straw hat, Norberto took the farm woman with a blade to the lower back. Then he yanked her around by one shoulder and shoved the knife into the soft flesh of her belly, pulling it upward as she shuddered and tried to twist away. As always, Norberto enjoyed the struggle. He kept his gaze locked on Ilsa Peterson's sky-blue eyes as the light drained out of them. As her life force faded, his seemed to increase. He felt the familiar rush of energy that came to him in these moments, the sense of power and destiny. He bounced on the soles of his feet as the woman sagged on his blade. He held her upright with the metal as her warm blood bathed his hands.

Paco felt no such elation. Killing was a job. A means to an end. He only did it because Ramon said he had to. Ramon was smart. He read books. He'd been to the city, even studied at one of the big universities. And he'd been right about everything so far. The map. The plan. He'd known exactly how to entice the white-haired Irishman into joining their group, convincing the fool there were treasures in Texas ripe for the taking and that he, Ramon, knew just how to find them. Kelso had taken the bait, as Ramon predicted. The fortune hunter had contacted men with an interest in the sacred things of their Mayan ancestors. In return for promises, he'd obtained the money they needed to finance the expedition. Ramon had even managed to convince Kelso that he, and not Ramon himself, was leading the search. Though he was still a young man, Ramon knew things old and magical. He seemed to have come from a different place. A different world, maybe. A better one. So Paco did as he was told. He killed.

The Peterson boys, Oscar, nine, and Frederick, seven, were more difficult to dispatch than their parents. Like frightened rabbits, they bolted in opposite directions. Paco and Norberto went after them, Paco a little less enthusiastically than his smaller comrade. He wasn't as fast as Norberto, and he knew if the child he was chasing made it more than a couple of hundred yards from the farmstead, he would have trouble finding him. Fortunately, he could hear the boy calling for his mother as he ran. Paco tripped over a root and pitched face-first into the dirt. He was certain he'd lost his chance. He was down on all fours, looking for the macahuitl he'd dropped and thinking about how angry Ramon was going to be if he returned to the farmhouse without the kid when it came again, the boy's frightened voice, as high-pitched and tremulous as the cry of a whippoorwill. And close. The big man launched himself in the direction of the sound. He had a single simple job to do. All other thoughts disappeared from his mind. He wouldn't fail, he told himself. He wouldn't fail Ramon, and he wouldn't fail the god they served. Not tonight. Not ever. He couldn't.

The two Mayans reappeared at the farmstead a few minutes later, each bearing one of the stunned and senseless Peterson boys over his shoulder like a woodsman returning from a hunt. It wasn't until then that Paco realized he'd lost the macahuitl somewhere out in the brush. That wasn't going to please Ramon. On the other hand, there was another one just like it back at the cave. Maybe, Paco figured, no one would notice.

By now the barn was an inferno, and the flames threw a garish light on the proceedings. Working quickly, the killers hung the adult Petersons by their ankles from the lowest limb of a nearby juniper, gathering the blood that flowed from the severed veins in their throats in clay beakers on the ground. They needed no such measures for the boys. Paco held them by the heels as Norberto, chuckling and humming to himself, sliced their jugular veins and positioned the containers to catch the fluid. When their bodies were bled out, the boys were dragged back into the farmhouse and arranged with the corpses of their parents as they might have been positioned while sleeping. Ramon carried a smoldering plank across the neatly raked dirt yard and set it just inside the door, in another puddle of lamp oil. It had been a dry autumn. The house went up so fast that it seemed as if it *wanted* to go—as if, dismayed by the deaths of its inhabitants, it saw no further purpose in remaining on earth. By dawn there was little to show of Nils and Ilsa Peterson, their two boys, and the lives they'd tried to fashion for themselves in the Texas outback.

What the killers hadn't noticed was easy to overlook. The little girl had a fever and had been confined to the house for the better part of two days. In fact, Lyssa Peterson was lying awake between her mother and a log wall of the little dugout when the men came down from the hills. She was the first to realize something very wrong was happening. She watched her father pull his trousers up over his long johns, wanting to warn him but unable to find the words for the dread she felt. She ignored her mother's whispered command and followed her to the door, then peeked around it just in time to see Paco bring his bladed club down on her father's head, not ten feet away. Too frightened to scream, she watched as her mother dashed outside. The boys must have shouldered past her at that point. Lyssa crawled under the big bed, thought better of it, and scrambled back out. She grabbed her favorite doll, the one with the red yarn for hair, and went to the door again. Outside she saw the bodies of her parents lying bloody and lifeless in the dirt of the yard. She also saw a ponytailed man, naked to the waist, standing with his back to her, watching the barn consume itself in the glow of the blaze. He was shouting something into the flames, but she couldn't tell what it was. He seemed to have snakes on his back—dark lines that twisted and flexed as he rejoiced in the destructive dance of the flames. From somewhere not too far away came a cry. One of her brothers, she realized. At almost the same moment, her father's milk cow burst through a charred wall of the burning barn and galloped into the stand of mesquite trees beyond the yard. The animal's back and hindquarters were on fire, and the cow bawled in panic and pain as it ran. It was a bizarre and fascinating spectacle, and the shirtless man stood transfixed as he watched it unfold. The little girl knew this was her chance. She bolted from the doorway and headed west, moving—almost flying—barefoot and silent along the sandy trail that led to the creek. Lyssa Peterson was a tiny thing, not much over three feet tall, all tousled blond hair and bony brown legs. But having older brothers had served her well. She could run. And Lord, as her poor mother had sometimes complained, Lyssa Peterson knew how to hide.

4. Freda

Austin, October 19

Otto Zenger had a secret life. He owned and operated a two-story stone and oak mercantile establishment just a few blocks northwest of the capitol. During the day, the store sold hardware, fabrics, and a generous selection of staples to the good citizens of Austin. Ladies could buy pecans, in season, and Southern Pride seeds and cheesecloth and sugar and cans of tomatoes and spinach. Kids could get bags of hard candy at the counter. Otto called his store Zenger's Dry Goods and Grocery. He was also known to refer to it as the Wonder of the West Side, the Modern Marvel of the Mercantile Arts, and the Larder of Liberty. Otto, bald, plump, and almost always cheerful, liked to talk. He was good at it—and he practiced.

In fact, one of the few subjects he managed to keep quiet about was another of his businesses. Downstairs, in a cellar carved out of the native limestone, Otto ran a less public establishment that sold cider and good pilsner beer to a restricted clientele. A door in the wall of the cellar led into a tunnel underneath Guadalupe Street. Using this tunnel, a man could walk unseen by the world to the basement of the bordello seventy-five feet to the west. And there, on the house's second floor, he could partake of the carnal favors of, among others, thirty-two-year-old Indian Jill, who was actually Irish; twenty-six-year-old Ann Marie Boudreaux—Cajun

Annie, they called her—who hailed from Cincinnati; and teen-aged twins from Hermosillo named Veronica and Alicia. Jill and Annie were boisterous, foul-mouthed, and fond of strangers. The twins by contrast were a watchful pair, sad-eyed and inconsolable, with an air of ruined plans and fallen grandeur. When they weren't working, Veronica played the guitar while Alicia sang tender ballads about the exploits of Sonoran bandits and the women who loved them. Only a few of their customers could understand these songs, but this was just as well, as many of them celebrated the violent deaths of multiple gringos and the re-establishment of Mexican dominion over the American Southwest.

There were fancier brothels in Austin. The Guy Town district boasted half a dozen, including Blanche Satterwhite's establishment, the Midnight Rose, which was the cream of the crop. A night with one of Blanche's best girls—Miss Regine Napoleon, for example—could set a man back more money than most cowhands made in a month. There were plenty of men who were willing to pay the tariff, though. Miss Regine was said to do things with her tongue that could make a man howl in ecstasy. There were also cheaper brothels closer to the Colorado River—half a dozen pine-plank brothels and saloons and, across the railroad tracks, another ten to twenty dirt-floor shacks populated by whores who lived out of whiskey bottles or shot themselves up with so much morphine on a daily basis that they barely knew where they were. Zenger's wasn't showy. In fact, the place was resolutely low-key. In all the many discussions taking place in Austin and indeed throughout the state about whether prostitution should be made illegal, a crime against Christianity, womanhood, and personal hygiene, Zenger's was never mentioned. It maintained an aura of propriety without any great pretension.

It was, admittedly, unorthodox to employ Hispanic women alongside whites, but the twins were quiet, and no one cared to object. Indeed, there were men—old Judge Elihu DeGroot, for example—who preferred them, alone or in tandem. Whether this was because of their exotic Spanish heritage or their tender years, he steadfastly declined to say.

The whorehouse didn't have a name, as such, but it was generally referred to as Zenger's Place or sometimes as the Mercantile. It was presided over by a stocky blond Czech woman named Freda Mikulska, who kept the place clean, its customers peaceful, and its sporting women disease-free and out of trouble with the city of Austin. Everyone knew prostitution was going to be outlawed eventually, and probably sooner rather than later. The tide of public sentiment had already turned against it. The best way for a brothel owner to delay the inevitable was to keep the place out of the newspapers and well hidden from the attentions of the progressive reformers who seemed to dominate city politics these days. Otto and Freda were good at both of these tasks.

Freda Mikulska's position in the Zenger organization was ill-defined but important. She wasn't just a madam. She shopped and planned meals for the Zenger family, and she maintained the household's, the store's, and the brothel's accounts. Otto Zenger was a born salesman and raconteur, but he wasn't much for details such as inventory and accounting. He frequently said Freda had the quickest head for numbers he'd ever seen. Since Otto's wife was sickly, his son was off at the Naval Academy in Annapolis, and neither of his daughters had any interest in the mercantile arts, Freda operated with little or no supervision. She was scrupulously honest, and she enjoyed the work. Hell, she enjoyed work, period, which was something Jewel Lightfoot could respect, if not necessarily emulate.

Over the course of four years, Jewel and Freda had come to be particular friends. The ranger kept a room at Miss Cora Spivey's boarding house at the west end of Pecan Street—bachelor's quarters with outhouse access, nothing more—because it was cheap and because he knew Miss Cora, seventy-two years old, fond of snuff, and nearly blind, liked the security of having a lawman on the premises. But it was also an exercise in respectability, a way to keep up appearances. In truth, he spent as much time as he could with Freda when he visited Austin. He brought her arrowheads and wildflowers, particularly bluebonnets, when they bloomed in March. She kept him fed and decently dressed and frequently sober. When he left town, she wrote him long conversational letters in her peculiar block script, heavy with news from the River City in general and the Zenger family in particular and inter-stitched with queries about his health and dietary habits. On occasion they also contained elaborate expressions of longing for his company, which the ranger appreciated but declined to acknowledge, mostly because they made him blush, but also because he thought his workmanlike prose unsuitable for the emotional embroidery she sought to summon from him.

Freda was a student of the ranger's behavior. Many men have been studied in this fashion, but few have ever really deserved the attention. She knew his habits and preferences, his significant strengths and mostly minor weaknesses. She knew, for example, that Lightfoot wore boots with slightly elevated heels—a concession to vanity he mistakenly assumed went unnoticed. He was not an attractive individual in the conventional sense, but there was something about his angular features and steel-gray eyes that Freda found compelling.

She was short, too, but warm where he was cold, stout where he was spare, ample in the bosom and hips. He listened to her sing. She put him to work. But as much as he liked spending time with Freda, the ranger sometimes wondered if his lady friend had plied the sheets as a *fille de joie* before proving herself more valuable to Otto Zenger's burgeoning business empire in other capacities. He couldn't prove it. Hell, he didn't want to prove it. This was a continent neither one of them cared to explore, though both of them were always aware of its proximity. He was just as protective of his past as she was of hers. But unlike Freda, Jewel Lightfoot talked in his sleep, or sometimes in that strange half-sleeping state that blurs dream and waking life, and through gentle questioning on quiet mornings she'd learned a few things about him in spite of his generally private nature.

He'd spent his early years in Louisiana, the illegitimate son of a pretty teenager named Mary LaSalle Lightfoot, kin to both the Virginia Lightfoots and the South Carolina Calhouns. Sally, as she was called, was born to a life of privilege: cotillions, French lessons, a pianoforte in the parlor. All of this paled in comparison with the blandishments of a rakish young man from Memphis named Anson Sweet, who, though down on his luck, claimed to have been a spy for the Confederacy during the War and in such capacity to have learned the whereabouts of hidden gold meant to finance a Southern revival at some undisclosed time in the future. Anson Sweet had curly dark hair and eyes that shone like moonlight on a slow river. He promised he'd cherish Sally forever. He gave her an enormous ruby ring that he joked was older than Jesus. He said he'd build her a mansion and dig her a pond that he would stock with turtles and many more outlandish and agreeable things, but he disappeared shortly after she announced, flush with equal parts horror and jubilation, that she was expecting his child. Sally never saw Anson Sweet again. She had her baby nonetheless—out of wedlock, out of money, and cast out by her respectable family in Ferriday.

Jewel never knew his father, but he knew his stepfather a little too well. Gideon Fitch was abusive, fond of Scripture and the bottle both, and volatile when under the influence of either, though for different reasons. The old man had a vicious temper, which his stepson soon learned to match, punch for punch. Fitch turned up dead one summer afternoon in 1881, just a half mile from home, killed by a blow to the head from a ball-peen hammer administered by an assailant or assailants unknown.

Not long afterward, Jewel Lightfoot decided to try his luck in Texas. His was a familiar story. Texas had settled down considerably since the wild and wooly days of Reconstruction, but it was still a magnet for refugees, bankrupts, and troublemakers of all kinds. It also attracted those who just plain didn't fit anywhere else, which was an apt description of Jewel Lightfoot as a young man.

Young Jewel found work in Nacogdoches pounding railroad spikes. He was a gandy dancer, jut-jawed and thin as a splinter, a rare white man in a colored man's world. The work—straightening track and replacing cross ties, compacting gravel for the track bed—was tough, and Jewel's hands grew hard as a consequence and his forearms thickened with corded muscle. In Corsicana he was noticed by a ranger named Al Woodard, who saw the kid put a yard boss on his back in a vicious fight. Woodard took a shine to the kid. He got him a place with the Austin Police Department for two months, and they worked together on a case that involved a series of particularly brutal murders of the city's Negro maids. The events predated Freda's arrival in Austin, though, and she could never find anyone who wanted to talk about them. Certainly Jewel wasn't interested in discussing the matter. She'd asked him half a dozen times and never gotten more than a shrug in response.

Eventually Al Woodard managed to get his young friend an invitation to join the Rangers. There the thread of the narrative frayed. Lightfoot didn't like discussing his time on the force. It wasn't that he was ashamed of it. To the contrary: He was so comprehensively a ranger that Freda wondered if he could survive without the badge. But she got the feeling there were things he didn't want to share with her even in his sleep. Was it because she wouldn't understand? Or was it because she would? She suspected these reminiscences were the dark materials of his dreams, when he bolted from bed, voice ragged with fear and confusion, or woke with his eyes wet with tears that she pretended not to notice. In the blackest of those nightmares he called for his mother, and Freda loved him all the more for his loneliness, even as she shook her head that he couldn't bring himself to call her name instead.

Two days after leaving Piedras Blancas, the ranger woke to the sight of Freda Mikulska propped on one elbow in her narrow bed, gazing at him as if she'd just won him at auction. Her massive breasts lay before her like a merchant's wares, great ripe jungle fruits spilling from the cornucopia of her unfastened corset. It was the fashion among Austin's society dames to wear their corsets tight—not the old-style corsets but the new, the ones that forced a woman's hips back and her breasts forward so that, viewed from the side, she presented an odd, S-shaped figure. Freda had no patience for such contortions. She unfastened herself whenever possible, which was generally fine with the ranger. Now, though, in the bright, blunt light of a hangover, with his mouth as dry as dirt and his head a rut in a very bad road, her breasts seemed less enticing than they had the night before, when he'd traversed them as if they were an undiscovered country, the faint blue veins a map of magical rivers and their tiny tributaries, all leading to the shining pink ponds of her nipples, now concave in the morning warmth, the soft skin chafed and raw from the repeated attentions of his teeth and tongue.

Freda read his expression and chuckled. She brushed a tendril of hair from his eyes.

"Tired," she said.

"Bone tired," he agreed.

"I know because you fell asleep early last night. Perhaps the drink is too strong?"

"Perhaps you is too strong. I feel like I been rode hard and put up wet."

"So. There is nothing wrong with your memory."

He might have grinned at this, if he'd had a single muscle in his face that didn't hurt. He hated it when she felt sprightly in the morning. The ranger didn't much appreciate sprightly at any time of the day, but morning seemed to him particularly unsuitable.

"No. My memory's a little too good."

"So? You remember dancing in the garden with me? Where I teach you the schottische?"

"Now I know you're lying."

Perhaps she thought this was an insult. He hadn't meant it as such, but then again, social intercourse wasn't his strong suit. The truth was, he didn't remember dancing. With her. With anyone. She frowned as she backed out of the bed. But Freda wasn't easily offended. By the time she'd finished buckling herself into the complicated machinery that functioned as her undergarments, she'd grown fond of the lawman again.

"Are you hungry this morning?"

Lightfoot winced. Freda's voice filled the room like too much coffee in a tiny cup. The ranger needed some quiet to soothe the pounding in his head. Freda's place was two rooms above Otto Zenger's carriage house, where the German kept his fine new phaeton and the horses that pulled it. The structure stood across the street from Zenger's mercantile store and just behind the bordello, linked by a gravel walkway and shaded by a giant sweetgum tree. It was little wonder the ranger preferred Freda's rooms to his bachelor's quarters. The mattress was softer. The air smelled sweetly of horses and hay, and the morning breeze sighed in the branches just outside the two windows.

Plus there was Freda.

"No," he said, without moving his lips. "I'm not hungry. Can you close that curtain?"

"I just opened the curtain."

"Then I guess you know how."

"Very well. Closed. So we will live in the darkness."

He mumbled something in response.

"You had dreams last night."

The ranger opened his eyes and gazed at the ceiling. "What kind of dreams?"

"Not good ones. Will you tell me what scares you?"

"Nothing scares me. And it ain't right for a woman to interrogate a man when he's naked."

"I'll ask you another time, then."

"And I won't answer another time."

Freda went to her wardrobe and started wriggling into her favorite blue dress. Her work dress, she called it. "How long do you stay?"

"I may be leaving this morning."

She stopped short. Her hands, which had been busy attaching an earring, descended slowly to her waist. "This morning?"

Lightfoot took the pillow away from his head. Jesus. He hadn't meant to veer off on this subject. He did his best to sit up.

"Aw, don't go looking like that. It ain't my choice. Hell, I may not even have a job next time you see me. But if I do, Al Woodard's gonna get me out of Austin as soon as he can."

"One night, Jewel?"

He shrugged. "It was a good night."

She averted her gaze, as if she'd been struck. "You promised me last time."

"Promised you what?"

"That you would stay. For more than just—"

"I would if I could, darling."

She sat down on the bed with her back to him. "No, you wouldn't. You're a leaf. A brown, dead leaf. Someone blows and you start skittering down the road."

"Hey, it's not like I want to. I go where they send me. That's my job. We're shorthanded these days."

"Stop letting them send you. It doesn't have to be your job. You're not a young man anymore."

"Don't get started on that. I can outride any one of them punks they've badged up the last few years."

She gazed down at her hands, appraising them front and back as if she were thinking of trading them for someone else's. "That's not the point."

"What's the point?"

"The point is, you can't marry your horse. Don't you want something a little more permanent? A wife? A home?"

Lightfoot went back to his pillow. It smelled like Freda. Not a bad thing. He liked the way Freda smelled: like fresh bread and talcum powder and Professor J. D. Salton's London Primrose & Lavender Soap. He thought about what she'd said. Last time he'd been here, it had actually been worse. She'd thrown a shoe at him. Called him sorry and no-count. Said he was just like every other mangy cowboy or railroad hand who wandered in off the street looking for a drunken fuck. And he readily agreed. He *was* just like the rest of them. That's why he'd stumbled into the Mercantile four years ago to begin with. But he didn't say it, and at some point she'd calmed down enough to tell him she'd bought a little piece of property on Shoal Creek, north of the city. Not far from where old Charlie Seider and his kin got killed by Comanches, he mentioned. She'd rolled her eyes and told him she wasn't interested in ancient history. She wanted someone to build a house with. Or no. That wasn't it. She knew he wasn't a carpenter. They'd find someone for that. What she wanted was someone to make a home with. She'd had plans drawn up by a certified architect—H. R. McMullen, on Brazos Street— on sheets of oversized paper, complete with measurements and angles and precise dimensions, all the way down to the privy. What she needed now was someone who could see the plans through. Someone who could handle himself. Someone who'd seen a few things.

Lightfoot shook his head when she talked like this. He'd seen a few things. Sure. That was the problem. Freda Mikulska didn't know half the things he'd seen, and what they'd done to him. Were *doing* to him. He'd killed seven men. When he thought of them, he thought also, and without prompting, of his justification for their deaths. It was an old argument, wholly internal and never-ending. Liberty Rosario. Notorious rapist and abuser of women. Cause of civil strife and at least two homicides. Franklin K. Suggs. Serial fornicator. Aggressive drunk. Murdered a San Antonio jeweler with a hoe and a fountain pen. That kid in Piedras Blancas. Jed Rosario. Liberty's cousin. Sixteen. Pretty Boy. Wrong place, wrong time. In some weird twist of memory, the faces seemed to grow more vivid with each passing year. This last one now visited his dreams. The drunken walk from the cantina. The three pairs of boots that stopped him. The farm boy nervous and sweating. Jed Rosario's expression as he realized he'd been shot. Surprise, yes—but then resignation. He was a kid and he'd never done this before, but he didn't have to look. He knew his job was to lie down and introduce himself to the dirt. And he breathed on for a few seconds there in the dust before he bled out, his breath growing fainter, his eyes losing focus, but they weren't good seconds. Maybe he had a sweetheart. Lightfoot hadn't asked. Lord knows he had parents, friends, family. All those good years robbed. His and theirs. The future an empty house.

Shut your eyes, Pretty Boy. Stop looking at me.

It wasn't my fault.

When he woke up again, Freda was gone, and a little Mexican girl was staring solemnly down at him, waiting to change the sheets.

"*Lo siento,*" she murmured. "I come back."

"No, it's all right. I'm all slept out."

"Miss Freda sent me."

"I'm sure she did. Miss Freda doesn't know how to sleep late, so she doesn't want no one else to neither."

The girl frowned.

"Aw, hell. Never mind. You ain't never gonna get nowhere listenin' to an old broke-dick lawman like me."

"Miss Freda," said the girl, before padding to the door and closing it behind her.

"*Entiendo,*" said Lightfoot, smoothing his hair back from his forehead. "Miss Freda." The ranger swung his stockinged feet out over the side of the bed. He stood to pull on his undergarments and brown wool pants, then buttoned up his favorite red gingham shirt and fortified it with a black waistcoat, pocket watch and chain attached. His other personal effects—jacket, firearms, ammunition belt—were neatly stowed in a wardrobe in the corner. He reached down for one of his boots and tried to slide it on. But something wasn't right. He heard a crackling sound as he pulled. He yanked the boot back off and peered down into it.

Dead leaves, he observed. A dozen of 'em.

5. John Nemo

Few men fought a mystery like Jewel Lightfoot. He didn't care for the damn things. Never had. It didn't matter if it was big or small, exotic or mundane; he fretted over what he couldn't understand. He was a man who needed to know the whys and wherefores of human behavior like others had to take an engine apart to see how it worked. Hidden motives and inconclusive endings irritated the ranger, which was why he so often tended to talk to John Nemo. Nemo was a problem he was determined to solve.

There was enough of a chill in the air this October morning to make a man appreciate the patches of sunshine he passed through. Lightfoot's breath steamed as he crossed Guadalupe Street to the grocery store, which was closed for business but receiving early deliveries. He rounded the north end of the building, crushing an acorn with every step, and strode around back, where a set of stone steps led down to the cellar. The ranger smelled wood smoke and bacon, and he heard the notes of the big Steinway drifting up out of the beer hall. A newer instrument sat in the parlor of the bordello across the street, but this one, though much abused over the years, was actually favored by the man who sat at the keyboard.

The cellar was so dark that Lightfoot had to pause for a moment before he could proceed past the doorway.

"Goddammit, John," he growled, "it's too early for music."

The piano player grinned without glancing up. "Never too early for music, Cap'n. Never too late, neither."

"What are you doing up at this hour?"

"Well, I ain't exactly up. I just never went down. Late night, last night."

The ranger waved at Jess, the big cook.

"Coffee?" said Jess.

"As much as you got."

"We got plenty. Have a seat, Cap'n."

Lightfoot eased himself down at a table behind the piano player's bench. He rolled his head to the left and right, massaged his eyes. The smell down here was the swampy aroma of fermenting lager, brewed to Otto Zenger's exacting specifications.

"I ain't a captain," the ranger complained to no one in particular. "I keep tellin' y'all that. I was a captain for about three months back in 1904, till someone realized the error of their ways. Sorry, John. You adding some new tunes to your repertoire?"

The blind man ran his hands along the worn keys of the piano. Not playing them. Just feeling. Counting them, maybe. He was dressed in a pair of black linen trousers, just a little too long, a sweat-stained white shirt, and a scarlet waistcoat. He wore a pair of black brogans without any socks. His brown skin seemed pale in the few shafts of morning light that reached the cellar. "That's right. I like to change 'em up. I'm proud you noticed."

"I ain't much for music. Calms the cattle, that's all I know."

"This here's called the 'Maple Leaf Rag.' Wrote by a man named Scott Joplin up in Missouri."

"Does it play any softer? I got a head today."

John Nemo chuckled. "Kicked by a mule, huh? Sure. It plays as soft as I do. You see Freda last night?"

Jess materialized with a spoon, a mismatched cup and saucer, and a pot of coffee. Lightfoot nodded and poured himself a serv-ing of the viscous black liquid. The ranger enjoyed the sensation of sitting in a chair, listening to the clink of metal against porce-lain as he stirred the liquid. It was almost like being a real person. Like one of those upstanding residents of Austin he saw on the streets of an afternoon, freshly barbered and wearing a clean cel-luloid collar, building a life in the busy, sawdust-filled capital city. He pictured himself living that other life for a moment. He tried it on like a new hat. Business to attend to. Ledgers to study. The fit seemed okay, till his headache spoiled it.

"Did I see Freda?" he said. "Maybe. Who's asking?"

"You gonna be around for a while?"

"I may not be around at all anymore, if some folks have their way."

"Oh, Lord. Then we're in for a rough week."

John Nemo held out his cup and the ranger filled it up, being careful not to spill any on the blind man's hand. "What's that supposed to mean?"

"Means Freda don't like the world so much when she sees you go ridin' off like you do. She's all right when you ain't here, and she's all right when you are. It's the ridin' off part that gets her."

Lightfoot took an experimental sip of the coffee. It was dark and hot and rich. He always enjoyed drinking Jess's coffee. "Man's gotta eat."

Nemo shrugged. "Yessir. And a woman's gotta make plans."

"So?"

"So she's a woman. Women ain't like us. They need things we don't need. And if they don't get 'em, they start to strangle up inside."

"She'll get over it. Plenty of fish in the sea. Younger, better-looking fish."

The blind man cocked his head toward the ceiling, his

customary pose when he sensed humor in the air. "You mean to tell me you ain't good-looking?"

"I give ugly nightmares."

John Nemo laughed. When he found something funny, he could laugh all day. It was hard not to join him. "I'm sure you do. She seems stuck on you, though."

"And that makes me question her judgment."

"Lord, that's right," said the piano player. He paused a moment before he turned around on his bench to resume playing. It was something in a minor key, lonesome and out of place on this bright morning. "I do too, Captain. I do too."

"John?"

"Yessir?"

"Why do you play so many damned sad songs?"

John Nemo's fingers kept moving. The notes drifted up from the piano, circled the room, grew faint, and died. Their memory hung like blue perfume in the air. "'Cause of what I lost, I guess."

"That's sort of what I'm gettin' at. You got amnesia, right? A textbook case. If you can't remember anything, what are you grieving for?"

Nemo picked out a brief arpeggio. "Oh, I know I lost something, Cap'n. Everybody has. I'm just not sure what it was."

6. Statistics and History

L ater that morning, two men sat in an ill-ventilated office on the third floor of the Texas capitol, trying not to get on each other's nerves. It should have been easy. The capitol was distraction enough. Completed twenty years earlier by a small army of convict laborers, the Italian Renaissance Revival building was constructed mostly of Hill Country limestone but clad for aesthetic purposes in the distinctive red granite quarried in Marble Falls, fifty miles northwest of Austin. Sprawling over two and a half acres, it contained 360,000 square feet of chambers, offices, and galleries, all built around a massive rotunda. Rising several feet taller than the nation's capitol and occupying the high ground just north of downtown, the structure felt like the geographic and political center of the state. It was often said that on a clear day, a man standing atop the capitol dome could see halfway to San Antonio, although, like much of what was said in the capitol, this was demonstrably false.

Today, though, the grandeur of the setting didn't seem to help. One of the men in the office was comfortable surrounded by people and paper. Major Deak Ross perched in a high-back chair that was drawn up close to a heavy oak desk. He was of middling height, with freshly trimmed blond hair, a neat moustache, and a blush in his cheeks. Though he wasn't obese— nothing like the Republican running for president, for example, a walrus-like figure who tipped the scales at over three hundred pounds—he'd grown stout in his middle years, thickening particularly in his belly and haunches. The flesh of his throat was noticeably pinched by his stiff collar. He was, in short, the picture of middle-class prosperity.

The other man in the room slouched behind the desk, obviously ill at ease. Colonel Al Woodard rarely met the eyes of his subordinate, preferring instead to turn his gaze outside, where the city of Austin was going about its business on a warm October morning. Woodard was slender about the shoulders and hips, with the beginnings of a paunch protruding over his bronze belt buckle. His white hair fell below his collar, and his large hands almost completely obscured the horseshoe he held. He had thick eyebrows, a beak nose, and thin lips hidden beneath a bushy moustache yellowed by tobacco smoke. His eyes, at one time a piercing blue, were now clouded by age. The ranger was only sixty years old, but the years had been hard ones, lived with few comforts and with the threat of violent extinction rarely far from his mind.

The neatly dressed man examined his pocket watch. "He said he was coming, Colonel?" asked Ross.

"Of course he said he was coming. Would I be sitting here on my backside if he hadn't? The man ain't punctual. If he was punctual, and polite, and ever what you want him to be, he wouldn't be worth a helluva lot to us out there."

"Out where?"

"Out there." The older man paused to spit into the galvanized bucket behind his desk. "Everything west of us. Every goddamned saguaro and rattlesnake and dry creek bed past the Colorado. What's that crazy sonofabitch done this time, anyway? I guess you'd better tell me."

"He got a boy killed, is what he did. Down in Robertson

County. Sir, I know you and the sergeant have an illustrious history together."

Woodard waved a hand as if this overture were an annoying insect. "Never mind our lustrous history. Who was the boy?"

"The boy was no one to speak of. But he had friends, and one of them was with him that night. A big fellow. Waylon Buckner. His father is on the county commissioners' court. Buckner says he and his companions hoped to have words with Sergeant Lightfoot in connection with an earlier shooting death."

"Words, huh? What kind of words?"

"With respect, does it matter? Lightfoot is responsible for the death of one of these young men. He shot another man's ear off, nearly dispatching him as well, and he beat the complainant, Buckner, who's only seventeen, with his own firearm, leaving him with several contusions and a rather severe concussion."

"Not severe enough. He didn't know not to mess with a ranger the first time, and I'll let him slide on that. But now he's messing with him again."

"He wasn't messing with—"

There was a knock at the door.

Woodard shook his head. "Get in here, you reprobate." Jewel Lightfoot stepped inside and gazed around the room.

He took in the sight of the tidy stranger with no obvious sign of emotion, but he stared at the grizzled figure behind the desk with the hint of a grin.

"I knew it!" he crowed. "You're gettin' fat riding that desk."

"And you're gettin' ugly riding that reputation. Shut the door and take a seat. You got your tit in the wringer again, Jewel."

"I figured you didn't call me in just to buy me a drink. Is this about Sam Millicent?"

"We'll get to that. This here's Major Ross. Former assistant superintendent of the Dallas Metropolitan Police Department.

Now my quartermaster and second-in-command, by order of the governor."

"Well, orders is orders. Proud to know you, Major."

"Sam Millicent is the man I mentioned to the governor," said Woodard, glancing over at Deak Ross. "Big sonofabitch. White hair. He's a former ranger who's now an assassin for hire. He murdered a constable named Ray Lanning last year down in Nogales. A friend of ours. Jewel's been tracking him ever since."

Ross pursed his lips, as if he'd tasted something unpleasant. "Well, I take it you haven't had much success. But no, that's not what this is about. You killed a young man, Sergeant Lightfoot. That's why we're here."

"Did he deserve it?"

If Jewel Lightfoot was bluffing, he didn't give much away. Though he was slightly built, he carried himself as if his spine had been welded in place, rigid and upright. Even now, looking half-drunk and unshaven, with a gash above one temple and an open wound—a powder burn, by the looks of it—on one cheek, he sat ramrod straight in his chair. He had sharp features on a narrow face, and his gray eyes had a piercing, birdlike aspect. His once dark hair was mostly silver now, and lines radiated from the corners of his eyes, but he was otherwise youthful in appearance, despite his years. He was in fact one of the oldest rangers on the force, a man of considerable accomplishment who'd let his fondness for alcohol and an unfashionable infatuation with the truth derail his professional progress. Though he was a sergeant and Al Woodard a colonel, and thus the highest-ranking ranger, there was little to separate their skills and general temperament but a slight seasoning of civility, which Woodard had and Lightfoot frequently lacked. It wasn't that Jewel Lightfoot was incapable of good behavior. It was more that he had an inability to walk away from a fight, or even an argument. Fights he generally won. He was legendary for his persistence in the face of a physical threat. Men said the more punishment he suffered, the more dangerous he became. But he was considerably less successful with verbal altercations. When riled, Lightfoot had a tendency to say too much and to the wrong person. He'd insulted legislators, municipal judges, even general officers of the U.S. Army. These weren't arguments anyone could win, at least in the long run, and Jewel Lightfoot's crippled career was proof.

"His name was Jed Rosario. He died in Piedras Blancas, in Robertson County, at approximately seven o'clock in the evening on October 7. You also shot his brother Charlie's ear off, and you nearly killed another boy, Waylon Buckner, by cracking his skull with the butt end of a shotgun. His own shotgun, according to the report."

The ranger winced as if the memory were a bright light. He rubbed his eyes and the bridge of his nose. The room was silent for several seconds. "That was a bad night," he conceded.

Woodard aimed a thin jet of spit at his bucket. "I ain't supposed to smoke anymore," he explained, to no one in particular. "Don't mean I can't chew."

Ross cleared his throat. "I assure you, there will be inquiries made, Sergeant. Inquiries of a very rigorous nature."

Lightfoot sighed. Before he could make up his mind to say something else, Woodard intervened. "That'll be all, Major. Why don't you leave me and the sergeant here to talk about a few things."

"As you wish, sir. Is there anything I can bring you?"

"Not a thing."

The two men listened as Deak Ross's footsteps faded down the hall.

Lightfoot squinted as if he were scouting a distant ridge. "Anything he can bring you? What does that mean? You feelin' okay?"

"Don't change the subject, Jewel. This ain't good."

"I'll give you that. But first, tell me what the hell that thing is."

Lightfoot pointed over the colonel's shoulder at a paper map of Texas pinned to the wall. Spread out around the map were brass thumbtacks, each with a numbered paper tag attached. Most of the tacks were arranged in clusters around the head-quarters of each of the four Ranger companies: Company A in Weatherford, where it belonged; Company D with that tough sonofabitch John Hughes in Ysleta, north of El Paso; Company B sweating it out down in Alice; and Lightfoot's own company, C, stationed right here in Austin. With his lips moving only a little bit, Lightfoot counted thirty-three thumbtacks.

Woodard leaned back in his chair and opened his hands. "That's our personnel tracking system. Tells me where everybody is. Well, not me so much. I already know where everybody is. But if anyone else wants to know, they can just check the map. You're number nine, by the way. I move you around a lot."

"Jesus," said Lightfoot.

"Ross's idea. The governor has one of these maps too. Old Shiny Boots may not be much in the field, but he knows how to fight here in Austin. You don't want to get on the wrong side of that one."

"I think that point's been settled. Why do we have six men in San Antone?"

"Revolutionaries. You heard about that bunch we grabbed in Del Rio, right?"

"Vicente Guerrero and them?"

"One and the same. They was the fighting arm of these here we're fixin' to round up down in Bexar County. Mexican socialists. The Land and Liberty Party. They want to overthrow Díaz and give farms to the poor and just generally put a pig in the parlor."

"I know I been gone a while, chief. But what do we care about revolution in Mexico?"

"Lot of money tied up down there. That's why we care. That's why anyone in this building cares about anything, as far as I can tell."

Woodard seemed to think better of his words. He examined the heel of one of his boots. He sniffed.

"Jewel," said the colonel. "You're no longer working for me. Officially, that is. You're on assignment." He pointed with his chin at a stack of papers at the edge of his desk. "Take a look at that file."

The ranger straightened in his chair. "Hold up, now. Assignment to who?"

"The commissioner of insurance, statistics, and history."

"Aw, come on now. What kind of happy horse shit is this? I don't want to work for no commissioner of insurance."

"You sit your ass back in that chair, and I'll tell you what kind of horse shit it is." Woodard paused to finger a fleck of tobacco off his lip. "It's a death case. Death by fire, most like. Only problem is, the dead couple had life insurance policies. Ten thousand face value each, issued by the Equitable of Texas, which is a brand-new insurance company based right here in Austin. The legislature is hell-bent on growing an insurance industry in our fair state, in case you hadn't heard. The Armstrong Committee got everybody all stirred up. People are tired of Yankee insurance companies taking all our money. There's some as want to keep that money here."

"I still don't follow."

"The commissioner of insurance ain't just a regulator. He's also a shareholder of the Equitable, along with several other individuals with some stroke around here, including Governor Campbell. And the commissioner wants to know why two ten-thousand-dollar policies are now due for payment five weeks after they were issued—and just seven weeks after the company got its charter."

"'Cause the insureds got killed? Ain't that how insurance works?"

"He's got that part. He wants to know how and why. Paying out on them policies is going to cost the company a big chunk of its capital and surplus. According to the law, it ain't even supposed to operate once it gets to that state. So your job is to figure out what happened. Make sure there ain't nothing crooked going on." Woodard scratched one cheek with his long fingernails. He searched his desk for something, found it, and picked up his horseshoe. "Take a look at the file. The dead folks were a farm family living just south of San Luis. You know San Luis?"

Lightfoot exhaled heavily. He didn't want to say the words. Didn't want to know the first thing about this case. "Up near Llano," he said.

"That's her. These folks was named Peterson. Came over from Sweden last year. They landed in Galveston, spent a couple of months in Houston, bought the property back in February after Nils Peterson, the husband, answered a newspaper advertisement. Tried farming, though that ain't the likeliest country. Peterson, his wife, and their two boys died, their bodies burned down to the bones. Their little girl got away somehow. Cowboy for the Circle H found her on Bull Creek five days later, buck naked and damn near starved. She wouldn't talk to no one for almost a week. When she finally commenced, what she said didn't make much sense."

Woodard glanced up from his horseshoe.

"Go on," said Lightfoot.

"Said three dark-skinned men killed her family. One of 'em had long hair and snakes on his back. The men hit her mama and daddy with a stick, turned them upside down, and then threw 'em in the fire. It's a strange story, but them little ones will say queer things when they've seen something bad." Woodard let his thoughts get the better of him. It was several seconds before he returned to the business at hand. "Burning was the cause of death, best they could tell."

"Best who could tell?"

"Local sheriff. Man named Hawley Reese."

"Hell, that don't make no sense. They take anything?"

"Who?"

"Whoever done the killing."

"Hold on, thunderbolt. I never said there was a killing. The little girl said something that made folks think maybe this wasn't just a fire, like it looked to be at first. So remember that: Al Woodard is not saying there was a murder. Anyway, there wasn't much to take, from what I can tell. A cow was found burned to death. Sheep and chickens was missing, but that don't mean they were stole. Coulda wandered off. Got et by varmints. No tellin'."

"All right. Don't seem like much to make a fuss about."

"Maybe not. Though it's goddamn bad luck to have your house and your barn catch fire both."

Lightfoot flipped a page. "You didn't mention that part. Any wind that night?"

"There's always wind out there. Coulda happened, I guess. But that ain't what makes it interesting. The sheriff up there found this at the scene."

The colonel reached behind his desk for a parcel wrapped in wax cloth. It was slender, a little under three feet long, apparently heavy. The cloth fell to the floor as he unwrapped it.

"Good Lord," said Lightfoot.

Woodard held the object up to the light, lengthening his neck as he gazed at it. "Some kind of a club, I expect. Someone wiped it off, but it was found with skin and blood on them blades."

"A club with blades. I don't believe I've seen its like before."

The colonel rose with some difficulty. Lightfoot stood to help. "Me neither. You look close, you can see pictures carved in the handle. See the little fella with the big headdress? Some kind of a trail boss, I reckon. All them other ones is following him."

Lightfoot squinted. "I'll be damned for a Baptist. They found this at the farmhouse? Is this some kind of Indian weapon?"

"Not at the farmhouse, exactly. Nearby. And I never knew no Indians to use one of these. Major Ross says the carving looks Aztec. He says there's a professor over at the university who might be able to help. Studies up on the kind of folks who mighta made it. It's called Mesoamerican history."

Lightfoot held the club up to the light of the window. Whoever had cleaned the weapon had missed a single hair, held in place by some gummy dark matter at the inside base of one of the stone teeth. A fair hair, fine, almost invisible in the sunshine. The ranger felt an old and unwelcome humming in his gut. It was the feeling he got when a situation didn't make sense: curiosity, mixed with fear. And there was another sensation churning down there as he handled the club. It was the red hot urge he got before he hit somebody as hard as he could. Alcohol couldn't come close to the sensation. It was a drug he manufactured himself, a buzz in the base of his brain, and he recognized for the hundredth time that he was unable to resist. Un*willing* to resist. Freda wasn't going to be happy.

"So you're saying this thing coulda been the murder weapon? Or *a* murder weapon?"

"I told you, I ain't saying nothing about a murder. That's your job to figure out. Fella at the university is named Kitzinger."

"I reckoned that's where you was headed with all this."

"It ain't where I'm headed; it's where you're headed. Llano first. After you talk to Kitzinger, I mean. You can take the train there these days. The seven a.m. will get you there right around noon. Pretty much have to rent a horse to get out to San Luis, though. Go down the hall to the Department of Insurance and see John MacKinnon. He's the clerk. He'll give you cash for the trip."

"Hell, I ain't even said I'd do it yet. But let me see if I've got this straight. The Petersons died close on to . . ." Lightfoot set the club down on the floor beside him and reached for the file again. "Ten days ago."

"That's right."

"So whoever done it could be five hundred miles away by now."

"Could be. But they ain't."

"How do you know?"

"Because," said Woodard, scratching the skin on the back of one hand, "there was another body found two nights ago. That's why I need you out there as soon as you can get your kit together and after you've talked to this fellow Kitzinger at the college. I've never met the man, but Deak Ross knows him, so he must be extremely important and fairly annoying. Mind your Ps and Qs."

Lightfoot rubbed his chin. "Hey, Al."

"Hey what?"

"I do this, I get to stay in the company, right?"

"I ain't promising, Jewel, because it ain't just me that has a say. But this assignment is going to get you out of the way for a while, and that's half the battle. And then if you do a decent job, you're gonna have the commissioner of insurance on your side. And with me and him beside you, Major Shiny Boots is gonna be outvoted."

Lightfoot nodded. What he needed to say didn't come easy. "Goddammit," he murmured instead.

Al Woodard knew what the profanity meant. He knew Lightfoot was hooked like a trout, because he and the wayward sergeant shared a number of traits. Now that Lightfoot was intrigued, he'd pick up the scent and keep following it till he came to the gates of hell, at which point he'd find a hammer and start working on the hinges. But this wasn't necessarily a good thing. Jewel Lightfoot wasn't just his best investigator, tough and persistent and downright nasty at times; he was also one of the colonel's closest friends—a *compadre*, as they said on the border. Do you send your *compadre* into a lightless house? Or do you send someone else? Someone with less fire, maybe, but more common sense? Woodard walked across the room to the window and gazed out toward the Balcones Escarpment, a line of green hills that stood like a wall erected to hold back the wild things that roamed in the west. The old man spat and watched the brown knot of tobacco juice travel down to the bed of azaleas at the base of the building. Most deaths made sense, he reflected. Even most killings made sense. But there was something he didn't like about this case, something in the pit of his stomach whispering that the few facts he knew about it didn't exactly add up. He'd seen his share of violence and a good bit more. He'd waded through tears and tracked blood across a dozen pine-plank floors. He'd catalogued the dismal work of jealous husbands and angry wives, drunken card sharps and idiot thieves. You got to know the stories after a while. You got to know the type of people who told them and the torn and tawdry pictures that illustrated their work, and these sad, every-day sins more or less folded into the encyclopedia of cynicism he kept in his head. But some crimes were different. The killings in 1885, for example. He'd worked them with a much younger version of the man who sat in his office now. The victims, unrelated domestic servants, surprised in the night and dragged from their beds. Violently raped. Their heads split open with an axe by a killer or killers the police tried for months to catch—or even to see. It was a case that he still wasn't sure he understood. One that ended badly, bizarrely, and unhappily, as both he and Jewel Lightfoot could attest.

And maybe that's what this one was going to be too.

Lightfoot stood to leave. Al Woodard turned away from the window and took his hand. And then, stiffly, he leaned in to embrace his companion.

"Cut it out," said Lightfoot, backing out of the awkward entanglement. "I can take care of myself."

"I know you can," said the colonel. "Just make sure you do."

7. The Professor

Lightfoot boarded an electric streetcar for the short ride from the capitol to the University of Texas. As he exited on 19th Street and strolled up the cement promenade to the Main Building, he glanced up at the view in front of him. Perched on a hill just a few blocks north of the capitol, the Gothic Revival structure was clad in yellow buff brick and embellished with parapets, buttresses, and arched windows, like some New York architect's medieval fever dream set down whole amid the snakeweed and mesquite of Central Texas. Dominated by a soaring central tower and twin turrets on its east and west ends, the building when seen from the south seemed to have a head and two wings, as if it were a giant bird of prey glimpsed in silhouette against the sun. The twenty-five-year-old edifice stood almost alone on the forty acres of campus, save for the modest chemistry laboratory behind it and the new engineering building, Gebauer Hall, a hundred yards to the east. Students called the Main Building the Haunted House. Old-timers just called it an eyesore.

Professor Ernst-Michael Kitzinger occupied a corner office on the second floor of the Main Building. Lightfoot presented himself, hat in hand, at the suite of offices assigned to the History Department. He didn't have a card, so he wrote a brief note on a piece of stationery set out near the door. "JEWEL T. LIGHTFOOT," he printed.

SERGEANT, TEXAS RANGERS.
REQUEST FOR INTERVUE—OLD INDIANS.

A secretary named Irma Shapiro, a thumb-shaped woman in a starched blouse, eyed the message as if it had blown in off the street. She seemed equally suspicious of the cloth bag Lightfoot carried. She asked the ranger to take a seat in one of the green leather chairs on the other side of the room. Here the lawman met the eyes of a tall, cadaverous student with a stiff collar and a furze of reddish facial hair. The kid gave Lightfoot a vaguely pitying smile—the glance all college students give to adults venturing onto campus—and palmed a lock of hair back from his forehead.

"Do you follow the Texas eleven, sir?" asked the scholar, by way of introduction. He held up a magazine with a halftone photograph on the cover of a football player gazing ruggedly out at the reader. The gridiron star had slicked-back dark hair and a brow like a Carpathian mountain range.

"I'm afraid not, son. I've been a little busy down south."

"Colorado College this weekend. Should be a real ripsnorter!"

"I'll be sorry to miss it."

"Oh, it'll be swell. Coach Metzenthin is set to roll out the passing attack, they say."

The ranger nodded companionably, though he had no idea what the comment meant. It was just as he'd feared. He'd only been on campus a few minutes and he already felt stupid. He hadn't had much of an education. His reading skills were rudimentary, and his knowledge of mathematics petered out at long division. Sitting in the warm waiting room, he felt like all of this information was printed on his cheeks. He tried reading the *Statesman* someone had left on the table, but the news was cheerless. Taft was ahead of his challenger, William Jennings Bryan, with just a few weeks left till the big election. Lightfoot wanted to believe a Democrat could win, but he wasn't going to bet on it. How many times had Bryan run for the presidency? As the slogan said, *Vote for Taft Now. You Can Vote for Bryan Anytime.* The British were fighting somebody or other in Africa, as they frequently were, and the German Empire had sent munitions and advisors to prop up the government of Mexico against the threat of rebellion. Among the weapons dispatched by the kaiser was a giant flying egg called a Zeppelin, explained by the newspaper as a newly developed, lighter-than-air flying ship filled with hydrogen. Courtesy of its diesel-fueled propellers, the Zeppelin was capable of traveling thousands of feet off the earth, far out of range of any projectile fired from the ground—a marvel, the reporter called it, of science, imagination, and Teutonic ingenuity. The more he read, the worse Lightfoot felt. It wasn't just the airship and the drumbeat of war. There was trouble all over. The paper carried news of famine in China and flooding in Tennessee, and it was getting a little too warm in the waiting room for the ranger's comfort. He was relieved when Mrs. Shapiro reappeared to announce that the professor was available to speak to him. She walked the lawman down a tiled hallway flanked by oak doors with frosted-glass windows. An elderly fellow dressed in porters' blues passed them, carrying a human skeleton as nonchalantly as if he were moving a coat rack.

"I didn't do it," said the ranger, raising his hands, but the remark failed to elicit a smile. Lightfoot could smell pipe tobacco and bleach—the latter probably some product used to clean the floors. The foyer was quiet except for the sound of someone practicing scales on a fiddle.

Violin, the ranger corrected himself.

Professor Kitzinger glanced up from his desk when Lightfoot appeared. "Ah, the good sergeant. I've just finished reading your note. Come in, please. This is a rare pleasure. A Texas Ranger, yes?"

Ernst-Michael Kitzinger was a switch of a man who wore his dark hair closely trimmed on the sides but longer on top, like a Russian composer. Narrow and tapering to a sharp aquiline nose, his face seemed custom-made for wedging into cracks and crevices. His heavily lidded eyes gazed out over a gold pince-nez. He was dressed in a brown tweed suit with a green velvet waistcoat, and he spoke with a pronounced old-world accent.

"Jewel Lightfoot, Professor. Here on state business."

Lightfoot surveyed the office. Two of the walls were lined from floor to ceiling with books. A third was decorated with animal heads—African animals, as best the lawman could tell. A lion. Something cowlike. A gazelle of some sort. The professor's windows were open, but the curtains were drawn, and the room was gloomy save for the electric lamp on the desk. Lightfoot could smell the aging pages of the books around him, full of ancient pronouncements and secret wisdom, and, filtering in from outside, the pungent smoke from the coal-fired power plant just north of the building.

"I assure you, Sergeant. I am unarmed." The learned man chuckled at his own jest.

"I appreciate that. I know you professors can be salty."

"Salty?" said Kitzinger. He tried to grin, but the expression died somewhere short of his eyes. "So? As in zesty?"

"I mean spirited. Cantankerous."

"Ah. Indeed. About as cantankerous as some of the Mexicans you and your comrades have dispatched down on *die Grenze*, yes? The border?"

"I'm sorry to disappoint you, sir, but I can't say I've killed a single Mexican."

"Apparently you are the exception then. My apologies."

"You think we got it in for them fellas?"

Kitzinger waved one hand dismissively. "I should think that

would be obvious by now. But it's not just your colleagues, of course. The United States has a long history of predatory practices toward its neighbor. You know what President Díaz has said."

"Díaz?"

"Porfirio Díaz. The president of the nation to your south, now, for thirty-three years."

"I know who the man is. I'm just not familiar with what he said."

Kitzinger nodded as if he'd expected as much. "'Poor Mexico. So far from God, so close to the United States.'"

"That's real catchy. But a gun'll shoot whichever way you aim it, you know. And some of 'em get aimed to the north."

Lightfoot had seen the leather-bound registry in Al Woodard's office. On its pages every ranger death in the line of duty was recorded in a spidery script, with a concise recitation of when, where, and how the event had occurred. There were plenty of men who'd been cut down by Comanches and Kiowas, of course, but just as many had died on the border. In Lightfoot's view, the war between Texas and Mexico had never really ended. No single battle satisfied the appetite for land and riches on the Anglo side or the injured pride of the dispossessed Mexicans on the other. Santa Anna's regulars killed Texans at the Alamo and Goliad, and Sam Houston's men butchered the Mexican army in the swamps of San Jacinto in return. The peace that was supposed to follow was shot to hell a dozen times. The American victories at Veracruz and Chapultepec in 1848 quieted things for a while, but there had been dozens of bloody feuds and assassinations along the Rio Grande since the Treaty of Guadalupe was signed, and Lightfoot figured there would be a hundred more before the killing stopped, if it ever did. Even now there were gangs of revolutionaries riding the border, looking for money and recruits to help them overthrow the corrupt and indescribably wealthy ruling class of Mexico. These insurrectionists were happy to take gold and guns offered voluntarily, but they were just as willing to rob and kill for what they wanted, and it didn't matter what side of the river a man lived on if he owned anything of value to them.

"I suppose you know," said Professor Kitzinger, "that I am a citizen of the Empire of Germany. The Deutsches Reich, as we call it. Our foreign ministry has taken an interest in the unfortunate state of relations between the United States and Mexico. It is the kaiser's studied opinion that the Treaty of Guadalupe Hidalgo was illegal pursuant to American covenants made in 1821 regarding Texas and other Spanish holdings; that the treaty was signed under duress, namely, the threat of further warfare with the United States, Mexico's larger and richer neighbor; and that the treaty's disposition of a substantial amount of Mexican territory was therefore fraudulent and *ungültig*. Voidable."

Lightfoot's face was impassive.

"Not good," added the professor.

"You're aiming a little high, Professor. You might want to let Governor Campbell know about the kaiser's opinion. Maybe he'll give it all back. They can have Brownsville, in my opinion."

"You make a joke, Sergeant."

"Bad habit."

"Perhaps you will not always find this subject so amusing. The United States treats Mexico like, how do you say it? A cheap whore. Your automobiles roll on Mexican rubber. Your telephone signals travel through Mexican copper. Your ice creams and candies are filled with Mexican sugar and vanilla and chicle. And yet always you Americans want more, for less. Soon I think your neighbors will wake up and realize they are being robbed. And they will have friends who will help them recover what they lost."

"Is that a fact?"

"I believe it is. Now, what is your business at the university, Sergeant? This is a place of learning. I'm sure you cannot feel completely comfortable here."

"Happy birthday to you too, Professor. But I didn't come for a picnic. I understand you've done some studying up on old savages."

"You could say this, yes. Thirty-one years of savages. I have examined the world of the Aztecs in particular, though in truth I find the mysteries of Mayan culture—particularly its language—somewhat more intriguing. You know of the Mayans? No? Their hieroglyphic system of writing is the only one known to have existed in the pre-Columbian world. These savages, as you say, developed advanced mathematics, architecture, and astronomy, and a complicated cosmology we are just now starting to under-stand. A thirteen-layered heaven, and a similarly elaborate hell. Scores—perhaps hundreds—of gods and spirits and demons, and a class of priests to catalogue and placate them all. And all of this was established a thousand years before the first Europeans set foot in the New World.

"The problem with studying the Mayans is that so much of their world simply vanished. They died or dispersed, and the jungle swallowed up their cities and tombs. Their pyramids still stand, covered in vines and vegetation, but they of course are mute, like great stone ghosts in the forest. As a result, there is precious little for us to use in trying to understand who these people were and why they disappeared."

"Disappeared," said the ranger.

"Just so. One of the world's great empires essentially vanished. We don't know why. Legend says they disobeyed their gods, and the gods grew angry. The god of darkness sowed anger and discontent among the various city-states of the empire, which turned against each other. Death and disease followed. It reminds one of ancient Greece, of course—if one is familiar with such things. At any rate, from the Mayan perspective, it was the gods that destroyed the empire."

"And the Aztecs?"

The professor sighed. "Oh, we know plenty about them. Theirs was a magnificent culture as well, as intricate and elaborate in its own way as anything devised by Western man. But it was derivative—borrowed—an imitation of their Mayan predecessors, neither as imaginative nor as vital."

"And a mite bloody, I've heard."

"*Bloody*, says the ranger." The professor turned and scanned the table behind his desk. He found a book and thumbed through the pages before passing it, open, to the ranger. Lightfoot took it with both hands and angled the tome to catch the weak light from the lamp. In the lithograph before him, an Indian priest wearing an elaborately feathered headdress was uttering some invocation or prayer over a naked male figure chained to an altar. The priest held a dagger in his right hand and a human heart in his left.

"Bloody indeed. Blood was a central feature of both the Mayan and the Aztec religions. The Mayans believed that providing the substance to their gods was necessary so that the gods would keep the earth in existence. Their kings offered up their own blood to commune with the divine. The monarch would pierce his penis with a blade or a stingray spine and drain the fluid into a ceremonial bowl, where it would be burned as an offering. But human sacrifice—as you see in the book—became increasingly important to the Mayans as they turned against each other. The typical offering would be a prisoner taken in battle, or perhaps a low-caste member of the tribe. Sometimes children could be bought for the purpose. After going through the necessary rituals, the high priest would remove the victim's heart while he or she was still alive. The

Mayans worried quite a lot about the end of the world and created for themselves an elaborate conception of the *Götterdämmerung*— the apocalypse. And of course, they were right to be worried. But I suspect it wasn't their gods who destroyed the civilizations of the New World; it was ours. The West's gods. Gold and glory. Christ and conquest." Kitzinger pulled a watch out of his waist-coat and examined it with exaggerated concern. "But all of this information is easily found in various books, both scholarly and popular. Our library has several. I would love to stay and shoot at the breeze, as you say, but I'm afraid I have to teach a class in exactly . . . six minutes. Is there anything else?"

"Not a whole lot, I guess."

"Very well. Then I must—"

"But there is one thing."

Lightfoot reached into his bag. He pulled out the wax cloth-wrapped package Al Woodard had given him and care-fully unbundled it. The object he revealed seemed to resonate with menace. Kitzinger had distracted himself with straightening the stacks of paper on his desk, but when Lightfoot held up the ancient club, the professor stared as if he'd seen a ghost. He rose from his chair.

"*Mein Gott.* Where . . . ?"

The ranger moved the weapon a little closer to the professor. "You know what this is?"

Kitzinger didn't answer immediately. He didn't have to. His eyes told the story. To the ranger, they seemed to hold a mixture of apprehension and avarice, intense interest and sudden confu-sion. The professor extended his hands, reverently, and Lightfoot let him take the object. "*Ja. Natürlich.* I know very well what it is. Where did you get it?"

"It was found about seventy-five miles west of here, as best I can figure. Northwest, anyway."

"Northwest," the professor repeated. "Northwest. Near what city? Who found it?"

"Well, there ain't really any cities out there to speak of."

"Yes, yes, of course. Too small. But what village?"

"We'll just leave that out for now."

"Leave it out?" The professor's voice took on an imperious tone. "What do you mean?"

"I'd prefer not to discuss the details, if it's all the same to you."

"It is not all the same to me. This object belongs in a museum. I strongly suggest you turn it over to the proper authorities. People who know what they are doing. And I would point out, Sergeant, that I am on speaking terms with a number of well-placed individuals in your state government."

"You got a leg up on me there. There ain't a one of them folks would care to be seen speaking to me. But I reckon I am the proper authorities for the time being. This here is evidence from a crime scene. Four murders. Possible murders, anyhow. Farm family. Father, mother. Two little boys."

Kitzinger blanched. He brought up his left hand and scratched a patch of skin just behind his left ear. "I don't understand. They are dead, this family?"

"Yessir. That's what happens when you get murdered in these parts."

"How?"

"How what?"

"How were they murdered?" Kitzinger persisted. He sucked in a mouthful of saliva. "With this weapon?"

"Possibly. I wasn't there, so I couldn't swear to it. But let me back you up just a minute. What is this thing?"

The professor licked his upper lip as he considered the question. His fingers probed the smooth face of the weapon, traced the filigree on its worn wooden handle. "This, Sergeant Lightfoot, is a macahuitl. Quite possibly authentic, though I would hesitate to offer an opinion in this regard without a chance to examine the object at greater length."

"It looks old."

"Indeed. A thousand years old, if authentic. Perhaps more."

"And what does it do?"

"The macahuitl was a battlefield weapon used by both the Mayans and the Aztecs. It is, of course, a striking instrument, rather than a thrusting one"—here the professor pantomimed swinging the club down like a railroad worker pounding a spike, though the blow generated by the professor's feeble effort would scarcely have harmed a potato bug—"and can be used as a club or a bludgeon. These insets along the edges are of obsidian—volcanic glass—and are therefore sharper than any metal. The macahuitl could slice a man's arm off quite handily."

"Any idea what those carvings on the blade mean? Is that Aztec writing?"

"Not at all. Those are Mayan glyphs. But neither I nor any man living—any white man, that is—knows what they mean. It is a subject of much study and debate." The professor softened his voice. "And this is what I am trying to tell you, Sergeant. This is the crucial point. You cannot be expected to know this—I am not casting aspersions—but what you have brought me is of extreme historical and linguistic significance. If this object does prove to be authentic, it will be the only item of its kind in existence. Everything else we know about such things has come to us in drawings. There was another weapon such as this, apparently genuine, but it was destroyed in a fire in Madrid in 1884. However, with time and a little effort, I am optimistic that we may be able to announce another macahuitl has been added to mankind's collection of the world's rarest and most beautiful antiquities."

With this, the professor placed the club behind his desk.

"Uh-uh," said the lawman, raising an admonitory finger. "That's gonna have to wait."

"Wait? *Warum*? For what?"

"Till I say so, that's what. As I said, that thing may be evidence in a criminal investigation."

"Surely you don't mean to say—"

"That's exactly what I mean to say. And get that look off your face, 'cause you ain't keepin' it."

Kitzinger's expression clouded. "This is a mistake. What you have found is essentially . . . *unbezahlbar*. Priceless. As I said, it belongs in a museum."

"A German museum?"

"No, not—not necessarily. The Smithsonian, perhaps. But not in the hands of state policemen with tin stars on their shirts."

"I'm sorry you feel that way, Professor. But the badge is silver, carved from a Mexican five-peso piece. And you can talk to whoever you want to about museums, just as soon as I'm finished with this thing."

The academic glanced down at the books on his desk. His hands clenched once and then again. When he looked up, he tried to nod. It was a feeble effort. His dark eyes glittered with malice as he handed the macahuitl back to the ranger.

"As you wish, Sergeant. But be careful with it. It is worth more than a roomful of rangers and your investigations."

"I'll be real careful," said the ranger. "Like I said. It's evidence. It's gonna stay right here in this wax cloth. Unless I need to do some pruning back at the house. Kind of curious to see how this obsidian glass works on a hackberry tree."

Ernst-Michael Kitzinger declined to return Lightfoot's smile. He watched his visitor leave without saying goodbye. Once he was sure the ranger had cleared the hallway, he walked to his window to watch some more. He pulled back the curtain and gazed intently as Lightfoot exited the Main Building and made his slow way south down the promenade, disappearing into the bustle of carriages and wagons on Congress Avenue. Only then did the professor turn away. He went to his desk, pulled out his best pen, and started to scratch out a note. The metal tip of the pen tore the paper, so he tossed his first page aside and reached for another.

He had to wait for his hand to stop trembling.

8. Dry Country

San Luis, October 20

The next morning, Lightfoot boarded the Austin & Northwestern for the trip to Llano, where he disembarked and rented a chestnut mare named Clementine from Joseph Patterson's livery stable. The journey was uneventful save for one detail: The ranger suspected he was being followed. A thick-set man in a black homburg bought a ticket on the same train just a few minutes after he did and got off in Llano. This in itself was unremarkable, as a handful of other men and two women did the same. But the ranger felt eyes upon him as he rode out of town. He turned in the saddle, and sure enough, the same man was watching him from the porch of a building fifty yards up the street. This was a little too coincidental, as far as Lightfoot was concerned, and he sniffed with irritation as he tried to place this mysterious watcher. On the other hand, there was no law against looking. When he failed to dredge up any memory of the man on the porch, Lightfoot resolved not to worry about it. He nudged Clementine into a canter and had put a good dent in the distance between Llano and his destination by the time the mare worked up a sweat.

It had been a strange year for weather. May brought torrential rain from the west that washed out the creeks and carried livestock and houses away. Summer was dry, though, and the

Colorado River was just a trickle after a particularly arid early
fall. Lightfoot crossed without getting his boots wet and continued west through a terrain of limestone bluffs dotted with
scrubby greasewood and cedar trees. Mornings were crisp out
here, but the days warmed up fast, and around noon the ranger
took off his jacket and stuffed it in one of his saddle bags. At
three o'clock he finished the last of the griddle cakes Freda had
grudgingly packed for him and went to work on the hard candy
she'd hidden in his shaving gear—the usual spot. He rode into
San Luis just before five, hungry and tired and in need of a drink.

Hawley Reese, the sheriff of Coulter County, wasn't content to
be the chief law enforcement officer of a county populated largely
by lizards and sheep, and occasionally it showed. At six feet, three
inches tall, he had a habit of looking over the head of whomever he was conversing with, as if he was trying to see his future
approaching along some distant stretch of standard-gauge track.
The future was moving slowly. In fact, some days it looked as if
it might have stalled out completely. But the deaths of Nils and
Ilsa Peterson and their boys were giving him hope that the train
might pick up speed in the near future. This case was extraordi-
nary. Hell, it even had Austin interested. This was his intention,
of course. The best way to get to be a Texas Ranger was to get to
know a ranger—someone who could vouch for your bona fides
to the officials in the capital who determined who got to wear the
silver star.

Even in his wildest speculation, though, Hawley Reese had never
counted on seeing the man who rode into town this afternoon.
Jewel Lightfoot was a figure of barroom bombast and campfire
legend. People said he'd ridden down some of the baddest men

on the border and faced them unafraid. They said he'd been shot three times—once straight through the head. They said he and Al Woodard had put an end to Austin's servant girl murders in 1885 under mysterious circumstances and never spoken a word in explanation since—as if the truth were too terrible, or unbelievable, to be divulged. And now he was standing in the dust of the street outside the sheriff's office, examining his horse's hooves.

The sheriff did a quick inventory of what he was seeing. The ranger was a slender man with piercing gray eyes and a predatory gaze. He wore a brown felt hat, a white collared shirt with a blue cravat, a black waistcoat, and brown wool trousers tucked into a pair of black boots. He carried a six-gun in a side holster rig, just behind a Bowie knife in a deer-hide sheath. A slide-action Winchester shotgun in a battered leather case hung from the saddle. The ranger straightened from examining the horse and looked over to where Hawley Reese stood in the window, as if he'd known the sheriff had been there the whole time. The sheriff offered him a companionable wave. Lightfoot spat. He gave the mare a pat on one shoulder and headed for the office.

Hawley Reese tried to keep his mind on his work. After proper introductions were made and a pot of coffee fetched from the Hopwood Hotel, the first order of business was the little girl. Reese summoned her from her lodgings with the local Methodist minister and his wife, both of whom accompanied her on the short walk to the jail.

Lyssa Peterson seemed calm enough, but her blue eyes had a tendency to wander, and she stared at the ranger's outstretched hand as if it were a dead thing dredged from the sea. She repeated what she'd told the sheriff a few days before. Men had come to the family farm. Three of them. She didn't know why, but they'd hurt her mommy and daddy, and Daddy still wasn't home yet. It was dark that night and the cow caught fire. No, she didn't know what the men said. They hadn't talked much, and they spoke in a funny way, neither English nor Swedish. Her mother was pretty and made her warm milk with cinnamon when she was sick. Her brothers were funny and tall and had yellow hair. Lyssa looked down at the little doll she carried, which was wearing a white pinafore similar to her own. She hummed.

"When is Daddy coming?" she asked.

Lightfoot had a sick feeling in the pit of his stomach. But he knew he had to do it. When he brought the macahuitl out of its bag, the girl's face stiffened. She bolted from her chair to hide behind the minister's wife.

"You've seen this?" asked the ranger.

The girl sank to her knees.

The ranger leaned forward, holding the weapon, which only made things worse. "Lyssa. Please. Look at me. Did the men have this with them?"

"Really, Sergeant," the minister said. "Do you have to ask?" Lightfoot wasn't partial to preachers, especially balding, thin-wristed ones who smelled of licorice. He generally found them to be officious, meddling souls, more concerned with chastity than charity. But this time, when the man spoke, the ranger acknowledged the wisdom of his words.

He sat back in his chair, his gaze still fixed on Lyssa. She was holding her hands over her ears, and bright tears streaked her cheeks. "No, sir. I reckon I don't. When she calms down some, tell her I'm sorry." He added, in a softer voice, "Tell her I'm real sorry."

Hawley Reese couldn't tell Lightfoot much about the Peterson murders that the ranger hadn't learned already from reading the sheriff's report. But he had more information about the second killing. Local laborer named Wexler, he said, handing the ranger a page of notes written in longhand. No steady employment, no known enemies. Borderline simpleton. Good mostly for digging trenches and cesspits. Found partially submerged in Hat Creek with wounds to his head and his body almost completely bled out. Pale as a fish. Oh, and one small detail: hands and feet hacked off and nowhere to be found.

"That wasn't in the file I saw down in Austin."

"Didn't want to get people scared," said the sheriff.

"Good luck scaring Al Woodard. Next time put it in."

"Yessir. I will."

The ranger sighed. "Nasty business. Says here he was tied to . . . What? A rock?"

"That's right. Someone was trying to keep him underwater. Didn't do a very good job, though. He come a-floatin' up again."

"But what makes you think this one has anything to do with the Petersons?"

The rawboned sheriff stood up, walked around his desk, and glanced outside his office—presumably, thought Lightfoot, on the off chance that someone in San Luis might actually be interested or enterprising enough to eavesdrop. Then he closed the door and returned to his chair. "One of the bodies out at the Peterson place didn't get burned all the way down. Little boy, maybe ten years old. Looked like he'd been drained of blood too."

Lightfoot ran a hand through his hair. He realized for the hundredth time that there wasn't as much hair there now as there had been a few years back, and then he noticed how well tended the sheriff kept his strawberry blond sideburns.

"Drained of blood," he said. "What's that supposed to mean?"

Sheriff Reese shrugged. "From what we could tell, anyhow. It didn't make a lot of sense, so—"

"So you left it out. Why the hell would anyone want to drain the blood out of a little boy? Or a grown man, for that matter? Drained into what?"

"That's not all. We dug Nils Peterson's bones out of the ashes. Looked like his collarbone was cut clean through."

"Might have cracked in the fire."

Reese nodded. "Might have."

Lightfoot continued. "You know of anyone who didn't like these folks?"

"The Petersons?"

"The Petersons. Pardon me. I ain't so good with names. And before I forget, what was this business about snakes on the back of one of the killers? That was in your report."

"It was, and I had a chance to talk to Lyssa about it. Best I can tell, what she saw was scars on the back of one of the men. Like he'd been whipped."

"Whipped. All right. I don't have a better explanation, so maybe so. What about the Petersons? Anyone have a beef with 'em? Any enemies?"

"I'm not sure many people even knew them. They'd only been here since February. Barely had time to get a crop in. I gather it didn't take, because Peterson bought himself a hundred Merinos in early April when Miles Murphy moved out to California. Got 'em cheap, too. Ol' Miles found himself a bride out there and was rarin' to get hitched. He—"

"Any questions about the land they were working? Were they behind on the rent?"

"Bought the place straight up, according to Tom Parnell. That's his land, and it was for sale four years before the Petersons came. That and another six thousand acres around it. I suspect he was glad to sell someone even a small parcel, like the Petersons got. It ain't good for much. Most of it doesn't have water."

"So the Petersons had some money? Is that what I'm hearing?"

"Must have. Bought the land. All them sheep. Not sure how much he had left, but he must have come with some savings. Bought them life insurance policies too."

"Exactly. Any chance this was a robbery?"

"Didn't look like a robbery to me."

Lightfoot grunted in agreement. "Goddamned bloody robbery, if it was one. Any suspects in mind? Any strangers hereabouts?"

The sheriff held up the index fingers of both hands, like a salesman making a pitch. "Well now, I'm glad you brought that up. No, there's no suspects exactly. But when you say strangers, yes. There's a man been seen in these parts a couple of times lately. Bought some groceries a while back. Sent a telegram—maybe two. He's a grifter. One of our locals said he'd seen him up north of here a few years back. I made some inquiries, and my friend Roy Biggs up in Cisco sent me this, from the *Cisco Scimitar*. I have a fair number of contacts in law enforcement in these parts—"

"I'm sure you do."

"And I was able to poke up a couple of leads. Look at these articles. One from out west. The other from Burnet just a couple of years ago."

Lightfoot paged through the clippings. As the minutes wore on, the sheriff started to reach for his nail clipper, but thought better of it.

"I get it," said the ranger, handing the papers back across the desk. "J. P. Kelso. Bogus prospector. Con man. He says he's hot on the trail of incredible treasure. He gets the locals worked up. He sells subscriptions or scrip for a share in the profits of whatever dig he's dead sure is about to strike it rich. He takes in a bucketful of cash, but he never quite finds what he's looking for. Then, when the money runs out, he disappears. Is that about right?"

"Except this character tends to disappear *before* the money runs out. In fact, I think he disappears with the money. It ain't exactly an original idea."

Lightfoot gave a what-the-hell shrug. "No, it ain't, though elsewhere it's other scams. In farm country you get these fellas claim they can make rain or find water with dousing sticks. Down south, near the border, they get excited about their *curanderos*, faith healers who claim they can bring folks back from the dead, as long as they get their money up front and a room near the railroad tracks. So he's been seen hereabouts. Anything else?"

"Gerald Sweeney was living in Burnet County around the time of the dig in that article. He saw Kelso here in town two or three weeks back and tried to talk to him. Kelso gave him the cold shoulder, but Gerald ain't exactly the type to be put off. His aunt lost some money in Burnet County, and he started asking about when it might be forthcoming. Kelso kept saying Gerald must have mistaken him for someone else. Got pretty hot about it. Gerald swears up and down it was him, though. And then, you know, he was around and then he wasn't. Kelso, I mean. And he's a con man. That's about it."

"No history of violence?"

"Violent exaggeration, maybe. Can't arrest a man for that."

"Wouldn't have any lawyers if you could. You tried to find him? What I'm getting at is, how do you know he's disappeared?"

"I've put out the word. Haven't heard much back yet."

"What if I was to go looking for Mr. Kelso? Where would I start?"

"The one pretty good piece of information I've got is that he was spotted heading out of town a while back more or less in the direction of the Peterson place. Him and a crew of Mexicans. A cart, couple of mules, picks, and shovels. Typical mining stuff."

"Hmm. Any mines out there?"

"Lord, there's mines all up in them hills. Lots of legends."

"Anyone I could talk to who might know those parts?"

"Just one that I know of. A Spanish fella name of Ernesto Zavala. He's a miner himself. Supposedly knows every dig in a hundred miles. He might could help you."

"Is that so?" said Lightfoot. "Tell me more about our friend Ernesto."

"Not a whole lot to tell. Pretty much a loner, though I've heard he was friends with Sheriff Angleton before the sheriff died four years ago. That's when I come out here, you know. I'm from Kansas. A little quieter here than I thought. Not that that's bad, mind you. I just—you know. Texas. Anyhow. Ernesto. He's an old-timer, maybe seventy years old. Wife died a few years ago. He lives out of town a piece. You take the Fredericksburg road south five or six miles, and head west right after you cross Cold Creek. There's a wagon trail leads back up thataway somewhere. It was marked the last time I was out there, and it hasn't rained much since. You'll find it."

"I'll find it," the ranger agreed. "That all you got?"

"How do you mean?"

"Has anything else happened around here lately that might seem odd or out of place?"

"Hmm. Lot of snakes out this year. It's been warm, though, so maybe . . . One of our schoolteachers disappeared for two weeks, but he came back. Don't really have an explanation for that one, but he's now looking for employment elsewhere. Someone stole a coffin."

"A coffin?"

"Never seen that before."

"I guess someone's planning ahead."

"Oh, and one other thing about Ernesto. He has a grandson."

"How old?"

"Sixteen, seventeen. Got a little pepper in him. I locked him up a year or so ago for drunk and disorderly. I know he's handy with a rifle. Brings a whitetail into Ray Stoddard's butcher shop every once in a while."

"Good to know. Is he gainfully employed?"

"I don't see how."

"I'll keep an eye out for him. I plan to head out that way tomorrow morning."

"Mind if I tag along?"

"I'd rather you not. You've done a fine job pulling all this information together, but I think I'll poke around by my lonesome for starters. Sometimes when nobody knows you, you hear a little bit more. If you know what I mean."

"I get it. Keep me posted, though, would you?"

"I'll do that. It's your case."

Hawley Reese dipped his chin. "I was hoping you'd remember that."

Lightfoot stood to leave. He wandered over to the window and lingered for a moment, gazing out over the dusty main street of San Luis. It was a dreary sight. The town was as dull as an Anglican hymnal. The street was empty save for a ragged dog sniffing the gutters for something to eat until a little man in a blue suit stepped out the front door of the Hopwood Hotel and surveyed the vicinity, as if looking for customers. Clementine shook her head and stomped a front hoof on the sunbaked dirt. The ranger knew just how the mare felt. He'd hoped he could wrap things up quickly in San Luis. He was beginning to think it might take a little longer.

"You wouldn't happen to know where a man could get a drink, would you?"

"I would," said the sheriff. "But it's the next county over."

"Dry," the ranger mused. "I knew there was something I didn't like about this town."

9. Prayers

This, Ramon reflected, is how you quicken the black heart of Death. This is how you send your voice echoing down the corridors of hell. He had spent years learning these words and gestures, a set of movements so intricate and precise they comprised a sort of dance with the divine. He felt sure he'd gotten them right, but the dark god still slumbered in its scarlet bath. He'd exhausted the blood the farm family supplied. They'd used up the fluid drained from the laborer Norberto killed near the creek—though Norberto had neglected to collect as much as he could have. The pitchers were almost empty when Paco reappeared that evening, carrying a collection of gourds with a new supply of the precious liquid still warm within.

"You were careful?" asked Ramon. The smoke from the herbs he'd been burning had turned his eyes red.

"Sí. A traveler. *Un Negro*. He never saw me."

"And you left nothing behind?"

Ramon's voice was harsher than he intended. Nevertheless, he didn't care to conceal his anger completely. Paco was a good man, obedient and reliable, as solid as stone, but losing one of the two macahuitls from the tomb was a dangerous error. Surely no one would connect the weapon with the deaths of the farm family or the disappearance of J. P. Kelso. It might never be found in the first place. Even if it was, the odds were overwhelming that no one in Central Texas was going to know what he or she was looking at. But Ramon didn't like leaving loose ends. He and his disciples were in hostile territory, with no shelter to be had until they reached San Antonio. He knew there were men there sympathetic to his cause, if not necessarily to the precise nature of his enterprise. They hated Díaz and his lackeys. But San Antonio was a week away, over dangerous country. Anglo country.

"I left nothing behind," Paco promised. With his lips tightly pursed, he looked like a giant child who was expecting a scolding.

"The body?"

"Weighted with rocks. At the bottom of a creek, like the last one."

Ramon waited a while before he let Paco relax. "Good," he said.

"Have you received word from Bexar?" the big man asked.

"No message for almost a week. It is very strange. I'll send Norberto to Mason tomorrow to check the telegraph office. It's a long trip, but we can't risk being seen in San Luis. If there is still no message, we will have to take care of ourselves."

"And the client?"

"I think he suspects the Irishman is no longer with us. He won't meet us in person. He tells us to go southwest, to the border, where he says we can deliver our cargo, and the money will be waiting. He has sent me compass coordinates. And he offers a good price. Twice the original."

"He is smarter than you thought, maybe."

"Smart enough to know we'll kill him if he brings the money himself. Smart enough to realize what we have. Not smart enough to know it's not for sale. The coordinates he sent are far away, back in Mexico. I found them on the Irishman's map."

"Will we go there?"

"If there is no answer from Bexar, yes. We'll go west. It might be the safest way, anyway."

"I wish we had stayed in the cave."

Ramon frowned. He glanced at the sagging timbers of the roof that sheltered them. They'd chosen to lay up in an old barn beside a ruined farmhouse. It wasn't ideal. The southeast corner of the roof was falling in, and they could see the lights of another farmhouse not more than a mile away. Still, the structure was isolated, and they were out of the wind. It would do.

"Norberto's on guard," he said.

This statement wasn't actually that reassuring. Norberto was reliably vicious. He could follow simple instructions. He was quick with the knife and other weapons. But diligence was not a trait he possessed in abundance, and neither Ramon nor Paco completely trusted him. It wasn't just that they were of the Ch'ol tribe—blood descendants of the Maya—and Norberto, by contrast, was Xinca, and therefore of a different lineage altogether. The Xincas were good fighters, but not much use for anything else. Norberto in particular was easily distracted. He was just as likely to follow a rabbit into the brush in hopes of an easy dinner as he was to stay alert at his post.

Torchlight danced on the sagging walls of the barn, the play of shadows on the knots and holes in the wood suggesting the presence of other faces and souls in the refuge with him: souls of the dead from years long past, perhaps, gathered to watch him at his work. From somewhere in the rafters came the sound of bats stirring in the early hours of morning. He knew the songs, written many hundreds of years ago by men much wiser than him. He lit another bead of the black nopal resin beloved of the gods, soaked cotton rags in the fresh blood, and resumed bathing the rough skin of the deity in the pine coffin. He used broad strokes on the gray-green flesh and bone of the chest and stomach, finer movements on the ridged features of the face and head. The important thing was to make sure every part of the body received nourishment. The god was still senseless, in this state. Desiccated and helpless. But venerated again. Cared for. Worshiped. And, as the ancients knew, a thing that is worshiped can never truly die.

Whispers drifted out of the corners of the barn. One in particular called to him, more insistent than the rest. It was like a voice speaking from a distant prison cell. Beyond thick walls. Begging to get out. And it seemed to him, as he bent to his work, that the whisperer was pleased.

Ramon waved another fly away. It was futile to think he could keep them all off, but he did the best he could. He frowned, now, as he watched one of the insects land on the god's stomach. He flicked his hand again, but the insect remained where it was, though its wings vibrated. He looked closer. The fly's legs had penetrated the flesh of the corpse. The insect tried again to move, to no avail. It sank farther, like a man in quicksand. It was, in fact, being absorbed. One wing broke off as the little creature disappeared beneath the skin of the sleeping deity. The whole process had taken less than a minute. Ramon shook his head, unsure if he was dreaming. He checked his surroundings. No. It was real. The candles burned. The incense smoked.

"The cave was safer," said Paco.

"Go back," Ramon snapped, "if that's what you want. But remember. No place is safe in this country."

"Forgive me. I meant no disrespect. Tell me again how the god came to be here in the north country. In *los Despoblados*."

"No one knows the whole story."

"Then tell part."

Ramon chuckled. Perhaps it was time for a respite from his vigil. He settled back against the wall of the barn alongside where Paco stood. "You know that we come from a very great people, yes?"

"You've taught me this much."

"I didn't have to teach you. You've seen the temples."

"*Claro*. Like mountains, made by men. Now buried in the jungle."

"Once they rose like stairs to the heavens. Our scientists would look at the stars and read their movements like a book. They wrote in a language almost no one now can understand. They made war. They made art. They built an empire."

Paco dipped his head. "But what happened to them? Why are they no longer here?"

"Our fathers displeased the gods. No one knows how or why, but the ancient ones became angry and turned on their worshipers. The god of darkness killed his followers. He destroyed whole cities and drove thousands of people into the jungle to live like animals. Warriors managed to trap the god in a temple consecrated to his worship. Trapped him without food or light for fourteen years. When they opened the doors, they found him sleeping, as if dead, just as you see him now. The high priests thought it a very great sin to kill one of the ancient ones. So they bound him in silver manacles and sealed him in a stone sarcophagus. They chose their best warriors to take him into the wild country, as far as they could travel, and they wove spells that would keep him from remembering the way home unless summoned. Forty warriors and forty craftsmen—stonemasons, engineers, and artists—set out from the jungles with the sleeping god and traveled many weeks to the north, into a country so tortured by wind and sun that it seemed to them unlikely ever to bloom. Here, in this dead country, they found a cave—a cavern you yourself have visited, yes? They spent months carving and painting the walls of the cave. The Comanche horse lords that were to torment the Spanish were still a weak and disorganized tribe at that time, and our people captured many for the priests, who cut out their hearts to offer them to the gods of this place. When the expedition left, four men stayed behind, sacrificed so their souls could guard against any desecration of the tomb. On the way back, the soldiers killed the stoneworkers so none could tell where the god lay. The priests then poisoned the soldiers and hid the maps that chronicled their journey. For hundreds of years, these maps, delicate things, fashioned from fig bark, were buried in clay pots deep in the jungle, passed down from one man to the next, each recipient careful to keep the secrets safe, each learning in turn the sacred script and the mysteries it describes and teaching them to one or two others. The Spanish learned of the god's tomb as well and wrote of it in the books they made of Mayan culture and history. And they searched, but they could never find it. In the centuries since, many legends have grown up about the tomb and its treasures. But the only true story says that the god will awaken in the time of troubles for his people and return to slay their enemies. Our enemies. He will drink their blood, and eat their souls, and send them all to the deepest hell. This is that time, my friend. And this is why we will awaken the ancient one."

Ah, but the waking. That was the difficult part. Ramon put his spectacles back on and returned to his study of the texts—both the original glyphs and the crabbed, sometimes smeared Spanish translation that ran alongside and beneath them. Perhaps there was something he'd missed. Something he hadn't said or done correctly. If the rituals weren't working, it had to be his fault. He wasn't worthy.

And yet . . . wait.

Ramon put down the parchment. He looked closer at the ancient corpse. It was dark in the barn, but surely there was a change in the color of the god's flesh. It looked brighter somehow. Ramon touched it. Yes. And smoother. No longer cracked and fissured. The corpse seemed to have grown in its wooden resting place. Its shoulders now touched both sides of the box.

"You will try again tonight?"

"Hmm?"

Paco pointed with his chin. "Try again?"

Ramon glanced up at his companion but seemed not to see him. His heart was pounding in his chest. He tried to keep his voice calm. "Of course. I will try until my breath gives out. It is our only hope."

Paco eased himself down on the dirt, his back against one wall of the little structure. He was hungry again. He was always hungry again. He was a big man, and a whole world away from home. Though their quest had gone well so far, he suspected hardship lay ahead. "Then may the god awaken," he said.

"Sí," came the response, but from far away. Ramon looked upon the silent corpse, and his eyes were wet with tears. "May the god awaken." And then, softer: "Very soon."

10. Ernesto and Antonio

Coulter County, October 21

You could tell a few things about a man from the condition of his dwelling. For example, Jewel Lightfoot knew immediately that Ernesto Zavala was not currently living in the blessed state of matrimony. No self-respecting woman would have put up with Ernesto's poor excuse for a dwelling. It was just a single room, maybe twenty feet wide and a few feet longer, roofed with a combination of cedar poles, mud, a canvas tarp, and several large bushes. A worn-out jacal stood listing and roofless just inside a fence made of deadfall and a few spindly mesquite posts, and two goats watched from the bed of a broken handcart as Lightfoot entered the scrubby front yard. The ranger dismounted a good distance from the door. He had a guest with him, and he helped the young man down from his mount and situated him, seated, in the shade of a massive live oak. It was the biggest tree Lightfoot had seen since he left Austin.

The ranger retrieved a package from where it was lashed behind his saddle. Then he went and knocked on the door. It was a flimsy thing made of cedar and acacia limbs, more a flap than a door and secured only by a loop of leather on the inside. When no one answered, Lightfoot pulled his revolver, reached inside to unlatch the leather thong, and nudged the door open with his right foot. Ernesto wasn't hard to find.

He was sitting in a shaft of sunlight that poured through a hole about two-thirds of the way up the southern wall. On the dirt floor around him lay picks and shovels, part of a wheelbarrow, two lanterns, and a pile of fist-size rocks. It took a minute for Lightfoot's eyes to adjust to the gloom. When he was satisfied no one else was present, he holstered his pistol and closed the door behind him.

"Ernesto Zavala?"

The old man glanced up through a shock of white hair. If he was surprised to see the gringo standing in his home, he didn't show it. "I am Ernesto."

"Sergeant Jewel Lightfoot, of the Rangers. Were you gonna open this door, or do you just not like visitors?"

"I've never had a visitor."

The statement was so odd and so solemnly put that the ranger had to laugh. "Is that right?"

"*Es la verdad.*"

"Well, I don't bite. And I'll try to mind my manners. You mind if I sit?"

Ernesto held out his hands. "Why not?" said the gesture.

"They tell me you're an expert on silver mining hereabouts," said Lightfoot.

"Silver?"

"*Plata.* It's a type of metal. Some folks think it's worth something."

The old man shrugged. He lowered a wooden spoon into a bowl of beans and slowly stirred. Lightfoot surveyed the room. As he expected, another bowl and spoon sat on a chair beside the little Dutch oven. The ranger eased himself down, facing Ernesto, on a stool that appeared to be tied together. To his right, in a recess in the stone wall, stood a faded wooden painting of a woman robed in blue and surrounded by what were either rays of light or giant spines. Her hands were clasped in prayer, and she was being held up in the air by a chubby boyish angel. Lightfoot wasn't much for icons, but even he knew the woman was the Virgin of Guadalupe, sacred to every Mexican he'd ever met. Supposedly the mother of Jesus had showed up to some local four hundred years ago on a hill near Mexico City. The Blessed Virgin told this hombre to build her a church, which Mexicans were known to do anyway, and then she'd miraculously healed some folks and later materialized on the inside of a quilt. It wasn't her on the quilt, exactly. This had been explained to him once in a Laredo barroom by an idealistic young priest who nevertheless enjoyed the occasional cerveza. It was an image of her—the footprint of her soul, or some such. But even this was enough to cause a commotion, and by now she was worshiped and adored by millions down south. Here, in a little valley in the back end of nowhere, eight hundred miles from Mexico City, the Virgin stood surrounded by a battery of paraffin candles, only two of which were burning, along with a number of round stones painted to look like grinning skulls. Mother of mercy. Bones of the dead. It was hard to figure what went through some people's heads.

"Don't turtle up on me, amigo. They tell me you've been digging silver out of this country for forty years."

"Who tells you this?"

"Whoever I ask, that's who."

Ernesto glanced at the hole in his wall. He raised his left hand to scratch the whiskers on his cheek. "Do I look like a man who has found *la plata*?"

Lightfoot gazed around the interior of the house. Hut was more like it. "You look like a man who ain't got a pot to piss in. Which is exactly how anyone mining silver out here had better look, if he don't want to get hisself robbed blind."

"You think I am rich because I look poor?"

"You could say that."

"I can't help you. I'm sorry."

"You can help me plenty. Is there a mine out here some-where? Some place a couple of bad men could hole up without being seen?"

"There are mines here, sí. Several in this country. Most of them, eh . . . *sealed*. *Barricado*."

"Sealed? Why?"

The old man turned up his palms.

"So there's nothin' in 'em? I mean, nothing worth taking out?"

"Some have silver. Not a lot." Ernesto glanced down at his weathered hands. Even in the gloom of the little house, the ranger could tell they were bent and stiff, like claws. The miner had a weather-stained but handsome face, deeply lined, with thick, slightly arched eyebrows. Like his hair and moustache, the brows had once been black but were now shot through with gray. He wore his faded cotton shirt buttoned to his throat, but a tuft of white hair peeked out over the collar. Ernesto's eyes were dark and partially obscured by sagging skin, but they focused on the ranger with intelligence and—naturally—concern.

"This," he concluded, "I tell you from my own experience."

"You're breaking my heart." The ranger stretched his legs out in front of him. "Where are these mines?"

"I don't remember."

"Sure you do."

"Not anymore. *Soy un hombre viejo*."

"You and me both. So tell me. How do you get along out here? I heard you had a grandson helps you out."

Ernesto shook his head.

"Name of Antonio?" said Lightfoot. "Is that right?"

Again with the head shake. Evidently Ernesto wasn't one for words.

"Hate to see any harm come to the boy. You talked to him lately?"

"I haven't seen him for a long time. I think he has gone to Mexico."

"Do tell."

"*Es la verdad.*"

"You must miss him."

"I do."

The ranger couldn't help but laugh. "Well then maybe you'd like to say howdy, Ernesto. 'Cause I got him trussed up right out in front."

There was silence between them for several long moments. The old man glanced over to where the Mother of Sorrows offered her mercy to the world. Then he stood, went to the door, and peered outside. Sure enough, in the dirt of the front yard, hands and feet tied, with a bandana stuffed in his mouth, sat his grandson, with holes in the knees of his trousers and long dark hair spilling from his hat down over his shoulders. Antonio was a troubled boy, always battling some internal weather that frequently showed on his face. Now his expression was angry enough to light a fire.

A goat was nibbling at his hat.

The old man returned to his seat. He looked at the ranger, and the ranger returned the gaze. Lightfoot expected to see hatred in Ernesto's eyes, as he'd seen it in the eyes of many men before. But tonight he saw only sorrow.

"What is it you want?" said the miner.

"Hallelujah," said the lawman. "I thought you'd never ask."

"So why was them mines shut up if there was silver in them?"

"*No sé.* It happened long ago. Back before the Anglos came.

The stories say the Benedictines, who were the first to bring the holy word to *los Indios*, used the people to dig these mines. The Jesuits came later. They were rivals of the Benedictines. Enemies, sometimes. The Benedictines did not want the Jesuits to take the silver, so they sealed the mines."

"But that's not what you say, is it?"

Ernesto gazed into the little fire. His shoulders sagged. "No. That is not what I say."

"I'm listening."

"There are certain things, *señor*, that . . . I don't know how to say these words. Certain things buried in this country are worth more than metal. To some people."

Lightfoot reached back to feel the hair on the nape of his neck. He needed a shave. Not just a knife shave. A real shave. A shave with lather and hot water and a sharpened razor. Maybe a towel laid over his face as he relaxed in a big leather chair. He was missing Freda Mikulska already. It was going to be a long night.

"That's about as clear as mud."

"My grandson," said the old man. "It is getting cold."

It was true. The evening was growing chilly as the sun set. "So?"

"I will put a blanket on him, yes?"

"Hell, you can cut him loose, if you like. I can find him again if I need to. Just tell him not to mess with my horse. That his rifle?"

"Sí."

Once Ernesto was outside, the ranger walked over and examined the weapon. It was a Remington Model 94, maybe a decade old, in fine shape except for a discoloration that looked like a burn on one side of the stock. Lightfoot looked around near the door. Sure enough, there, beside a bedroll and a tin cup, stood two boxes of black-powder shells. The ranger returned to his stool and stood the rifle up against the wall beside where he'd laid the wax cloth package he'd brought in with him. He eased himself back down and had a look at his boots, which were worn considerably at the heels. He could hear the two men arguing outside.

Ernesto returned a few minutes later, his grandson just behind him. Antonio was tall and lean and, like most young men his age, looked like he could use a bath. He had a beginner's moustache that didn't suit him and the long fingers of a natural musician. His dark eyes were clear, and he moved with the unself-conscious ease of someone who'd spent much of his life outdoors. He sat in the dirt in a far corner of the room and eyed the ranger with obvious malice. Next he looked for his rifle. It only took him a moment to figure out Lightfoot had confiscated it. The ranger could see the kid's jaw working with frustration.

"He survived, I see."

"He was cold."

"I wasn't cold," said Antonio.

"I'm sorry to hear it. Son, your grandfather ain't a big talker, but he's coming around."

The boy glared.

"Ernesto, you tell your boy if he wants a fight, he can have it whenever he's ready. Otherwise, he needs to quit staring at me. Makes me nervous."

"*Los Rinches* don't fight fair," the boy spat.

"*¡Cállete!*" said Ernesto, with sudden vehemence.

"Not if we can help it," Lightfoot confirmed. He pulled his holster over to where it was sitting in plain sight in his lap. He grasped the butt of the Colt. "You fight fair, you get yourself killed. Where were we, Ernesto? We were talking about what might be down in them mines, right?"

"Sí. That's what we were talking about."

"Well? Go on."

The old man leaned over and dug a bottle out of the wooden crate that sat beside him. It was pulque, a milky liquor produced in central Mexico from the fermented sap of agave leaves. Pulque was a poor man's drink and hard to find this far north, which was just as well. The ranger had suffered one of the worst hangovers in his life as a result of drinking the stuff. He'd woken up on the south bank of the Rio Grande two days after he started his binge, naked but for his shirt and gun belt and mystified as to his activities in the meantime. One of the villagers who found him claimed he'd gotten himself married. Another congratulated him on converting to the One True Faith. Eventually the onlookers laughed and brought him some pants, size extra large, and he figured it was all a joke, though to this day he wasn't quite sure. He watched as Ernesto took a sip of the liquor and washed it down with water.

"The conquistadores," said Ernesto, "found great wealth in the New World. But they also found things they should not have found, deep in the tombs they stole from."

"What tombs?"

"The tombs of the Maya. The great empire of the south."

"What did they find? Gold, you mean?"

"Sí. Gold. And also legends. Histories. Secret writings."

"Secret writings. What does all this have to do with silver mines in Coulter County?"

"*Tal vez nada*," said the old man. "Maybe something."

Now it was Lightfoot's turn to produce an item from stowage. He reached behind him and unwrapped the black club. "All right. Play possum on me. You ever seen something like this before?"

Surprise and confusion played across Ernesto's features as he gazed at the weapon There was something else in his expression as well. It was—unless the ranger was very much mistaken—dread. Interesting, this. The German professor's eyes had lit up when he first saw the weapon. Ernesto, by contrast, had winced.

"Where did you find this thing?"

"We think it might have come from somewhere around here.

It's a maca— Hell, I can't remember exactly what it's called. It's a club, used by—"

"I know what it is. The Aztecs used such a weapon."

"And the Mayans?"

"The Mayans invented it. *¿Pero a dónde?* Where did you find it?"

"It was found at a murder scene, not far from here."

Ernesto crossed himself. "Murder," he whispered.

Lightfoot hadn't come up with a list of suspects yet, but if he had, he'd have taken Ernesto off of it. The old man spoke of homicide with genuine disgust. The ranger tried to hand the weapon to his host. "Pretty hefty," he said. "Feel it."

"No," said Ernesto. "I do not want it. Please. Put it down."

The ranger did as he was asked. "Family named Peterson," he said. "Swedish. New to these parts. Did you know them?"

"I don't know anyone. They lived near here?"

"A few miles west. I went by their place this morning. What's left of it, anyway. No reason for anyone to have a quarrel with them, as best I can tell. All I know is this thing showed up not far from their farmhouse, and a bunch of grifters were seen trying to dig up an old mine hereabouts. It's not much of a link, but it's all we got. So I guess what I'm asking is this: I need you to show me a mine." Lightfoot paused to emphasize his point. "Only I ain't asking."

Ernesto Zavala met the ranger's gaze. He took another long slug of the pulque, crossed himself, and stood up.

"You have a gun?" he asked.

"Ernesto," said Lightfoot, touching the pistol in his lap. "I'm a Ranger. I can put my hands on a firearm or two."

Ernesto considered Lightfoot's revolver with a rueful smile. His eyes drifted back toward the obsidian-studded club.

"If we find the place this came from, I am afraid you will want something bigger."

11. The Meeting

Austin, October 22

Any cop or constable will confess this dismal truth: Human life is cheap. The high priests knew it. They paid thirty pieces of silver for Jesus. In Texas, such a sum would have more than covered the lives of three men and a horse. Not that Austinites regularly pondered such unhappy transactions. It was Indian summer in Central Texas, and most days you could find the city's young and young at heart daring themselves into the frigid waters of Barton Springs, southwest of town. Billy Barton was long dead, but the current landowner, Andrew Zilker, still let folks swim in the pool created by the Big Spring for a nickel a head, and he wasn't all that diligent about collecting the fee. Every year, gangs of boys built dams to capture the flow—tens of thousands of gallons a day of cold, clear water—from deep underground. They'd pile chunks of limestone from one bank to the other and plug the gaps with Spanish moss. These barriers would last until the next big flood, usually in February of the following year, and the process would start all over again as soon as the weather warmed up.

There were picnic tables set up under the cottonwoods on the north side of the creek, but it was early in the day and the tables were mostly empty. The meeting that took place this morning was unremarkable save for the formal attire of the older of the two men who stood facing each other over one of the tables. This gentleman was dressed in a brown tweed suit and a forest green waistcoat. He was carrying an elegant walking stick with an ivory handle. A thick-set, bald individual who looked something like an animated tree stump observed the proceedings from another table a few feet away. He watched as the older man exchanged greetings with a tall, fair-haired stranger in shirtsleeves and blue dungarees.

"I appreciate your meeting me like this, Mr. Millicent," said the gentleman, adding a slight tilt of his head. "Especially on such short notice."

Sam Millicent took a last bite of the apple he was holding. He wiped his mouth on his shirtsleeve and gestured to the older man to sit. "You got my attention, that's a fact. Cash will do that."

"This is good to know. And I understand you have spoken with my assistant, Herr Fromm." The older man gestured toward the bald individual who sat watching them. "You understand the nature of the project?"

The blond man tossed his apple core into the grass beside them. "I understand fine. You want me to track down this hombre who took a runner on you. Irishman. Older gent."

"That is one way to put it. Indeed. A runner. The gentleman's name is Kelso. He is in my debt, and he has for some reason broken off communications. He was meant to cable me every Monday afternoon from San Luis. It has now been several weeks since last I heard from him. I have heard instead from someone else. At first this mysterious substitute pretended to be Mr. Kelso. However, as he has now failed on two separate occasions to use the code words I had worked out with Kelso, I suspect this substitute has interfered with my project and is now trying to, how do you say it? *Lure me out*, for some reason—possibly to do me harm, if I were foolish enough to actually try to deliver a certain sum of money myself."

"Yeah? What sum would that be?"

"Never mind that for now. Mr. Kelso and I agreed to the payment of a percentage of fees up front, as they say, to finance an expedition he was leading. He was to collect a somewhat larger sum upon completion of the project and delivery to me of a particular item."

"And he—or whoever is wiring you—says he's done, and he wants the rest of the cash."

"Just so. As you can understand, I am anxious to know Mr. Kelso's whereabouts and the status of his work."

"You say you heard from your man when he was in San Luis? You know for a fact he was there?"

"I do. He sent me a message, with the code words included, from San Luis. He wrote that he had put together a team of assistants—three foreign nationals, I believe, one of whom was the owner of a map that was to guide him in his search—and was preparing to begin. He indicated that there was cause for optimism."

"Foreign nationals?"

"Citizens of the Free State of Yucatan. The nation formerly known as Chan Santa Cruz."

"You mean the one that don't exist anymore? I've spent some time in Mexico. They don't recognize any such country."

"I understand. Neither do the British, nor your own government. Nevertheless, there are those in the Yucatan who continue to fight for an independent Mayan state, and there are governments in other nations who are interested in their struggle." The older gentleman paused. He licked his lips. Millicent noticed the unconscious expression of nervous energy and calculated accordingly. "Be that as it may, the people I work for funded this endeavor, and they expect a return on their investment. I suspect the next two telegrams came from an imposter. One at least came from a wholly different location: the town of Mason. The sender indicated that he had what I was looking for and proposed that we meet to make an exchange. As I said, my money for the . . . item."

"So you had your man looking for silver in those hills. You ain't the first."

"Not exactly. Not silver. My interests are of a more academic nature. But the object my agent was assigned to recover is just as valuable—to me, at least, and to my investors."

"I get it. Bones and the like. And you think your man found something and hightailed it, maybe scouting around for a better offer."

"Perhaps you get it, and perhaps you do not. But I think you see my dilemma."

The big man shrugged.

"I need you to locate this man and find out what is happening."

"What's his full name?"

"Full name? John Patrick Kelso."

"Any aliases?"

"Not that I know of."

"And yours?"

"Mine?"

"That's right. I don't work for people I can't find."

"Very well. My name is Kitzinger. Ernst-Michael Kitzinger. You may have heard of me. I expect you to hold this information in the strictest confidence."

If Kitzinger had expected the announcement of his name to bring the scenes of frivolity around him to a sudden stop, he was sorely mistaken. His companion seemed unimpressed.

"What about these foreign nationals? The Mayans."

The professor straightened his cravat. "I have no interest in these individuals, save for any knowledge they might have regarding Kelso. They are evidently uneducated, but fortunate enough, or underhanded enough, to have come into possession of a very singular map. Kelso sent me a copy of this document, so its owners are of no further use to me."

"How do you know it ain't them who ran off with your bones?"

"Whoever sent me the most recent telegrams uses impeccable English. Not what I would expect from a crew of manual laborers. No. I suspect whoever is contacting me is a confederate of Mr. Kelso's, playing a game of some sort. It will be up to you to figure out what it is."

"Why not use your goon over there?"

"Herr Fromm?"

"If that's what you call him."

"Herr Fromm likes to break things. He knows how to kick a door open, but he is not so good at persuading people to ask him inside. He tends to stick out."

"Try the zoo. Give him a banana, and he'd fit right in."

"We seem to have lost the thread of this conversation."

Millicent nodded. "There was three of 'em, right? Any description?"

"A total of four—my man, plus the three laborers. Kelso is a portly individual of roughly sixty years. Of Irish origin and somewhat profane. White-haired, with a full beard and a slight limp. Thick arms and hands, as I recall, and the classic Gaelic features: pug nose, broad cheeks, prognathic brow. He wears rosary beads around his left wrist. I'm told he is a prodigious drunk, though he was sober enough the day we met. I'm afraid I can't help with the Mayans, as I've never seen them."

"Are you fond of Mr. Kelso?"

"I beg your pardon?"

The big man stared across the table without blinking. "Sometimes this line of work gets a little physical."

"Oh. Yes. Physical. Whatever fondness I had for Mr. Kelso—and there was precious little to begin with—is rapidly diminishing. Do what you think is necessary."

"And if he does have something that belongs to you?"

The words came quickly. "Bring it back."

Sam Millicent sucked at his teeth. "You want to add that to the job?"

Kitzinger gave a little snort of irritation. "I see. Forgive me. I am unaccustomed to such frank discussions of compensation."

"You'll get used to it."

"Perhaps I shall. How about twenty percent of whatever you manage to recover?"

"Forty."

"A third?"

"See? You're used to it already. A third will work. You have my money?"

"Half now, half upon successful completion of the project."

"And a third of whatever I bring back."

"Ah," said the professor. "Then we have a deal. Shall we shake on it, as they say?"

"Let's not."

The older man's cheeks and forehead flushed a deep red at this off-handed rebuke. Sam Millicent turned and spat something off the tip of his tongue. The professor worked up the ghost of a smile. He produced a brown envelope from an inside pocket of his jacket and passed it across the table. Millicent opened it and counted the bills, unaware of or indifferent to the professor's discomfort at the sight of the cash. Kitzinger gazed around but noticed that no one in the vicinity seemed to be interested in the sheaf of currency that now lay in plain sight.

Austin. It was hard to figure what the citizens of this bustling little backwater did care about, aside from clear water and sunny

skies. Heathens. An infantile rabble. And that was just his students. Back home in Stuttgart, a man of education was widely
respected. Envied, even. Children tipped their caps to him when
they passed in the street. Not like here. Here the children threw
the spiky little seed pods they called sweetgum balls at the back
of his head and called him, ludicrously, a "Dutchman." But at
least the little ones reacted. Among his lethargic, semiliterate
neighbors, he might as well have been invisible. And wasn't that
the point? He chided himself. Vanity aside, it was wholly appropriate that Austin remained ignorant of the extent of his learning
and the ends to which he aimed to put it. So the city and the raw
untutored state it led and the nation in which it thrived slumbered
on, unaware of the great gears of history that were turning even
now, as the machinery of politics and war reshaped Europe, and
indeed the world, in Germany's image. Ernst-Michael Kitzinger
was engaged in a project that could alter the course of human
events forever. The people who mattered would see the fruits of
his labor soon enough. And his rewards would follow.

"No offense," said Millicent, folding the stack of bills and
placing it in his breast pocket.

"None taken, I assure you. I look forward to our next meeting. I've heard you are quite efficient at . . . what you do."

"I get by. I'll send word in a couple of weeks."

"Excellent. Then I shall be on my way. Herr Fromm?" The
professor stood to leave. The balding man at the table a few feet
away rose as well. But the professor paused. He ducked his head
as if he'd just remembered something important.

"By the way," he said. "There is one complication."

Millicent gazed off down the green slope toward the springs.
Female sunbathers sprawled on the grassy banks of Barton Creek,
calves and ankles exposed. Three boys were racing up the opposite bank, chasing a dog. "There always is."

"There may be someone else looking for Mr. Kelso."

"Is that so?"

"A state policeman. An unpleasant little fellow named Lightfoot. Slight of build. Gray eyes. Nervous disposition."

Millicent chuckled mirthlessly. "Lightfoot, you say?"

"I do indeed."

"Professor," he said, "that ain't a complication. That's what they call a fringe benefit."

"Excellent. I was hoping you would feel that way. You dislike this man?"

"Let's just say he's developed an unhealthy interest in my affairs. He thinks I killed his friend, a fat-ass sonofabitch named Ray Lanning. I've sent Sergeant Lightfoot a couple of warnings, but he's slow on the uptake. Does he keep a place up here?"

The German placed a folder on the table. "Just a room, as far as we can tell, but he does frequent the habitation of a madam, not far from the university. Here's what we know about him. Where he stays. Who he sees. Herr Fromm has been doing the legwork, as you say. You are welcome to it."

Millicent took the folder without looking at it. "And why are the Rangers after your man Kelso?"

"This I don't know. I suggest it only as a possibility. Evidently there has been some unpleasantness in the area, and he has—so I have heard—been asked to conduct an inquiry. I have since learned that Mr. Kelso has been involved in a number of unsuccessful mining expeditions in the past. These failures resulted in several lawsuits and at least two criminal complaints."

"He's a grifter," said Millicent.

"I beg your pardon?"

"A cheat. A thief."

Kitzinger winced at the word. "Let us hope not—for all of our sakes. But perhaps you will furnish the best evidence of whether this is so. *Auf wiedersehen*, Mr. Millicent. And happy hunting."

"Back at you," said Sam Millicent, watching the little professor as he made his way back to his carriage. The big man knew what he was, and he was content with this knowledge. He was a hired gun. An assassin. He took money from his clients, and he did unpleasant things to people in return. He made sure his clients got their money's worth. But he didn't have to like them. And he didn't like this client in particular.

Under his breath, he added, "You kraut-eating sonofabitch." He pulled the wad of bills out of his pocket. Wouldn't hurt, he figured, to count it again.

He didn't notice the professor's return until the professor was standing right in front of him.

"And did you?" the older man asked, a little triangle of tongue protruding from between his thin lips. Millicent knew the type. Excited by violence. Probably wouldn't mind getting slapped around some himself. But not here. Not now.

"Did I what?"

"Kill the ranger's friend?"

"Oh yeah," said Sam Millicent. "I killed him deader than hell."

12. Crime Scene

Coulter County, October 22

L ightfoot found tracks near the burnt-out Peterson farmhouse. The footprints—three pairs of them, as best he could tell—led southwest through broken country before disappearing on a ridge of exposed limestone. Sheriff Reese had meanwhile learned that two men, strangers in the area, paid cash for a horse in San Luis not long before the night of the murders. A fellow named George Lipp owned the only livery stable in town, so it was easy to track down the details. Lipp said one of the strangers was a slightly built individual with bad teeth and a nervous laugh. The other was severe in aspect, above average in height, and remarkable chiefly for his long black hair. The men spoke Spanish, and Lipp figured they were Mexican. They were reluctant to answer questions, but the skinny one said something about mining when asked what the horse was to be used for. The long-haired man shut him up with a single word. They purchased a horse named Lucky, a fourteen-year-old gelding with a strong back and one chipped hoof. Lipp watched the men leave town, headed east. The man with the long hair rode while his companion walked beside the horse.

Lightfoot played the facts out in his mind a dozen times. The con man named Kelso spotted in town but disinclined to publicize whatever new venture he'd embarked upon—though publicity was essential for the success of his crackpot treasure-hunting schemes. The unknown Mexicans mentioning mining in connection with their purchase of a horse, which they then took east, in roughly the direction of the Peterson homestead. And, finally, the tracks of the killers of the Peterson family, leading southwest. The distance between San Luis and the Peterson place was eleven miles. According to Ernesto, there were abandoned digs just east of the halfway point. Lightfoot knew there wouldn't be much of a trail left, but he figured with the limited information he had, and Ernesto's knowledge of the mines, they might at least be able to get close to whatever refuge or rendezvous the killers were using. But were the Mexicans really miners? And were the miners the men who'd killed the Petersons? Why would a man like Kelso, by all accounts an unscrupulous swindler but by no means violent, be involved with something so brutal and bloody? It was a slender collection of clues. Not even clues, really—more like circumstances. It might not lead anywhere. But it was all he had, and he was a man unaccustomed to contemplation.

He and Ernesto set out early the next morning, riding with the sun on their backs through uncultivated country choked with cat-claw and creosote bushes and unmarked by any road or habitation. Lightfoot was mounted on Clementine, a sure-footed animal he was starting to appreciate. Ernesto rode a mule he called Rosita, a sweet-tempered creature greatly devoted to him. Just a few years ago, Ernesto had prospected for silver here on land nestled in a pocket canyon carved out of the earth by a creek so obscure it didn't have a name—at least, none that Ernesto knew. One of the two old Spanish mines was just a little way down into the canyon. The two men reckoned this was as good a place as any to start.

"You ever hear of a man name of Kelso?" called the ranger, pushing the stopper back in his canteen as he watched Ernesto's mule make her way up a little ridge toward him. He could feel a film of sweat on the small of his back. "Sets himself up as a treasure hunter? Or a mining engineer?"

Ernesto waited until he had reached the crest of the ridge before he answered. He was a man who valued economies of effort. "Sorry, Capitán. No."

"Just a stab in the dark. And by the way, I ain't a captain."

"It's easy to talk about *la plata*," said Ernesto. He wiped the sweat from his forehead with a grimy red rag. "It's just hard to find it."

"You notice who's behind us?"

"I did."

"Are you gonna tell him to go home," said the ranger, "or should I?"

"He is hard-headed, my grandson. Like my wife. We can both tell him. He won't listen."

"If I was to give him his rifle back, would he shoot me?"

The old miner measured his words carefully. "I believe he would, yes. You embarrassed him."

"Good to know. Here. I'll keep the rifle. You take my pistol. It's got two rounds in it. Fire it if you find something."

"Like what?"

"Hell, Ernesto. I don't know. People. Pirates. Anything out of the ordinary."

"Pirates," sighed Ernesto.

The entrance to the canyon was unpromising, a vision of tortured rock and long, ragged fissures like claw marks in the earth. The land was as barren and resentful as everything else within a hundred square miles, so desolate and drained of sound it seemed as if no man of any shape or shade had ever set foot on it. And yet this was not quite true, for occasionally Lightfoot found evidence of human transit. A piece of bridle leather. A rusted tin can lying in the weeds.

Ernesto gave Rosita a nudge with his heels and descended into the canyon to search the sites he knew. He waved to Antonio to follow him, but the boy remained where he was. The ranger meanwhile spent the afternoon and early evening making a large and very imperfect circuit of the area, cutting for sign. Eventually he found faint evidence of the passage of two men on foot, with two horses—or possibly mules—pulling a wood-wheeled wagon and another animal walking beside the conveyance. The tracks were headed away from where he'd left Ernesto. The ranger followed the traces of trail. He lost it, doubled back, thought he found a second, clearer set of markings just a hundred yards or so away. The likelihood that enough of it remained to lead him somewhere was slim, but he didn't have anything better to do, so for an hour he scouted, his mood alternating between a growing conviction that he'd located something important on the one hand and a nagging suspicion on the other that he was making up patterns in the dirt that didn't really exist. That he'd lost the trail. That he was right back where he started from: nowhere. That's when he heard the pistol shot.

The old man sat on a cube of limestone beside what looked like a wound in the side of the canyon. The hole was partially covered by mesquite and scrub oak limbs, but the leaves on the cuttings had gone brown, so the camouflage was no longer very effective. In fact, it was the color of the dead leaves that had attracted Ernesto's attention in the first place.

The old man fanned himself with his hat. "I found something," he said.

Lightfoot dismounted and surveyed the ground around the opening. He knelt and picked up a piece of charred wood.

He crushed it, sniffed it, sifted the grit through his fingers. He wandered a few feet each way from the stone, and soon he saw a faint but unmistakable trail through the brush up out of the canyon. Two animals pulling a wagon or cart. A chipped hoof barely visible in one of the prints. Two men had walked alongside the cart, one in flat-soled shoes or sandals, the other barefoot. There would have to have been another driving the wagon, and that would make three. But he was looking for four. Could there have been two people in the wagon? That might make sense on level ground, but climbing out of the canyon? Any sensible drover would have tried to lighten the load on the animals.

"I've been in this place many times," said Ernesto, nodding toward the wound in the earth. "Never have I seen this."

"No way you could have. This rock must have sealed the cave like a cork in a bottle. I'm thinking it took a fair amount of muscle to get it out."

The ranger pulled the dead limbs out of the way and tossed them to one side. The smell of decay hung heavy in the air of the entrance. Lightfoot spat to one side. He went to his saddle bag and pulled out a blue bandana, which he wrapped around his nose and mouth. Ernesto unpacked the two lanterns he'd brought.

"Something bad has happened here," the old man said, gazing up at the sky.

"It's Texas, Ernesto. Something bad has happened everywhere." The ranger squatted to peer into the hole. "Probably just a sheep fell in from above. I pulled a boy out of a cave like this down in Wimberley a few years back. Fell in while he was out hunting squirrels. He'd been there three days when we found him."

"Still alive, I am hoping?"

"Still alive. He ate a lizard."

"Whatever is in there now," said Ernesto, "ran out of lizards."

"That would be my guess. This limestone is tricky. Gets hollowed out underneath, and . . . hell, you know better than I do. Let's make sure we don't do any falling of our own. You want to fire up them lanterns?"

"No. Not really."

But he did it anyway, and soon the two men were on their hands and knees, moving out of the sunlight into the darkness of the cave. The temperature dropped once they were inside. The ranger was able to stand up again after only a few yards of crawling, but even with the aid of the lantern, it took several moments before he could make out shapes in the gloom of the cavern. A colony of bats circled above the two men and cycled up toward the ceiling of the cave, where a few slits of gray light were visible. The air was even cooler here in the chamber, and more pungent. Ordinarily, on a day like this, a break from the heat would have seemed like a blessing. But not here, and not now. The air was dank and polluted and heavy on the skin. It was as if the two men were in the grip of the darkness itself.

Ernesto batted a fly away from his face, then pulled his shirt up around his mouth. The insects were everywhere.

Lightfoot was first to see the figure. It knelt at the base of a set of steps that led up to a sort of throne—a huge stone seat carved into the wall of the cave. The figure's back was turned to the men, and it remained still as the ranger drew his pistol.

"*Madre de Dios*," whispered Ernesto, following Lightfoot's gaze. He crossed himself. It was a strange tableau. The kneeling man seemed to be hunched in prayer.

Lightfoot held his palm out toward Ernesto, as if to hold him in place. The ranger's pulse pounded as he moved toward the figure. He passed what looked like a stone rowboat with several fragments of rock beside it. He inspected the shards of bone that littered the cavern floor and took in the spears and helmets that lay at the base of the nearest wall. Still he moved forward, each step a picture of concentrated effort, until he was standing directly behind the supplicant. This was when he noticed the face staring back at him from the foot of the throne. It was the face of an older man, white-haired and pudgy-cheeked, with a pair of bushy sideburns. The eye sockets were filled with flies, but the face looked strangely peaceful in the flickering light—almost as if it had asked to be separated from the torso that supported it.

The ranger lifted a boot and nudged the corpse over.

Sure enough. Headless. The abdomen ripped open. Body drained of blood.

And the air alive with insects.

The ranger spoke without turning around. Oddly, this seemed important. To keep his eyes on the horror in front of him, as if it might stand up and move toward him. He felt like he was keeping his soul facing forward as well.

"Ernesto," he said. "I think we found Mr. Kelso."

As he backed away from the steps, Lightfoot looked up to take in the strange pageant carved into the wall above him. Snakes and screaming faces. An army of slaves moving like ants across the rock. A giant creature with curved teeth and malevolent, bulging eyes holding a severed human head in one hand, a scepter in the other. When the ranger collided with what he still imagined was the sculpture of a boat, he turned and held his lantern over the edge. A film of some congealed liquid, black and viscous, covered the bottom of the rock basin. Lightfoot knew what it was. He knew the smell.

"Blood," he said. "It's some kind of crypt." He found it hard to make the words. His voice seemed to die in his throat.

"Capitán," whispered Ernesto, who was suddenly standing beside him. "I think it best that we go. This is not a place for the living."

"Ernesto, look. These manacles. Cut clean through. Someone was bolted down here. I just want to—"

"Please! No more talk. I know this place. And we have to leave. *Ahora.*"

The ranger raised his lantern and canvassed the cave. Just in front of him was a large flat rock. It too was smeared with gore. Carved out of the wall beyond it was the figure of an immense creature that might have been a bat or a man, or possibly some combination of the species. It was two-legged, but possessed of wings rather than arms, which it held folded in front of it, and a head more demonic than mortal, with a pug nose, elongated ears, and large eyes. Around the creature, men in elaborate headgear—priests, perhaps—held daggers, as if hoping to employ them in service to the creature that loomed above them. In the flickering light of the lanterns, the figure seemed to be alive, trembling, about to lunge.

Ernesto was already heading for the tunnel, his rusty lantern squealing as it swung in his hand.

"¡Vamos!" he shouted.

Lightfoot saw the leather satchel as he was leaving. It lay between two rocks on the cavern floor, its contents strewn around it. The ranger couldn't help himself. He fell to his knees and gathered up the papers. He stuffed them in the battered bag and hugged the satchel to his chest with one arm. The gust surprised him. It was a peculiar blast of dirty, dank air, as if the cave were exhaling. The flame in his lantern sputtered and there was a low-pitched rumble behind him, like the groan of something very large stirring from a troublesome dream. For a moment Lightfoot felt a spasm of flat-out panic. It was a sensation he hadn't felt in years, and it was just as unpleasant now as it had ever been.

That's when the first bat hit him. It wasn't much—not enough to knock him off-balance. It felt as if someone had pitched a ball of mud at his head. The little animal was stunned by the impact and fell at the ranger's feet. Strange, but nothing to worry about.

Then it happened again.

And again.

The bats slammed into his head and his back with increasing force. The ranger was momentarily blinded by the flurry of wings. But there: He could see light ahead of him. And Ernesto's voice was calling. The ranger forced himself to take a deep breath. He dropped to his knees, left the lantern behind, and started crawling toward the sliver of daylight. All the while he felt as if something was behind him, creeping up on him, wishing him nothing but cold days and death. He reached the entrance to the tunnel, lunged into the open air, and collapsed in the dirt outside the cave, slapping at his head, clawing his hair. Bats carried hydrophobia, and hydrophobia meant a slow, agonizing death. But he felt nothing on him, and his hands brought back no blood, so perhaps he was safe. The bats hadn't followed. In fact . . . Lightfoot scanned the ground around him. There wasn't a bat to be seen. He opened the fist he'd made of his left hand, and a single fly emerged. It rose, circled once, and disappeared into the cave.

Ernesto and Antonio sat together on the limestone block, watching the ranger's strange dance of panic subside. The men gazed at each other as the last bruised hints of sunlight faded from the opposite wall of the arroyo. Darkness gathered around them.

"Capitán," said Ernesto, stooping to help the ranger to his feet. "We have much to discuss. But maybe it would be better not to do it here. Not after sundown."

13. Intelligence

Washington, D.C., October 22

The British ambassador's second-in-command, Roger Fellowes, glanced up from his paperwork with a barely noticeable frown. Young George March stood in the doorway, shiny as a new shilling and altogether too chipper for this humid Washington morning. First Secretary Fellowes let his eyebrows extend a grudging invitation.

March offered his superior a slight nod as he entered the room. "Sorry to bother, sir. But I've just read the strangest dispatch."

"Indeed? Have a seat, March. Just push those things aside. Enlighten me."

"It's our friends the Huns."

"Good Lord. On the rampage again? Testing the legions?"

"You'll recall that Whitehall authorized intercepts of all cables in and out of the German embassy here once we got wind of the dispatch of the Wehrmacht's new flying machine to Mexico."

"Ah yes. The flying egg. Any idea what the devil the Krauts are up to down there?"

"Testing, evidently. Mexico has a great deal of unoccupied land. Flat, dry land, as it turns out. It's perfect for putting the new machine—the Zeppelin, they call it, after the esteemed Count Ferdinand—through its paces. It's the LZ-4, quite like the model that crashed back in June, but supposedly improved.

Aluminium skeleton. Rubberized cotton cells for the hydrogen gas. Two external engines and top speed of around thirty miles per hour. They want to give it a go in a region that's warm and largely untroubled by Northern European storms. And where there aren't any spies around to take notes, incidentally."

"Except ours, of course."

"Quite. I think I mentioned we've seen a bit of an uptick in communications between the consulates recently. The German embassy here exchanging cables with their counterparts in Mexico City. And vice versa."

Roger Fellowes laid his pipe in its holder. The British embassy, which stood on Connecticut Avenue, in the heart of the city, was an old and difficult building, ill-suited to contemplation. It didn't help that a tram line ran in front of the house. The older man waited, now, as the hellish contraption rattled and squealed past his open window. No sense talking while it passed. It was difficult even to hear himself think.

"Ah," he said when the noise subsided. "The wonders of modernity. You did indeed mention an uptick, as you put it. What are we finding out?"

"One of their people in Texas—"

"The Germans have people in Texas?"

"They do indeed."

"Good Lord. Why?"

"I've no idea, sir. But he's a voluble sort. Sends a message or two each week. He's been telling the embassy staff here that his work has been successful and that he's managed to find some sort of relic in the American outback. Texas, that is. This in turn seems to have set off a flurry of communiques with Germany's consular office in Mexico City. Our friend Ambassador Stoltz writes that the Zeppelin has been placed at the disposal of the Mexican government, along with a crew of German Army scouts and spotters."

"I'm not sure I follow. Why are they sending the airship? That doesn't sound like testing to me."

"Apparently they're looking for something."

"Don't be tiresome, George. I appreciate a bit of intrigue as much as the next man, but I have a meeting with the American secretary of war in less than an hour and a fat lot of paper to get through beforehand. What are they looking for?"

"Three Mexican nationals, sir. Believed to be Mayans, with ties to resistance fighters in the Yucatan. They're traveling with some sort of treasure."

Roger Fellowes repeated the word as if he wasn't sure his colleague understood what it meant. "Treasure."

"Indeed. This fellow in Austin has been damned cryptic about it, but yes. It's something he considers to be of immense value. And the orders to the expedition being sent north are to recover this treasure at whatever cost."

"And these insurgents who are transporting it? What's to become of them?"

"Apparently they're expendable."

"Good heavens. Sounds dastardly and unaccountable. Just the ticket for you and your crew. Keep at it, then. Let's find out what this treasure is, and why the kaiser is so determined to help his Latin friends get it."

"Very good, sir. I'll do just that."

"Anything else?"

"No indeed," said the younger man.

"Right," said the first secretary. "Carry on, March. And see if you can locate that woman with the tea while you're at it. That's the mystery that has me truly worried this morning."

14. Reflections of a Revolutionary

Llano County, October 22

hy had fate punished his people?

What made the white man wealthy and the brown man poor? Who or what had allowed the Spanish priests to come and strip his ancestors of their beliefs? Of their lands? Of their gods?

Ramon knew the answers had to do with the gods themselves. They'd grown bored with the lukewarm devotions of their adherents, their petty squabbles, their preference for comfort over conquest. The ancient ones must have known what would happen when the white men came with their swords and crosses. And so the gods went away and left the Mayans to suffer. In all the many centuries since, his people, once the rulers of an immense and fertile empire, fearsome warriors who took slaves from the jungle like fruit from the trees, became lowly subsistence farmers pushed from one jungle tract to the next by their European overlords. Success in this world reflected one's ability to ape the manners and mores of the Spanish. The lighter one's skin, the easier it was to make the pantomime convincing.

Ramon knew. He'd played the game. He'd attracted the attention and then the favor of the priests. He'd attended and

excelled at the best of southern Mexico's schools, eventually earning admission to the Universidad Michoacana de San Nicolás
de Hidalgo. He could speak French by the age of thirteen and
English the following year. He'd read Shakespeare, Hobbes,
and Rousseau. Outraged by the plight of the *campesinos* under
the Díaz government, which not only permitted but also encour-
aged native and foreign business interests alike to seize Indian
property under protection of the laws regarding *terrenos baldio*,
or "unused land," he flirted with the ideas of Marx and Bakunin
in his teens, going so far as to draw up the organizational documents of the Mexican Students' Revolutionary Socialist Party in
1897. In those heady days he was convinced that religion of all
sorts was a set of blinkers that shielded the wearer from the harsh
truths of exploitation and economic slavery in every corner of the
world. But something never quite let go of him. He could never
quit reviewing the dimensions of the Pyramid of the Magician in
Uxmal or envisioning the fierce figures that paraded across the
frescos in Mexico City's Museo Nacional de Historia. This was
the work of his forefathers, and his forefathers had been magnificent: ambitious and bloody and uncompromising. So why
had the world walked over his people? And why had his people
allowed it to happen?

He drifted away from his Marxist study group. Harsh words
were exchanged. He was called a revisionist, a traitor, and worse,
and bitterly denounced in the group's newspaper. But by this time
he didn't care. His former friends were fighting over table scraps.
Their prescriptions for how to change the apparatus of ownership—even the bloodiest of those prescriptions—still tacitly
accepted the notion that industrialization was a desirable thing,
that ownership was liberation, that Westernization was progress.

He was no longer sure any of this was true.

And so Ramon took to the jungle, called back to the sources

of his ancestors' triumphs by voices that beckoned to him down long corridors of time. He wandered, and he read, and he listened. In unpolluted green places far from the Spanish towns and churches, he discovered that traces of the old beliefs endured, hidden from the pale men but still glowing dully like embers on a frosty morning, waiting to be fanned back to life. He sat for hours before a hundred tribal fires, absorbing the counsel of the elders and the complaints of the young. Until finally he started to speak. Why do we wait for gifts from Díaz, he asked, rather than taking what is rightfully ours? Why do we wear the white man's clothes and bow to his murdered God, when our own gods are waiting for us to call them forth? He found listeners. He found disciples, and more importantly he found teachers—wizened, sun-stained men who communed with ancient powers who they claimed still lived in the earth, anxious to rise again. From his teachers he learned to read and speak the antique tongues. Some among these shamans permitted him to study their secret texts, and others began to treat him as an equal, as a priest of the old deities. And perhaps it was true. From scraps of long-forgotten prayers and legends, he wrote a history in his head. From scattered embers in the jungle, he built an inner fire. Ramon's fervor grew stronger. It had burned brighter through all the long years of hardship and tribulation since. Years when he'd fought the Mexican army in the Yucatan to defend the Mayan nation, Chan Santa Cruz. Years that included two stays in federal prison and a dozen beatings by Díaz's secret police. The pain and hunger and humiliation had hardened him. He could feel the beatings every time he bent over, feel them in his damaged bones and the shiny lines of raised tissue that ribboned his back.

But he was happy for the beatings now. It showed they knew. Them. All of them. The Catholic curates and the murderous *federales* and the hard-eyed men who worked for the patrons, eager to strangle any sign of dissent or dissatisfaction. They'd killed his father and his little sister, Itzel, just because they fed the Cruzoob, the Mayan rebels. The soldiers had herded them into the jungle along with forty of their fellow villagers, where a captain named Quintero ordered the captives to dig their own mass grave and then lined them up—men, women, and children alike—and shot them down where they stood. There was no examination made of the bodies. Those who were wounded but still alive were buried with the rest. Desperate measures, to be sure. And effective, in the short run. But not in the long run. Because every murder bred resentment, and every loss cried out for revenge. Blood called for blood, and in every breath of anger Ramon could hear the whispers of the fallen. The end was coming. Not, as some thought, in the cult of the talking cross, but in something deeper, more powerful, and more deadly.

And so it came to pass.

The pewter flask that once contained John Patrick Kelso's whiskey now held the blood of a nine-year-old girl, a pretty thing, ivory-skinned, with dark hair that gleamed in the candlelight. She'd been taken in the night by Norberto on a visit to a farmhouse three miles to the west and brought alive to their place of refuge for the ritual. Perhaps her cries of panic awakened the creature. Perhaps it finally heard the words of the ritual, far away in the dream realm of the eternals, neither black nor white, alive nor dead, where time slowed and spread like a sluggish river and the stars ceased their repetitive journeys through the skies and wandered aimlessly instead like a child's tuneless song. But more likely it smelled the scent of her open veins and felt the warmth on the flesh of its face and chest.

Because now, finally, the god drank the blood of its people's enemies.

Now, finally, the god opened its eyes, yellowed and dry from the centuries of sleep. The long tongue flexed and curled between the parched lips, retrieving the few drops of spilled blood at the corner of its mouth, probing as well perhaps for some dimly remembered taste or odor. The deity's fingers reached out and grasped the wooden sides of the box, scoring the surface with sharp claws. Small eyes searched from side to side before they came to rest on Ramon.

Restoration.

Renewal.

The steel wheels of time squealing as they turned.

The priest sank to his knees. He bowed his head in prayer and thanksgiving. He'd done it. The god had returned. But protesting beneath the hymn of triumph in his head was a small voice. A questioning voice. He'd always assumed the return of the deity would be cause for celebration. But now the god had awakened, and it was not at all clear he was pleased.

Ramon rose from his knees. He glanced across the dark chamber and saw Paco and Norberto standing with their eyes averted. He took a step backward. He needed to escape the god's sight. Something about it was hurting his head. He tried but was unable to lift his foot. The god instructed him to stand where he was. Not in words. No words were uttered. And yet it happened, and so Ramon stayed where he was, rooted to the spot. The creature he had recalled from a slumber in the cellar of creation rose from the wooden box and stretched its arms wide. The face was long and stark and eternal. Snakelike nostrils flared to take in the scents of the night; the ocher eyes glittered with malice. The hairless flesh of the creature's wings blotted out the light of the candles, and Ramon stood cowed and immobile in the dark. He heard the god call.

He had to answer. He had no choice. "Lord," he whispered. "I am yours."

The barn was silent. Even the wind seemed to still. Ramon shut his eyes tight, sure that he was about to feel some crushing blow. But nothing came. He tilted his head to see the god leaning toward the table in the corner that they'd used as their altar. Where the little girl lay. The creature could smell it. The *blood*. It bent, now, as it moved toward the body, shuffling like a bat, its wings dragging the ground. The creature paused and glared at the men who stood nearby. Ramon watched as it pulled itself upon the table. He watched as the god he'd summoned chuffed and grunted, ripped skin from bone, and started to feed.

15. Ernesto

Coulter County

"What I am going to tell," said Ernesto, "may sound crazy." Lightfoot and Ernesto sat facing each other in the miner's little house. It was almost midnight, and a north wind had kicked up outside. Ernesto was boiling water for coffee. In the meantime, he took a slug of the pulque. Antonio sat on the dirt floor with his back against the west wall of the house. He pretended to study the pages of a battered Sears, Roebuck and Company catalogue, but it was clear he was listening. The kid seemed to have forgotten his grudge. Perhaps it was the sight of the ranger pawing at himself at the mouth of the cave, frantic in the dust. Maybe he figured they'd been equally embarrassed now.

Lightfoot eyed the jug. "You mind?"

"*Con calma*," cautioned Ernesto as he watched the ranger take a long pull of the liquor.

"If I wanted a wife," said Lightfoot, "I reckon I could get one."

Ernesto muttered something in Spanish.

"What's that?" said the ranger.

"I said, it's easy to get one. The hard part is when you want to give her back."

Lightfoot passed the jug back to his companion. "I take it you've been married."

"I have."

"*Mi abuela*," interrupted Antonio. "She died six years ago, and he cries about her every night. He just likes to sound macho."

Ernesto turned to glare at his grandson.

"You all can work this out later," said Lightfoot. "You want to talk about what happened back there?"

"Do you?" asked Ernesto.

"I do," said Antonio, smirking. "I never saw a ranger scared."

"You ain't never seen one mad neither." Lightfoot reached for the jug again. The pulque was a foul potion, half smoke and half poison. It was a little like swallowing a railroad spike. But he felt the muscles in his neck loosen up as a familiar warmth rose in his spine. "I'm glad to be shed of the place. I'll give you that."

"The Mayans had many gods," said Ernesto. "Like the Egyptians. One of them was a god of violence and disease."

"You mean the Mayans from a thousand years ago? The ones who died off? I did some legwork on those fellas before I left Austin. They don't get around much anymore."

Ernesto nodded. "They died off. Yes. The people wore out, but their gods did not. The Aztecs took them for their own. And when the Spanish came, the gods went away."

"Why are you telling me this?"

"Because there are those who think the gods can be brought back to life, to destroy the enemies of the children of the Maya."

"What children of the Maya?"

"*Los Indios.* The Indians. We are all descendants of the Maya, in a way. You know that Mexico is ruled by a very bad man, sí?"

"Díaz? My folks like him all right. He keeps the peace, at least."

"*Claro.* The gringos like him very much. He is fine for *los Estados Unidos.* For the French and the Germans as well. But not for *los Indios.* They are losing their farms to the foreigners Díaz does business with. The Europeans buy up the land for their ranches and orchards, and they pay their money to the government. So Díaz gets rich, and his friends get rich. The Europeans and *los Americanos* get rich. But some of those lands are Indian lands, and the Indians get *nada*. The Indians are forced to leave."

At the mention of Porfirio Díaz, Antonio seemed to be jolted by an electric shock. He tossed his hair back with a flick of his head. "He is a pig, Díaz. A greedy pig."

Lightfoot grunted companionably. "Thank you, Antonio. Turns out you're full of opinions. But what does all this have to do with . . . whatever the hell we're talking about?"

Ernesto paused to consider his words. "The Indians want many things. They want a new government—or at least a new *presidente*. They want justice. *La justicia*. But some believe this can never come by peaceful means. Some have turned to the old beliefs instead. They worship the god of shadows and darkness and ruin. The bat god. His name—I will write it for you."

Ernesto found a piece of charcoal and scrawled the name on one of the slips of paper Lightfoot had foraged from the late J. P. Kelso's satchel. Lightfoot bent forward to study it. Once the ranger sat back, Ernesto tossed the paper into the fire.

Lightfoot watched it ignite, amused to think that a grown man could be so frightened of a name that he'd written it down rather than say it aloud. His eyes focused on the little scrap of paper as it curled and darkened at the edges. It looked like a telegram.

"Wait!" he cried, bolting from his chair. "That's—"

He fell over his feet trying to get to the fire. The pulque didn't help. Lightfoot pulled the burning scrap from the flames and stomped it out with his boot. Then he picked the paper up and held it close to the lantern. Yes, a telegram. Most of it was gone now, charred beyond recognition. But at the bottom, listed as the sender of the message, was a name the ranger recognized: "Kitzinger." It hit him like a fist.

He was silent as he stared down at the blackened paper he held in his hands. When he looked up, he asked for coffee. Black. And sure enough it came, fished out of a moth-eaten burlap bag, dark as a night in hell and tasting like dirt mixed with cinders. But it worked. It sobered him up as he shuffled through the rest of the papers he'd found in the cave that held J. P. Kelso's muti-lated corpse. There were receipts for shovels and rope and tack. There was a map of Texas, two sticks of new dynamite—no crys-tallized nitroglycerine to be seen—and the first chapter of a dime novel Western, ripped from the spine of the book. At the bottom of the stack was a schedule of trains into and out of San Antonio and six pages of a handwritten letter, many years old, from some-one named Noreen in County Clare, Ireland. There was also a piece of newspaper from the *Albuquerque Record* with the head-line "Kelso Finds Gold." It was dated April 13, 1905.

The moon was low in the sky, and the night hung like a frigid blanket over Ernesto's cabin. The ranger had located at least three separate drafts of cold air. Still he sat and tried to understand the picture his instincts were painting. When he finally spoke, Antonio was just finishing up a plate of stewed beans and fried corn tortillas. His grandfather was scraping rust off his tools and wiping them down with an oily rag.

Lightfoot's voice was startling in the silence. "Ernesto, I'm going to quit beating around the bush. I got a stack of dead bodies to deal with, not to mention a little orphan gal about the size of a hackberry switch that survived a night from hell by some means I ain't quite got a handle on yet. I got a Mayan war weapon in my saddle bag and an empty cave out here in the ass-end of nowhere that the devil himself seems to know on an intimate basis. Evidently it was closed up for a long, long time before someone figured out where it was and how to open it, and there ain't as much of that someone coming out of that cave as ever went in. There were three men working with our mining grifter, Mr. Kelso, and I'm starting to get a bad feeling about them. They may be headed back south. At least, I would be if I was them, because they ain't gonna last very long in these parts. So what do they have and why do they want it? You spare me the Mayan ghost stories and we may be able to save some lives. You keep drinking that firewater, you're gonna end up choking on your own insides."

Ernesto took a last long draught and thumbed the corncob stopper back into the jug. He leaned so far forward that the ranger could smell the liquor on his breath. "It is my belief, Capitán, that they found the tomb of the god of darkness."

"Dammit, Ernesto. You say tomb. A tomb's where you put a dead body. If we're talking about a god, how could it be dead?"

The old man held his head in one hand. "The god *no es muerto*. Its physical form is . . . at rest. It is not dead."

Lightfoot blew his disgust out in a long exhalation. "So let me see if I'm following you here. The bat god is here in Texas?" Ernesto held up both hands. He glanced over to Antonio. The young man was clearly embarrassed.

"What you call Texas, yes. But remember, Capitán. This land was here long before any Anglo came along. It has had many names."

"Go back to the god."

"Sí. He was here. Buried deep beneath the earth. Sealed. Hidden."

"But now someone's found him, and they want to bring him back home. You're going to have to tell me how you know all this."

Ernesto glanced down at his ruined hands. "I have not always been a prospector. Many years ago, I too came looking for the tomb of . . . this thing."

"Good Lord. Why?"

Ernesto sniffed. "What do you know about the *Florentine Codex*?"

The ranger rocked forward on his rickety stool and placed

his sheaf of papers on the table. He reached down into his saddle bag and brought out the little red notebook Freda had given him. He'd mentioned to Freda how Major Deak Ross used his pencil like a weapon, jabbing and slashing at the paper as he listened to whoever was speaking. Freda had laughed and bought him a notepad from Otto's store, along with two sturdy Brit Boy pencils. "About as much as I know about the canals on Mars. Talk slow."

"The *Codex* is a book compiled by a Spanish priest named Bernardino de Sahagún. It was written in the Spanish and Nahuatl languages and tells everything of importance about Aztec culture and beliefs before the arrival of the Spanish."

"Fair enough. I gather the Spaniards weren't exactly gentle with their conquests."

"*Claro*. The Aztecs never recovered from their meeting with the Spanish. Smallpox and cholera took many. War took others. The rest became slaves—and so we remain, as some would say. There are twelve known books of the *Codex*. But there is also an unknown book. A volume that seemed too *extraño*—too strange—to include with the rest. The thirteenth book was a collection of prophecies, passed down from the Maya to the Aztecs. It contained stories and legends about the dark gods of those ancient peoples. The king of darkness was the bat god. The one whose name I will not say. The old tales say he was buried somewhere far away in the night lands to the north, but that he would wake up in the end times to bring death and destruction to the enemies of his people. As the Aztecs lost ground to the Spanish, the Mayan prophecies became more popular. In fact, the prophecies became something the Spanish tried to suppress so they would not become fuel for the fire of rebellion."

"They tried to hide the book?"

"Yes—the Spanish. But in particular, the priests. The Church.

They knew that just beneath the rituals of the Holy Church observed by the Indians, the old beliefs survived. In the Yucatan today, for example, old and new live side by side. God as the sun. The Virgin as the moon. And as long as these old beliefs survive, they are dangerous. Even though the priests managed to lock up or burn almost every copy of the thirteenth book, some say a copy survived. The Church knew of the legend and took it seriously. But the stories in the *Codex* were never clear enough to allow the priests to find the tomb. It took more than the Aztec stories for someone to do that. Perhaps your Kelso found a copy of the Mayan map. The real map, hidden away in the jungles for centuries. Or maybe the men who were with him found the map, or the old texts, and used *Señor* Kelso. With him they could travel north in the company of a gringo. With him their movements might not arouse interest. They might not even be noticed."

"But you were looking for the same thing."

"I was at one time. I have heard the stories. But I lost my desire. In fact, I thought it was a myth. A myth that left me a very poor man."

"And now?"

"And now I think maybe the myth was something else."

"So I gather. You think these folks found their god, Cama—"

"Do not. Please."

"And took his statue or whatever back to Mexico?"

"Not his statue. Not an image. Him."

"Him."

"Sí, Capitán. The god himself. They are trying to wake him up."

"Wake him up and do what? And how do you . . . ? What does it eat?"

"*No sé.* It is not my god. But in those days—long ago—it is said that he fed on human souls."

"Jesus. What are they trying to accomplish? What could they possibly gain from doing something like this?"

Ernesto frowned. "Death. Hatred. The blood of one people on the hands of another, and children crying in the streets. And if this god can summon others, perhaps—" The fire popped, and they all turned to watch it. "Perhaps," Ernesto continued, "the stories were right. The ones about the end of the world."

The ranger might have lost his taste for the pulque, but suddenly the old man reached for more. A lot more—and right away. Lightfoot let him drink. Hell, he'd have done it himself, but he had thinking to do. He glanced past Ernesto toward where Antonio sat, watching intently. Outside, the wind was picking up. It whistled through the chinks in Ernesto's walls like a tea kettle coming to boil. A draft stirred the flames in the little stone hearth, and shadows leaned this way and that on the walls. Lightfoot shivered as another gust of cold air reached up under his shirt.

"Antonio," said the ranger. He waited for the boy to look up. "I hear you can shoot."

16. A Social Call

Austin, October 23

"Good afternoon," said Freda, struggling to control her breathing as she entered the parlor. She had almost tripped on the stairs and come rolling into the room. That would have made for a graceful introduction. "I'm so sorry to keep you waiting."

The tall blond man before her stood up from the sofa. He was fair-skinned with green eyes and a touch of sunburn on his nose and cheeks. His wrinkled shirt and battered boots contrasted with the fine felt Stetson he'd left on the sofa. He gazed at Freda like a cat watching a mouse emerge from its hole.

"Not at all, ma'am. Not at all. I was just conversing with this delightful young thing. A Cajun princess, I believe. As pretty as the day is long."

"Annie Boudreaux," the princess said. "It was my pleasure." Nodding to Freda, she exited the room with the scent of ruin and rosewater trailing in her wake.

"If you'd rather I come back later?" asked Freda.

"Please. No. It's you I came to see. Or, rather, a particular friend of yours. But I understand Sergeant Lightfoot is not at home?"

"Oh, this isn't his home. He is here on occasion, but I'm afraid you missed him. He'll be sorry to hear that, Mr.—?"

"I beg your pardon," said the man. He ran a big hand through his hair. It was the lightest shade of blond she'd ever seen. Close to white. "Sam. Sam Millicent. Could be he's spoke of me?"

"I'm sure he has," said Freda. "But I confess, my memory's not what it used to be. How are the two of you acquainted?"

"We rangered together a few years back."

"Oh, splendid! You do have the look of a ranger about you."

"Do I now? I'll take that as a compliment, sure enough. Just as long as I no longer have the smell of a ranger about me. Horse sweat and ten-cent tobacco."

Freda felt the heat of a blush in her cheeks. She wasn't sure whether it was embarrassment at the stranger's forwardness or the first stirrings of resentment at what seemed like—did she imagine it?—the disdain in his voice. "I'm sure you two have a few stories to tell. Do you care for more coffee?"

"I'm just about coffeed up, thank you. I understand from Al Woodard that Jewel's on assignment. Is that so? The colonel wasn't clear on whether he'd left yet."

"He is indeed. On assignment, I mean. He left three days ago."

"Headed for Llano, right?"

"For Llano, I believe, and parts farther west. From what I could gather."

"Have you heard from him since he left?"

"Unfortunately, no. He's not much for telegrams."

"Or the telephone?"

Freda felt a tinge of uncertainty in some corner of her mind. Millicent? Was that it? Sam Millicent. The name didn't ring any bells. And though Jewel was tight-lipped when it came to his work, he was generally happy to talk about his friends. Al Woodard. John Nemo. Ray Lanning, rest his soul. Surely she would have heard something of this man who presented himself as Jewel's compadre. Jewel didn't have many compadres, for one thing. "Lord, I'm not sure that man knows how to use a telephone, even if he could find one out there."

Sam Millicent laughed. It seemed not so much an answer as

an offer. Would she join him in chuckling at the old-fangled ways of the little ranger? Not likely. Freda stood facing him for several moments, aware that he was looking her up and down in a manner that she found familiar and frankly offensive. She folded her arms to cover her breasts.

"Is there a message I could give him?" she asked at last.

Again with the laugh, though Freda could see nothing amusing in the situation. Millicent shook his head. "Hmm? Oh, no. No. I'd rather give him the message myself. I expect I'll see him soon. And I'd like for it to be a surprise."

17. The Bulletin

WESTERN UNION
1908 OCT 24 811 PM

FROM: COL. AL WOODARD, TEXAS RANGERS

ATTN: SHERIFFS, MILLS, LLANO, MASON, SAN SABA,
McCULLOCH, GILLESPIE, MENARD, COULTON, FAIRFIELD,
EASTER, CARNEY COUNTIES

Rangers seek 3 Mexican nats suspected murder moving SSW
from San Luis. Dark-skinned, poss. Indian. Report if seen.
Armed and dangerous. Do not approach.

18. The Stone Fort

Gillespie County, October 26

he plan was simple. Executing turned out to be a little more difficult.

A deputy sheriff in Gillespie County read Al Woodard's bulletin about the fugitives and knew he had something important to tell his boss. A local rancher named Sam Alexander had mentioned seeing the men. They looked like *hijadores*—itinerant sheep shearers—to him, but they were oddly unresponsive when Alexander offered them work crutching his flock for good cash money. He tried a second time with a higher price, but the men ignored him. It wasn't the sort of behavior a man expected from hired hands, and it struck the rancher as odd and ungrateful. Alexander passed this information on to the deputy, not thinking much of it other than as a sign of the nation's downward trajectory. The deputy proudly reported the news to the sheriff. There were three men, he said—one of them of exceptional size. They traveled with a horse and two mules that pulled a wood-wheeled cart. Sheriff A. C. Gottesman wired the information back to Austin, and Al Woodard relayed it to San Luis.

Jewel Lightfoot muttered as he read the dispatch. He'd expected the sighting farther to the west. He'd figured his suspects would head out into the parched and empty country of the Trans-Pecos, angling for the vast unpeopled borderland between Del Rio and Presidio. A man could ride for days in that region without seeing another soul. It was the logical route for anyone looking to cross the border without attracting attention. Instead the group had made slow progress, and seemed to be moving south—toward San Antonio, for some reason.

Hawley Reese asked the ranger what he made of the news as the train lurched out of Llano, but it took the ranger most of the day to answer.

"Tells me two things," Lightfoot mused as the passenger car rattled and jolted through the gently rolling countryside near Hye. This was farm country, quilted with neatly sown fields. In the middle distance, a team was harvesting wheat. Six mules pushed a McCormick header, with four of the asymmetrical wagons called barges in close proximity. He counted seven men operating the wagons and machinery, all in shirtsleeves and straw hats, their figures dwarfed by the vast swaying sea of yellow around them. Seated across from the two peace officers in the stuffy compartment, Ernesto and Antonio had seemed to be asleep. But their eyes opened when the lawmen started talking.

"First," the ranger continued, "they're moving slow. Part of that is because of what they got with 'em."

"Which is what?"

The ranger and Ernesto locked eyes.

"They found something in a dig out on the Milstead tract," said the ranger. "Let's leave it at that. So they're carrying cargo. But even so, they ain't in a hurry. That says they don't think anyone's on to them. Second, it means they've got friends in San Antonio. That or they know they can get on the IGN line to Laredo there. Now, the friend part may be a little troublesome for 'em, seeing as how a whole passel of socialist hotheads just got themselves rounded up by the law last week. That may be the bunch our boys was hoping to meet up with. But the train is still a problem. They get on the IGN, and they're at the border just a few hours later. And once they're over the border, they're home free. Them *federales* catch us trying to track fugitives in Coahuila, they're liable to throw us in prison before we can spit, and a Mexican prison ain't no place to bring a picnic. Either way, we need to stop our boys from getting anywhere close to the Alamo. That make sense to you, Ernesto?"

The old man nodded. The ranger and the tall Anglo stared at him. "*Claro*," he said. "They need to get back across *el Bravo*. As you say, the Rio Grande."

The sheriff pulled his canvas rifle case down from the overhead compartment and produced a rag from the side pocket of his valise. This was by now a familiar operation to the men who sat watching. Hawley Reese's gun was going to be the cleanest firearm in Texas by the time they made it to Fredericksburg.

"That," he announced, "ain't gonna happen."

Antonio rolled his eyes. It was clear to Lightfoot that the boy disliked the sheriff, who, for his part, preferred not to address either Antonio or his grandfather directly. But the kid knew not to complain. He was here on sufferance of the ranger, who'd brought him along because he spoke Spanish fluently and could handle a rifle, skills that might be needed if they caught up with the men they were seeking. Ernesto had insisted on coming as well. Antonio had resisted, but his grandfather swore his motives had nothing to do with playing nursemaid to a young man who he knew wouldn't listen to a word he said. Finally the ranger had shrugged and bought him a ticket on the train as well even though the old man never clearly stated why he wanted to go with them. Mexicans weren't welcome in the passenger cars of Texas trains, but Lightfoot didn't particularly care. He stared down all challenges from the drummers and stockmen he passed as he ushered his companions to their berth, and he slammed the door shut behind them.

Lightfoot had mixed feelings about the sheriff of Coulter County. He talked too much, and the ranger generally disliked talkative men, though he found the trait endearing in women. He had a halting, high-pitched laugh that sounded like maybe the sheriff hadn't quite learned how to produce the normal expression of mirth and was still practicing. Or maybe he just hadn't laughed much lately; there was a woman in the picture, a wife, the ranger gathered, but she was no longer in San Luis, and Reese hadn't volunteered any information as to why. Mostly what Lightfoot thought about the sheriff was that it was painful to see a man so set on becoming something he didn't really want. The ranger had met individuals like Reese before. He was smart enough, and he seemed to know his job. But he had a mixed-up notion of what being a ranger was all about. He'd heard the stories, and maybe seen a lurid lithograph or two, and so on quiet afternoons when it was too hot for the dogs to bark, he pictured himself riding some lonely high-country trail in search of murderous Kiowas or a gang of renegade bandits. There would be rain dripping down off of the brim of his hat and wolves howling all around him at night, but the ranger would slowly gain on his quarry. Eventually he'd force the bad men into a final symphonic shootout and walk out of the smoke and dust as the victor—to the surprise of no one, since the Texas Rangers always won these fights.

But of course, the reality was different, and never quite as glamorous as some chicken-necked newspaperman imagined while drinking watered-down rotgut in a tenement building somewhere in Brooklyn. The reality was poor pay, shoddy accommodations, and an over-familiarity with the Texas climate, which could go from barely tolerable to homicidal in the course of an afternoon's ride. Lightfoot himself had spent more time wrangling with lawyers and legislators than he ever had with dangerous desperadoes, and he'd once wasted two weeks trying to prove up the contents of a request for expenses he'd submitted while working the Monk Gibson case. Everyone wanted a ranger when there was trouble, but there weren't a lot of party invites when things were peaceful. So much for symphonic shootouts.

But try telling all this to a man like Hawley Reese. The more you mentioned the hardships and risks and pitiful recompense, the better the job sounded to someone who'd never experienced it. He was a decent sort, Sheriff Reese. It seemed like he knew his people and was good at what he did. The ranger didn't blame the man for having some of the same delusions he himself had harbored when he was young and foolish. But Lightfoot couldn't help feeling that Hawley Reese should have sent a deputy and stayed home in Coulter County, waving to widows and engaging in serious consultation with the mayor of San Luis about the worrisome rise in coyote sightings.

The ranger sniffed, as if to dismiss such thoughts. Not his lookout, he told himself. *I've got enough to worry about on my own.* Or maybe not worry about. Just figure out. The rest of his life, for example. Here was the thing about Freda Mikulska. She wasn't prettier than other girls. Hell, she wasn't a girl, when you came right down to it. She wasn't younger or prettier or richer than other women. She was just Freda. She could cook a little, if you gave her some time and a fair amount of cast iron. She kept a clean house, though she wasn't overly concerned how her blankets lay or her curtains hung. She was busier than the average woman, and Jewel had heard tell, without either believing or disbelieving, since neither was called for, that she could read a ledger like a parson reads a prayer book. But that wasn't what kept him with Freda. What kept him with Freda was the night they'd ventured out to attend a revival of *One Night in Chinatown* at the Paramount. Jewel had promised Freda his full attention. The only previous time they'd visited the theatre, they'd seen a touring production of *The Black Crook*, one of New York City's most famous shows, which neither of them knew had a running time of just over five hours. He'd grown restless not long after the dancing sylphs, clad only in flesh-colored body stockings, carried the protagonist off to their forest lair to enchant and beguile him and whatnot. By Act Three, just past ten p.m., the body stockings were a distant memory and Lightfoot was feeling downright cantankerous. Freda wasn't entirely pleased by the running time, either, but she at least managed to sit still like a grown-up and not groan every time a song started. The ranger's bad behavior was the subject of contention for a month afterward, though now they could usually laugh about it. Hoping to soothe any remaining hard feelings, Lightfoot had promised to enjoy himself at the theatre this time and to make pleasant conversation if called upon to do so, even if it was with a man with moist hands or with whom he was not previously acquainted.

They set out at seven. They'd made it just a few steps when they heard a cry of distress from the alley behind the carriage house. There they found a Negro boy lying faceup in the mud. His mount, a fractious old plow horse, blind in one eye, stood a few yards down the narrow path, looking frightened and guilty. Lightfoot went to fetch the animal. It took him three tries. When he returned, leading the mare behind him, he found Freda splayed out in the wet alley beside the kid, the skirt of her new taffeta dress parasoled out around her like a giant lily pad. She was holding the boy's hand and reassuring him as he tried not to cry.

"Horse saw a rat and pitched him right off," she said. Freda was no great admirer of horses. She gave the creature a look that could have curdled milk. "Shame on you. It looks like he broke his leg."

The ranger was puzzled by what he saw. Freda was a fastidious woman, known for her insistence on cleanliness in her employees and associates. What had compelled her to set herself down in the muck of this back alley to comfort a little boy?

Lightfoot struck a match and leaned down for a better look. He pursed his lips. "It's broke all right. Bone's poked plumb through the skin. See?"

"Jewel!" Freda hissed.

"What?"

"Do you mind?"

The boy stared up at Lightfoot through his injury, breathing heavily through his mouth, his eyes wide with pain. He wasn't even a teenager yet. The ranger wondered why the kid might have been riding through the back alleys of west Austin at night when the streets in this part of town were clear, graded, and at least dimly lit. He didn't have anything against the boy. Jewel Lightfoot wasn't a race-baiter. When he was a kid—younger than this one, in fact—he and his mother had been kept alive by furtive donations from two families nearby, one of them Negro. His stepfather would have killed everyone concerned had he known his young wife and stepson were taking charity, but it was true. A colored woman named Calliope left greens, sweet potatoes, and occasionally even a fresh-shot possum on their back porch when Jewel's stepfather was away. Jewel was too young to be proud. His mother was too poor. And they were both too hungry to feel anything but grateful. On the other hand, Lightfoot didn't have much sympathy for the broke-legged ten-year-old in front of him. A man who couldn't handle his horse was going to get thrown sooner or later. Best to do it in town, where the odds were better someone might find you afterward.

"He was bringing his mama some supper," said Freda, almost as if she'd read his mind. "She's helping Mrs. Mallory with her daughter's confinement."

"Supper, huh?"

"Don't you dare start asking questions," snapped Freda. "This boy needs a doctor. Go get Collins. He's in that big house on West with the red door. Two blocks south, I think. He'll come."

Eric Collins was one of Austin's best physicians, a prominent Methodist and sometime visitor to the Mercantile, especially when his wife was up north visiting family. Sure enough, when the ranger asked, the doctor fetched his medical bag and followed Lightfoot back to the alley. He made arrangements to have the kid—Mose, his name was—transported to the colored hospital on East Pecan. He even followed him there, riding the one-eyed horse.

Lightfoot wondered about this occasion more often than he could understand. It turned out Freda hadn't known the kid. Hadn't known a thing about him. She hadn't wanted to get her dress dirty, either. But the boy was hurt. And after all, it was only mud.

"And manure," Lightfoot noted.

He wasn't expecting a response to that observation, but it came anyway, from somewhere far away.

"Captain," said the sheriff.

"Hmm?" answered the ranger, wincing at the sunlight streaming through the window. He realized he'd been asleep.

Hawley Reese grinned. "We're here."

Provisioning for four was a little more complicated than it was for one, and Lightfoot had grown unaccustomed to the task. Indeed, for a moment he found himself wishing he'd brought Freda along to attend to such details. Freda was a top hand for planning. At times the ranger wondered if she actually thought in numbers. He got out his notebook and pencil to make a list, but he soon grew bored with ciphering and reverted to pointing and rough estimates instead. He spent almost nine dollars on bacon and beans, flour, butter, coffee, and salt for a week's scout. Ernesto was fine with a mule, but Antonio insisted on a horse and was picky to boot. In the end, Lightfoot was annoyed to realize that the boy's gelding was easily the equal of the bay mare he'd picked out and the older, larger gelding Reese favored. They left Fredericksburg just before noon the day after they arrived and set out to find the spot where Sam Alexander had encountered the fugitives two days before.

The ranger was a careful tracker and seemed to move forward only when no other direction would do. They picked up the trail not long after they started, and the next afternoon they found the fugitives twenty miles north of town in green, unsettled country. On October 28—a temperate evening, unusually humid—they saw firelight flickering in the ruins of an old stone fort that stood on a bluff overlooking Mission Creek. There was more stone than fort. In fact, only two walls and half the façade of the structure still stood, and even these remnants were considerably diminished. A good part of the edifice had been pulled down and hauled off over the years by the industrious German settlers who lived in this country and used the stone to build their homes and barns.

Lightfoot crept close enough to verify that these were the men he was looking for. When he returned to the group, the ranger sent Ernesto and his grandson back across the ridge they'd just crossed. They'd watch the animals, he said, while he and the sheriff made the arrests. Antonio protested. He kicked up a cloud of dust and rocks at one point, but the ranger was in no mood for discussion, and finally the boy and his grandfather relented.

"*Cuidado*, Capitán," said Ernesto. "I know you doubt me, as perhaps I would do if I was in your place. But these men are dangerous. Believe me. And the thing they travel with is more dangerous still."

Ordinarily the ranger would have dismissed the old man's warning with a barely perceptible shrug. With his experience in the cave still fresh in his mind, though, he was less cavalier. He nudged the barrel of the sheriff's rifle downward with two fingers. "I'll bear that in mind. We're going to sit and wait until that campfire goes out before we go in. With any luck, they're passing around a bottle right now and convincing themselves they're home free. Sheriff, you hold your fire till I either say so or start shooting first. If I'm going to get shot tonight, I'd rather it not be by my own man."

Ernesto scraped the back of one hand against the stubble on his cheek.

"Say it," said the ranger.

"It seems . . . it seems too easy, maybe?"

"It ain't never easy. But I've done this before. Men don't fight so good when they're asleep. I'll fire my sidearm twice when it's safe to come up. We'll need a hand getting these hombres trussed up. Got it?"

"Sí. I understand." The old man had to search for the words. "*Buena suerte.*"

"We don't need luck," said the sheriff, brandishing his rifle. "We got these."

Lightfoot and Reese advanced the half mile to the fort on foot. When they had closed to within a hundred yards, the ranger instructed Reese to take up a position on the north side of the clearing in front of the structure, situating the sheriff in such a way that both men had clear lines of fire toward the ruins, with little chance of hitting each other. Then he settled down behind a scrubby live oak with his Winchester cradled in his arms. He knew not to focus on the campfire. That was a good way to nod off—and to make yourself night-blind before you did. The plan was to wait until an hour had passed after the fugitives' fire went out. The men would be asleep, and possibly drunk, and he and the sheriff would take their quarry without a fight. But the wait took longer than expected. A late wind picked up, and the sky grew cloudy. That wasn't going to help matters, he realized. They needed to move. But when the ranger signaled to Reese to advance, around midnight, the sheriff didn't respond.

Lightfoot hooted again.

Nothing.

His knees ached when he stood. He took a step forward, moving cautiously in the dry autumn grass. The sheriff had probably fallen asleep. The ranger weighed the risks of crossing the clearing to investigate. It would be quicker, and probably quieter as well, but the night was so dark that he might trip and fall, or step on something and give away his movements. The better plan would be to retreat and then circle around the clearing through the brush that ringed it.

"Goddammit!" he muttered. "Give a man a simple job . . ."

Lightfoot started walking, retracing his route through the tangled mesquite and cedar trees. He heard a sharp whistle from off to his right. Before he could tell himself something was wrong, that he ought not to be looking toward where the whistle had come from, he felt a blow to the back of his head. He was dimly aware of stars spiraling around in the sky as he fell. The ground rushed up to meet him, and the world went black.

19. The View from Above

Washington, D.C., October 28

"Looking a bit down in the mouth today, March," Roger Fellowes said to his assistant. "All right?"

"Fine, sir, thank you. Just sifting through the cables. Some rather interesting communications today between our German friends and their consul in Mexico."

"Indeed? How so?"

"Interesting in their persistence. I mentioned recently the troop of Mexican cavalry sent north to recover some sort of contraband being transported from Texas."

"You did?"

"Indeed. With the airship?"

Roger Fellowes stroked his fine moustache. "Ah, yes. The flying egg. What news?"

"Nothing as yet. But as you know, both the Germans and the Latins are keen to acquire whatever's being brought south. Their efforts seem to be focused on an individual named Ramon Garcia Marquez. Our sources say he's Mayan, and evidently is or was an officer in the militia of Chan Santa Cruz, the Mayan republic that Díaz's army recently crushed. Marquez was captured, probably tortured, but later escaped. He's now one of Mexico's most wanted men. Fancies himself a prophet—sort of a Mesoamerican druid. Very dangerous. He's the one believed to be in possession of this treasure."

"Though we don't know what that might be."

"No. They're being very tight-lipped about it. Even for the Germans."

"Interesting. Better keep informed, then. No good can come from the Gothic influence in Mexico, Zeppelins or no. Are we in agreement?"

"Quite."

"Not that you should mention this to the ambassador, you know. Not yet, anyway."

"I'm aware of the ambassador's fondness for our northern friends. Teutonic freedom and all that. Germany, Britain, and the United States all living in harmony. I shan't trouble him with rumors and sketchy intelligence."

"Good man, March. I only hope he's right."

"Right? About what, sir?"

"About the Hun. I wonder, sometimes. Their navy is almost as big as ours these days, as they're fond of reminding us, and their army is considerably bigger. Do they not seem a bit pushy?"

March nodded. "You mean in Africa. Well, perhaps they're jealous."

"I'm sure they are. Everyone's jealous of Britain. Cain was jealous of Abel, March. No good came of that."

20. The God Revealed

Gillespie County

Darkness. Confusion. An ache like an angry black planet revolving in his head, grinding against the bone of his skull.

Lightfoot woke with his hands tied behind his back and blood caked in his hair. A rag was stuffed in his mouth, and he found it difficult to breathe without feeling like he was going to vomit. After he'd regained some semblance of consciousness, he became aware of the voices. He heard English and occasional Spanish, but he was puzzled by the words and rhythm of a tongue he'd never encountered before. He could tell he'd been insensible for some time. A cold wind was blowing from the northwest, and the moon was nowhere to be seen. The ranger worked up the strength to roll over. When he did, he came to rest directly in front of Hawley Reese. Blood masked the right side of the sheriff's face.

"Reese!" said the ranger. Muffled by the rag, his voice was just a sequence of unintelligible sounds. "Wake up!"

No answer. The man was out cold. It was hard to tell if he was even breathing. Lightfoot stretched his neck to one side and managed to catch a corner of his gag on the ground. He scooted himself away from Reese's body and worked his head back and forth. Spitting and dragging the cloth on the stony ground, he eased the gag out of his mouth and filled his lungs with air. He felt like he'd been hit by a streetcar. His head was throbbing and he wanted to rest, but he knew any slumber he allowed himself tonight was liable to be his last. *Think*, he told himself. He tried to conjure up a picture of his situation. He was lying between the supine body of Hawley Reese and the last stones of a low wall. The voices he'd heard were coming from just a few feet away. He could see the glow of a fire and smell the smoke. He couldn't see it well from here, but if he pushed himself just a little farther back, he'd be able to touch the wall and get a look at the men who had captured him. Not too fast, though. They probably thought he was dead. And hell, they weren't far off.

There was a fire all right. It seemed to be burning brighter than when he'd first regained consciousness. Lightfoot counted three figures on the far side of the blaze. His fugitives, he reckoned. The leader of the group was a slender, shirtless individual with a hank of long dark hair. He didn't say much, but then again he didn't have to. Whenever he spoke, the two men with him sprang to obey his directives. His chief lieutenant was a giant whose coarse hair, cut short, rose in a burr above his head. Even from this poor vantage point, Lightfoot could see that the man's two front teeth were gold. Periodically, he held what looked to be another macahuitl—all black, like the specimen Lightfoot had in his saddle bag—up in the firelight and examined the blades that lined its edges. A third figure, scrawny and unkempt, with a jade ornament pinned in his left ear, looked to be the junior man in the outfit. He was the one who gathered firewood and did chores for the other two. The big man grunted instructions—or, more properly, relayed instructions, since the long-haired leader was their source—and the little fellow scurried to carry them out.

More curious were the white men who sat on the near side of the fire. There was something familiar about the biggest of them, but it took Lightfoot several minutes before he made the connection, and then only because the figure turned to look over at him.

A chill ran up his spine. Even in the dim light of the dancing flames, he knew those eyes.

Sam Millicent.

Lightfoot tried to clear his head. Millicent had made his name as the best horseman on the force. He'd done good work in the Milam County War that left six men dead in 1901, but he'd never been one to follow orders, on account of which he'd never qualified for promotion. He was clever and ambitious but restless, constantly getting himself into minor scrapes and frequently just a step ahead of a jealous husband or spurned lover. He'd been drummed out of Company B for theft in 1905 and made his living since as a gun for hire. In March of 1907 he'd killed Lightfoot's friend Ray Lanning in Nogales, putting two slugs through Ray's forehead as he stepped out of the general store with a bag of Arbuckle's coffee in one arm and a can of beans in the other. The Rangers—Lightfoot in particular—had been looking for Millicent ever since. Lightfoot had missed him twice. The first time was in San Antonio, when he'd been tipped off by a newspaper editor who told him Millicent could be found at the Menger Hotel. By the time the ranger got there, Millicent had fled, apparently to avoid a gambling debt.

More recently, Lightfoot had traveled to Del Rio on a tip from an anonymous informant, who wrote to headquarters alleging Millicent had carried out the assassination of a local rancher on behalf of a client who'd wanted the rancher's wife and his land, though not necessarily in that order. This time the ranger missed his quarry by a matter of days. Lightfoot had detoured to Piedras Blancas on his way back to Austin, tried to drink his frustrations into submission, and wound up with three young men lying on a dusty street around him. Three young men he'd never seen before but now talked to most nights in his dreams. Three young men who'd known, somehow, where he'd be that evening in Piedras

In The Land of Dead Horses   149

Blancas, and in what condition. Lightfoot pondered the matter. He was sickened by the sudden suspicion—no, the sudden
conviction—that it was Millicent who'd ambushed him and
delivered him, bound and beaten, to the fugitives he was tracking. Maybe not Millicent himself. He had two men with him.
But Millicent was behind it. Of this the ranger had no doubt.

He could barely hear the conversation at the campfire and
had no idea what it concerned. As best he could tell, though,
Millicent had gone from asking to demanding. Lightfoot had
involved himself in a number of negotiations with hostile parties
over the years. He didn't enjoy the process, but he knew how it
worked. Demanding was never a good position to be in.

"I'll say it one more time," said Millicent, raising his voice.
"It's very simple. You have an item that belongs to my employer.
I'm willing to buy it from you. But make no mistake, Ramon. I
will take it, if need be."

The fugitives let the one Millicent called Ramon—their leader—
do their talking. His big lieutenant looked on impassively, as if the
conversation taking place was village gossip. When the skinny man
returned to the fireside, he stooped to whisper in the big fellow's
ear. He was promptly sent out again on some new errand.

"You are interfering," said Ramon, "in affairs you cannot possibly understand. We have nothing that belongs to you, gringo."

"Oh, I suspect you do. You have that box—that coffin, is what
it looks like from here. My employer paid a man named Kelso to
find and recover the contents of a burial site sixty miles north of
here. Kelso's done disappeared, and y'all are headed south with
something I'm guessing you didn't have when you started. That
makes you thieves, in my book. Mexican bandits. And Mexican
bandits don't last long in these parts. I've offered you guns. I've
offered you cash. Hell, I've even given you captives. Now I need
you to make a decision."

"*Señor, escúchame.* We are not thieves. What we have does not belong in a white man's museum. It belongs to our people, and that is where it's going. Back to our people."

"Horse shit. Whatever it is, it don't belong to you, because you're sneaking around out here in the ass-end of nowhere with it, hoping the law don't find you before you get home to frijole land."

Ramon picked up a handful of sand and filtered it through his fingers. He pointed with his chin toward where Jewel Lightfoot and Hawley Reese lay bound, thirty feet away. "Tell me again. Why do you bring me these men?"

"I didn't bring 'em. They were out there watching you. Waiting for you all to fall asleep, most like. Then they would have snuck in and slit your throats. I did you a favor."

"We didn't ask for a favor. Why give them up? Your own people."

Millicent glanced over at Lightfoot. "Let's just say my employer don't like one of 'em. And I ain't so partial to him myself. The short one, with the powder burn on his cheek. He's dangerous. Don't underestimate him."

"He is a warrior?"

Millicent grunted. "He's a ranger."

Damn straight, thought Lightfoot. He'd located a flat sharp rock and was trying to get it situated in his fingers. There was a pause in the conversation, and the ranger shut his eyes. Had they seen his movements? Were they coming to stop him?

"You want what we found in the cavern, sí?"

"Exactly. Whatever was in the cavern. You need to make a decision."

"And if my decision is no?"

Millicent inhaled loudly. The little fire crackled and hissed. "Then my man in the hills puts a lead slug in your skull."

"Your man in the hills," said Ramon. There was a hint of amusement in his voice.

"You want a demonstration?"

Ramon shrugged. "Do you?"

"What's that supposed to mean?"

"Norberto!" Ramon called out.

"Sí?"

Millicent and his companions turned to try to locate the source of the voice.

"You found him?" said Ramon.

"I did."

"Step forward."

The scrawny man advanced into the circle of firelight. In one hand, suspended by a hank of dark hair, he held a severed human head. He tossed the grisly trophy toward the men sitting around the fire.

Millicent's sniper, thought Lightfoot. What else would explain the stunned silence?

Ramon nodded gravely. "You're not looking for a box, gringo. You're looking for what's inside the box. And that is something you can never possess. We will give you nothing. In fact, since you are here, you will give to us. Look closely, unbelievers. It lives."

Whatever the men saw, it stood just beyond Lightfoot's field of vision. But it was clearly something unexpected. And unpleasant. The ranger could sense it. Even struggling with the pain in his head and his wrists, he felt a darkness descend on the ruins of the fort, a darkness that wasn't the absence of light alone but rather some tangible manifestation of evil and confusion. The air grew cold, as if the night had stooped to gather them in, to crush them in its black embrace. From the heavens a whirlwind of bats swept through the ruined fort, their wings roaring like a waterfall in the sky. No. Not *bats*. Leaves caught up in the wind. A breeze like the breath of death swept across the clearing dominated by the ruined fort, and from somewhere to the north came the muffled boom of thunder. Lightfoot smelled rain. He tried to decide if this was good or bad, if it would be a help or a hindrance. He heard the shriek of something unholy and obscene and squeezed his eyes shut. He opened them to see Sam Millicent staring with his mouth agape as the gale suddenly ceased.

"Jesus," said Millicent. He reached for his gun.

That's when the skinny man reappeared in the circle of firelight and plunged a knife into the base of Sam Millicent's neck. The big Mexican—the one who'd been sitting next to the leader— leapt to his feet. He hurdled the flames and struck the closest of Millicent's companions with the black macahuitl. The man's head rocked back on his shoulders, held only by the soft skin at the nape of his neck, as he slumped to one side. The third man was so startled that he couldn't free his pistol from its holster. Norberto was on him quickly. He cradled the man's skull, lifted his chin, and drew his slender blade across his throat. Blood spurted in great rhythmic gouts from the wound, hissing as it hit the flames. Millicent tried to stand, but Paco brought the club down flat on the back of his skull, and the man fell and lay still.

Ramon sat motionless as the mayhem raged around him, apparently indifferent, gazing into the fire with his glittering dark eyes. It was as if he knew the outcome of the fight already. As if he'd seen it in a dream. Finished with their butchery, the fugitives crouched and gazed up into the surrounding hills, likely wondering if there was another gunman hiding somewhere in the brush. But no shot rang out, and eventually the killers went back about their business. First they examined the men they'd attacked. Millicent, it seemed, was still alive. His hands were tied behind his back, and he was half dragged, half carried over to where Lightfoot and the sheriff lay.

The ranger's instincts shrieked in protest at the sensation of being helpless in such close proximity to the enemy. He'd seen the mutilated corpse of John Patrick Kelso, and he had a bad feeling about what was to come next. His legs were free. He knew he could stand up and run if he wanted. But how far would he get with his hands tied behind his back? It was better to stay still. Better to solve the problem than just delay the result. The little stone he'd picked up wasn't working. But then he realized a better solution might be within reach. He shoved himself backward another few inches. *There*. He could feel it. This portion of the wall was uneven, and the protruding surface was just sharp enough that it might work. A raindrop bounced off his forehead, and thunder rumbled through the little valley. It had to work. He started on the rope.

"Lightfoot," Millicent whispered. The ranger ignored him. "Hey! Lightfoot. Look here."

"Shut up."

"We need to work together, amigo. You almost loose?"

"The hell we do."

"Goddammit, Lightfoot. You ain't thinking right. You didn't see what I saw. Don't leave me here with that thing."

"I'm thinking just fine. Now close your mouth before you get us both killed."

Millicent scoffed. "Idiot. Don't say I didn't try."

"I could say a whole lot of things about you, Millicent, but that ain't one of 'em. You killed Ray Lanning, you sonofabitch. And if we get out of here alive, I'm coming for you. Count on it."

"That's how you want it, huh?"

"Got nothing to do with *want*. That's how it is."

"I'll remember that."

"Yeah. See that you do."

Half an hour later, Paco and Norberto seized Hawley Reese by his ankles and dragged him toward the fire, his face bouncing off weeds and stones as he went. The sheriff was still apparently unconscious, but as the men laid him on his back on a long, flat rock, he uttered a high-pitched moan, as if he sensed his peril.

Ramon had transformed himself. He was no longer an itinerant laborer. He was a priest. He'd daubed his face with stripes of red and blue and black. He'd donned a headdress fashioned of jade and turquoise, with a tuft of bright blue feathers and what looked to be swaths of a jaguar pelt hanging from the back. He drew a stone-bladed dagger from the scabbard at his waist and held it up for his companions to observe. The weapon was ten inches long. Its handle was shaped like a question mark. The wind was fiercer now, and a bolt of lightning struck a tree only a few hundred yards away, splitting the night with its detonation and sizzle. Ramon spoke for almost a minute in a language Lightfoot couldn't comprehend, and the words came faster as he proceeded. His companions voiced the last several phrases with him. He finished with something that sounded like a wail, and Paco and Norberto sang out in response.

The priest raised his knife in both hands. He glanced toward the heavens as if seeking command or confirmation from some source beyond the earth. Sure enough, another tongue of lightning snaked through the clouds, and Ramon slammed the blade into Hawley Reese's belly. The sheriff screamed—an eerie, hysterical sound, rendered even stranger by the fact that he never moved. Ramon made a long, straight cut toward the sternum, then straightened and handed the dripping blade to Paco. He plunged his right hand under the rib cage and into the sheriff's chest and yanked out Hawley Reese's heart. Then, oddly, the priest turned. He held the steaming organ toward something Lightfoot couldn't see. At least at first.

As the ranger watched, a piece of the darkness separated itself from the shadows and crawled out from a corner of the old fort. It was neither man nor beast but a creature in between, monstrous in aspect and uncatalogued in any inventory of the animate known to Lightfoot. It approached the spot where Ramon stood, pausing to sniff at the air and the earth around it, slowly surveying the faces in its immediate vicinity. Finally, it craned its misshapen neck forward and allowed Ramon to squeeze the fluids from Hawley Reese's severed heart into its gaping mouth. When the organ was drained of blood, the creature crawled forward, pulled itself up onto the stone, and mounted the sheriff's corpse. It bent its head to the gaping cavity in the dead man's abdomen, rooting in the body for the sustenance it held. Lightfoot heard grunts of satisfaction and the clicks of the night thing's teeth, heard flesh being separated from bone as the creature fed. It sounded like pages being torn from a very old book.

The ranger might have missed a portion of the grisly ceremony at this point. The rain was coming in spurts, and he was concentrating on the ropes that held his wrists, scraping them harder against the ridge of rock in the wall behind him. He was making progress. He could feel it. Just another minute. That was all he needed.

But no. They were here.

Paco and Norberto bent to take Sam Millicent. Before they could move him, though, the blond man spat.

"Fucking bean-eaters," he hissed. "Take the ranger! He's almost through his ropes."

The Mexicans paused to consider this information. Norberto reached out a foot and kicked Lightfoot over onto his belly.

"¡Chingón!" he said. "El tiene recho."

"I told you," Millicent added, his gaze meeting Lightfoot's. "He's a snake. Let me up, and I'll gut him for you."

"Shut up, güero," said Norberto, grinning through his wispy moustache. He and Paco hoisted the ranger to his feet. "You're dead already."

"Then I'll see you in hell," said Millicent.

Lightfoot couldn't resist. He lunged sideways and managed to plant a boot in Sam Millicent's ribs. Paco and Norberto laughed as they manhandled the ranger over to the same flat rock where Hawley Reese had lain. Lightfoot only had a moment to wonder what had happened to the sheriff before he saw him lying on the earth a few feet away, gutted like an animal. Whatever foul thing had feasted on him was gone. It might have been nearby, but the rain was intensifying by the minute and there was nothing to be seen in the immediate vicinity but cold stone, dead bodies, and the killers who gathered around him.

Lightfoot kicked as hard as he could. All he got for his effort was one of Paco's fists to his face. The big man held his legs—lay on them, really, to keep them still—as Norberto seized the ranger by the hair. Ramon loomed above him, uttering the same glottal pronouncements he'd spoken before in a language clawed from the earth like a pupal insect and, to the ranger's ears, as ugly and repugnant. He was still wearing the headdress and bizarre mask, but the pigments were smeared from the rain and the colors were mixed and blurred like an insane man's attempt at painting life and death in some obscene embrace. Lightfoot swore to himself. He wasn't in hell yet, but he figured he was in the neighborhood. Ramon tore the ranger's waistcoat open. Then his shirt. He fingered the ruby ring the lawman wore on a chain around his neck, and then the stone knife went to a spot just below Lightfoot's rib cage.

The ranger focused his gaze on the swirling lines of rain above him. What was it the professor had said about obsidian? Sharper than any man-made blade. At least it would be quick. Lightfoot poured every ounce of his will into the task of remaining silent. He refused to beg. He wasn't going to die ugly. He didn't have much to be proud of in his crook-legged life, but he had his own cussedness still, and his death wasn't going to give anyone a reason for sport. He felt the chill of stone on the skin of his belly and closed his eyes until it all went away.

That's when the shot rang out. A bullet ricocheted off the ruined wall just a few feet behind them.

Lightfoot guessed Millicent had another gunman up in the hills. He'd finally worked up the nerve to fire.

Ramon met Lightfoot's gaze for just a moment before the priest snarled and ran for cover.

The ranger was nobody's fool. He knew he was a dead man given a chance to live again. He worked the rope that bound his wrists as hard as he could against the stone beneath him. Another round whined overhead. Norberto dove behind a portion of the stone wall. Paco grabbed a shotgun from the corpse of one of Millicent's men and pointed it out into the rain.

A voice called from out of the trees that surrounded the ruins. "Put down your weapons! You don't have to die!"

It was Antonio Ramos.

Lightfoot broke through the rope. He rolled himself off the stone, gathered his legs beneath him, and reeled off toward the southwest wall of the fort. A gust of wind caught him as he pulled himself up on the rock wall and he slipped off the far side, twisting his knee as he landed awkwardly on the uneven ground below.

Beyond the confines of the fort, the clearing dropped off into a ravine that cut a ragged groove in the earth heading north-west. Lightfoot ducked as another bullet ricocheted off the stone behind him. He cocked his head, listening for movement, and realized the round hadn't been meant for him. It was intended for Norberto, who had broken cover and was now moving toward him while holding what looked like a musical instrument—a flute, maybe?—in one hand.

In a flash of lightning Lightfoot saw something indistinct and unknowable spread its wings as it stared at him from its perch atop the corner of the two remaining walls of the fort. In the murky half-light, it looked like a gargoyle had crept down off the parapets of some ancient church and taken up residence in this lonely place. If this was the thing Ramon had taken from the sarcophagus back in San Luis, it had grown. The torso was at least human in size, and its wings now stretched ten feet from tip to tip. Its features were wolfish, with a grotesquely elongated lower jaw and a turned-up, batlike nose. Through the silver curtain of the storm, the creature's close-set dark eyes gleamed with aggression or intelligence or maybe a combination of the two, and its lips curled in a snarl to reveal a set of long canine teeth. Its mouth was smeared red from consumption of the bloody mass of organ and tissue clutched in its clawed hands. It was a monstrous dream made real, or surreal, a demon from a medieval nightmare.

If not for the adrenaline flooding his bloodstream, Lightfoot might have stopped where he was, so intense was the creature's gaze. It seemed to command obedience. No. More than obedience. Worship. But the ranger wasn't the worshipping type. Some internal voice was shouting warnings to his brain, and finally he heard it. Lightfoot shook—literally shook, as his body convulsed with the effort—the visions out of his head. He was vaguely aware of Norberto raising the pipe he held to his lips. The next instant, the ranger felt a sharp pain in the left side of his neck. A dart, he realized. He'd been hit by a goddamned dart—like the headhunters used in the novels. *Murder in Bolivia. Lost Gold of the Incas. Dead Lawman of the Hill Country.*

He slid down the slope of the ravine, clawing the feathered object out of the flesh of his neck as he descended. Warm blood rushed from the wound. The damn thing must have punctured a vein. He could hear Norberto's yips of excitement close behind him, like the cries of a dog on a scent, closer with each second.

Instinctively, he crouched, and the little man went tumbling over his shoulder. The ranger lifted his boot and brought it down on Norberto's face, snapping his nose with an audible crunch of cartilage. He leaned down, plucked the knife from Norberto's hand, and barely avoided the swing of Paco's macahuitl. He heard the whoosh of the toothed blade as it missed his head. The momentum of the swing carried Paco forward over a little ledge, and he landed in the mud a few feet down the slope, cursing loudly.

The ranger didn't like to run, but he could do it when he had to. Now, for instance. His knee was throbbing, but it still worked. He stumbled off at an angle from his pursuers, first to the bottom of the ravine, already boiling with runoff, and then back up the opposite slope, grabbing bushes and small trees to pull himself forward where the earth was steepest. He stopped when he reached level ground again, his chest heaving with pain and exertion. He thought for a moment his pursuers had given up. But no. He could hear them down below, shouting in their odd dialect, making their way up the wall of the ravine toward him.

Lightfoot was hungry, thirsty, and tired. His breath came in great ragged gulps. His knee ached, and his hand went reflexively to the spot where the dart had pierced his flesh. He felt dizzy, and not just because of the earlier blow to his head. He realized the dart had been treated with some substance that was draining the sense right out of his skull. He wondered if the game was up. He wondered if he was dying, if every step was his last. Part of him did, anyway. The other part was concerned with one thing only: survival. His brain was singing an opera with a single note and a succession of surging, frantic words. "Run," it said. "Move. Go. NOW!"

21. The Rock

Enchanted Rock rose from the earth like the crown of a giant skull, its several hundred acres of rose-white granite glowing like a ghost against the empty sky and the dark hues of the cedar and snakeweed that encircled its base. It was a sacred place, revered for years beyond counting by the people who lived in this harsh land as home to spirits of uncertain disposition, strange figures in seeming half human and half moonlight who rose silent from the rock to gaze out over the hundred miles of Hill Country spread before them. These shimmering specters offered no commerce to those who came to visit and who left offerings—feathers, blankets, turquoise beads—in small hollows in the stone but neither was there outright hostility. Rather the small clan of covert beings cared for itself only and for the rituals it practiced to keep the world in place, though it was not necessarily the world anyone else could see. And so the legends said that the notes of wooden flutes could be heard at times on the rock and the chanting of old voices, but most heard only the wind and some indeed laughed at the notion of anything real that could not be touched or talked to or induced to trade. But still the offerings were made, and disappeared, and still some nights the notes of a stark sonata filtered over the luminous rock like the plaintive rattle of red leaves blowing in an autumn forest.

Jewel Lightfoot had other matters to consider at the moment. The little ranger was still being chased, and his strength was dwindling fast. He needed to stay low, hide, get lost in the scrubby vegetation. But his mind wouldn't let him. Maybe it was the poison of Norberto's dart talking, but he felt threatened down here. Hemmed in. Surrounded. He needed to get up on top of it all, away from the confusion of brush and boulders and wrinkled earth. He had to be able to see what was coming. His knee was starting to lock up, and whatever strange toxin had entered his veins was making him see vague shapes flare and flutter in the corners of his eyes. He heard voices calling to him that weren't really there. At least he didn't think they were there. And they had nothing helpful to say, so what did it matter?

He needed clarity. Elevation.

The storm had eased, leaving only puddles to mark its passing. Lightfoot staggered around the house-size boulders at the base of the giant dome and hauled himself up the steep pitch of the granite face, his wet clothes flapping as he pushed himself higher. His boots were no help. The smooth soles slipped on the wet rock, so he sat and pulled them off. Then the socks. His pale feet seemed luminous in the darkness, like fish dredged up from an underground lake. Finally, he peeled off his cold shirt and his rain-heavy trousers, leaving him clad only in his long johns. This was better. He could move faster, and he didn't make a sound. At the crest of the slope, he circled to his left, moving west, searching for someplace to hide. Nothing. He might as well have been standing on the moon. He stopped to catch his breath and found himself facing a band of men huddled around a fire. The ranger sank to one knee, trying to make sense of what he was seeing.

"You fellows are a sight for sore eyes," he said. "I'm in dire need of assistance."

Good Lord. He couldn't even talk right.

There was no response. The men were barefooted, like him, dressed in simple trousers but naked from the waist up. Several held blankets around their shoulders.

"Where are you going?" asked one of the figures.

"Friend, I'd be pleased to visit with you, but I ain't got time at the moment." The ranger bent at the waist, taking in air through his nose in long, intentional draws. Someone had told him once that the Chinese did it this way. It calmed their emotions, helped them think clearly. It couldn't hurt to try. "There's some hombres comin' you don't want to meet. Anybody here have a firearm?"

"Jewel Lightfoot. Why are you so eager to die?"

So far, none of the figures had moved an inch in response to the ranger's warning. He wondered again what he was seeing. Was this some sort of religious group? Hard-shell Baptists, maybe, on a midnight vigil?

"Jesus," he said. "Suit yourself." Lightfoot turned to run, but he never made it. He tried again. For some reason he couldn't explain even to himself, he stood staring into the light. After a few moments, he crouched. He could do that much, at least. Who were these people? How did they know his name?

"You've been trying to die for years," said the figure closest to him. The one with his back turned. His voice was calm, almost soothing. "You just aren't very good at it."

"I think I might be catching on."

"You've done terrible things."

"More than I care to discuss."

"You've stolen. Lied. Fornicated."

"Not as often as I'd have liked, all things considered."

"You've killed six men and a boy."

"How did you know that?"

"A couple of them worth saving. Or might have been, given time."

Lightfoot's lower jaw shot out. "Don't get horsey on me, god-dammit. That boy wasn't a boy. Not the way people usually mean. And I wasn't the one—"

"You going to shoot me again, Jewel?" said another of the seated figures. His voice sounded vaguely familiar. "Or stab me in the eye, like you did that gambler in Galveston?"

The ranger grasped for words. The incident in Galveston had happened a long time ago. In '97, maybe. Or '98. Who could remember that far back? He recalled sitting in Al Woodard's office in Austin, listening to Deak Ross warn him about an investigation of his shooting of the Rosario kid.

"He was with the fellows that jumped me," he stammered, responding to an allegation no one had made. He narrowed his eyes. "You're on the committee."

"In a manner of speaking."

"Who sent you? And what are you doing up here?"

"We're here because you have a skill."

"Or a flaw."

"And because you're about to die."

Lightfoot spat. It was a reflex. Whenever challenged. "We'll see about that."

"You are unarmed, Sergeant."

"I took a knife off that skinny one. And there's plenty of rocks hereabouts. Maybe you've noticed."

"You've been shot twice. Your left knee is just about useless."

"Damned inconvenient, I know. But they're just pellets. That big sonofabitch has a scatter gun."

"Your enemies are close."

"That's where the rocks come in."

"Step into the light, Jewel."

"Step into—?"

"Here in front of us. They're getting closer."

A blast rang out from somewhere below him. A round of shot hissed past the ranger's head. He heard voices. Paco and Norberto, closing in.

"Thank you, but I don't care to stand in the only light for twenty miles."

"No one will see you."

"That ain't how light works."

"It's your only chance. Step into the light, Jewel. Are you afraid?"

Another peal of man-made thunder. A piece of steel shot ricocheted up off the stone and tore off a piece of the ranger's shoulder. Lightfoot winced at the wound. It felt like a bee sting, only the bee was the size of a blue jay. He heard his pursuers. They'd broken cover and were yelling to each other. A sign of confidence. Maybe overconfidence. If he could just circle back around one of them. Come at him from behind. Take his gun. But what were the odds? His knee was locking up. Even through the adrenaline rush of his panic, he could feel the pain welling up in great sharp surges of red. He glanced again at the men who sat huddled around the fire. Except that there was no fire. Only light.

The seven men looked back at him, immovable and unexcited, and their eyes reflected the radiance. Lightfoot recognized them. The faces of the men he'd killed. Antoine LeFevre, the Galveston gambler, gazing up at him with his one good eye, the other a gaping red socket. Randolph Batson, rancher and cattle rustler, as big and dumb and angry now as the moment he'd died with a cleaver in his hand, a lead slug from Lightfoot's .45 slicing through the flesh of his soft palate and exiting the back of his skull. And long-haired Jed Rosario, beautiful and doomed, as slender as a child's sigh, watching him, now, as he crouched on the rock. It wasn't fair that he was here. How was that one his fault? Haystack was the one holding the gun. At the far end of the loose circle sat an older man, bearded, his head down as if he were contemplating some scripture written on the rock itself. Long, greasy hair. Ropy veins on his forearms and a scar on the back of one hand. Lightfoot knew this man but was neither sorry nor saddened to see him here. Nor did he care to look upon his face.

The ranger knew he was out of options. In some corner of his mind, he was furious at his own passivity in the face of the approaching danger. The Mexicans, yes. But maybe also that thing they traveled with. The thing that had feasted on Hawley Reese. Darkness visible. Some walking combination of nightmare god and man-size monster. And if he were to be captured, and taken back? It didn't bear thinking about.

Lightfoot made for the light. He stepped into the circle as buckshot filled the air around him, an angry tide of shot, scalding hot and hungry for his blood, a steel storm manufactured just for him. He looked up and saw the pellets suspended like a swarm of yellowjackets frozen in midflight. He emitted a small cry, surprised but uncomplaining.

And disappeared.

The light was all around him. It was on him, in him. For a moment, nothing hurt. Then an angel appeared. "I told you, Jewel," she said. "I told you."

It was Freda. She was saying something, and it was probably the truth, but he had no idea what she was talking about. *Told me what?* he tried to say to her. *What did you tell me?*

But Freda wouldn't answer. Her brown eyes glistened.

She was calling as she moved away from him, down a hall or a street or clean across the state, and it didn't much matter because wherever she was, she couldn't hear him. He had the sense of having just missed something important, as if her words were a place he was supposed to be but couldn't quite get to. The ranger tried to still his senses. Eventually he realized he was flat on his back, staring up. In the predawn darkness he could see a narrow band of stars directly in front of him. Occasionally this view was blotted out for a moment, as if blocked by a moving object. A man. Two men. They were up there above him, calling to each other in that strange language of theirs, and their words were angry. Accusatory. What were they looking for?

It took him a moment to figure it out.

They wouldn't be able to find him because he was deep in a crack in the rock, and this was good—it was miraculous, and he was unhurt, as far as he could tell, which was even more miraculous—except he wasn't sure he could move. He was safe from his pursuers but in a peril he could barely name, wedged in a tiny space that held him like a difficult lover, cold and unyielding and unwilling to give him up. He was Jonah in the whale, trapped and immobilized but still sentient, still breathing, and starting to realize that he was getting closer, with every breath, to his last.

He had no idea how long he lay there, shivering between wrinkles in the rock, wondering how he'd come to take for granted the freedom to move his legs. What could it have meant, he wondered, his journey into the light, where men and women who stood in showers of color told him he was meant for something profound and unintelligible? And now to find himself sealed in this subterranean crypt. He felt like his skull was going to split. All he wanted was to be up and moving, and when he realized it wasn't going to happen, possibly ever again, he thrashed and pitched himself so violently against the rock that held him that he tore the flesh from his hands and forehead but to no avail, and now his anxiety about being discovered left him and his fear of the nightmare thing he'd seen or hallucinated the previous evening too and all he felt was panic at the thought of never seeing or feeling the sun again. He screamed until his lungs hurt.

And that's when he felt the morning breeze. Fresh air filtered up from below him and moved around the left side of his rib cage. He wedged himself farther into the crevice to that side and with his hand ascertained that beyond its narrowest point, the adjoining rocks opened up so that the lower one formed a sort of shelf, tilted downward at a thirty-degree angle. There was an opening down there. There had to be, to admit the flow of air. But an opening into what? He wasn't sure he wanted to find out. It might just be a deeper hole in the rock. Another basement in the crypt. He looked up at a sliver of pale blue sky. Maybe his last glimpse, he realized. He used his right elbow to push himself farther to the left. He tried to recall what men did in times like these, when their whole miserable lives depended on the outcome of a single questionable decision.

Ah, he remembered.

"Jesus," he whispered. "I wonder if I could ask you a favor."

He waited. He listened. He felt nothing but the frigid grip of the rock and the dull pains in his head and his hands and his knee. As far as he could tell, Jesus declined to answer. The ranger rolled anyway, and it was just as he expected. He fell. A long way. Lord, did it hurt. Then the shadows found him, and he suffered no more.

22. Official Reports

Date: *November 1, 1908*
Colonel Alfred P. Woodard, Texas Rangers
State Capitol, Austin

Sir: In October of this year, I was seconded to the service of the
Commissioner of Insurance, Statistics, and History and assigned
to investigate the deaths of Mr. and Mrs. Nils Peterson and their
two sons, late of San Luis, Coulter County, who died on or about
October 10; and the suspected slaying of Mr. Lyle Wexler, also of
San Luis, on or about October 20.

Acting on information obtained from local law enforcement offi-
cials in Gillespie County, and enlisting the aid of the sheriff of
Coulter County, Hawley Reese, and two able-bodied civilians
which I deputized in the field, I managed to track three suspects
in the Peterson deaths to the ruins of an abandoned Spanish
fort approximately twenty miles north of Fredericksburg. There
we thought to take the perpetrators by surprise and bring them
to justice. Unfortunately, our sortie on the evening was compro-
mised. Sheriff Reese and I were taken hostage by Sam Millicent,
a known felon and murderer, and three accomplices, who were

evidently acting in concert with the perpetrators of the crimes in Coulter County.

Hawley J. Reese was killed in the line of duty. It is my privilege to report that he exhibited great fortitude and industry in the execution of his official duties. In addition, my deputies, Mr. Ernesto Zavala and his grandson, Antonio Ramos, performed with exemplary courage. During a timely exchange of gunfire initiated by Deputy Ramos, I escaped to the granite dome the locals call Enchanted Rock, pursued by the suspects. However, I was able to evade my attackers among the crevices of that geological feature. The means of my egress from the rock are unclear to me, as I was found unconscious by a party of pick-nickers late the following a.m.

I have since been in the care of Dr. E. L. Hauwert of this municipality, to whom the State of Texas is indebted in the amount of $21.78 for services rendered and medicines, etc. expertly administered. (In all candor, this seems a mite high to me.) There is also a matter which you may hear of involving a certain amount of broken window glass, and some random other accidental damage, but I will attempt to pay for such things personally. Dr. Hauwert pulled six pellets of buckshot from me during my period of unconsciousness. He says I took a few licks, which I already knew, but I am perfectly fit for duty, so I aim to return to Austin forthwith.

I regret to report that the suspects in the Coulter County killings remain at large. I believe they will probably move west by southwest in an attempt to reach Old Mexico. I will continue this report in person when I get to Austin. It is also my intention to discuss certain developments with an individual of particular interest to my investigation who is employed at the state university.

Respectfully,
Jewel T. Lightfoot

To Whom It May Concern:

It has been my privilege to care for Sergeant J. T. Lightfoot of your Ranger Company C, on special assignment, who was brought to me three days ago by local citizens who found him dehydrated, hypothermic, and unconscious on a shelf of stone at nearby Enchanted Rock. Sergeant Lightfoot is eager to return to Austin and to "take up the reins" again, as he says. However, I have warned him against resuming his official duties at this time, due to the severe nature of the injuries he has incurred and the evident stress it has put on his nervous system.

He suffered a major concussion prior to his having been delivered to me, as well as severe bruises to his left hip and knee. He was punctured six times by buckshot, all of which pellets I have removed, and lost a significant amount of blood as a result of such wounds. He was also injured by what the sergeant believes to have been a poisonous dart or other projectile. If this is so, it is quite possible the copious bleeding from the wound caused by this projectile saved his life, as it evacuated the toxin, though traces of it were sufficient to necrotize a portion of the flesh of his neck. The patient's return to a waking state was not without incident. On the second day of his stay in my infirmary, shortly after he regained consciousness, he attempted to flee. Restrained and apparently subdued, he then slipped from the grasp of my orderly and leapt through a second-story window, landing quite near an elderly milliner of this town, who had to be dissuaded from filing charges. He seemed delirious, and twice thereafter in his sleep spoke of monsters and shadows and his need to escape such menaces. There were words also about angels and a sort of holy war, none of which made any particular sense, but all of which caused unhealthy excitement in the patient and vexed him greatly.

I have been unable to obtain any more practical description from Sergeant Lightfoot of what actually transpired on the rock and who it was that caused his grievous wounds, reports of which have inspired considerable indignation among the citizenry here. The local police found most of his clothing and his badge in the vicinity of Enchanted Rock, and he has been reunited with such possessions. His firearms have not been located. Furthermore, his rented horse and the horses of the three men who rode out of town several days ago are also missing, as are their riders, though one at least among them is claimed by Lightfoot to be among the corpses found some distance north of this city.

It is my professional opinion that Sergeant Lightfoot needs rest—sixty days, at the least—and that he should be restricted from duty for the foreseeable future so that his mind and body may heal. He is a stubborn specimen, very boney, and possessed of a remarkable resistance to the strictures of common sense. He has received your cable instructing him to return to Austin. He intends to comply, and I cannot hold him. But he is, after all, only human. His reasoning faculties have been much disturbed and appear to be impaired. He needs rest—and possibly a course of laudanum or some other narcotizing sedative. I would be happy to discuss

Sergeant Lightfoot's injuries and prognosis further, at your convenience. In the meantime, I remain at your service, etc.

Ernst L. Hauwert, M.D., Fredericksburg

P.S. I enclose my bill for professional services rendered and for physical damages caused to my surgical facilities. Please remit payment upon receipt.

23. Colloquy

Austin, November 3

ightfoot knew Freda would meet him at the station. He picked
her out of the crowd at a distance and started toward her with
his head down. He had a lot to tell her. Too much, maybe. He
wasn't sure where to start. The cave near San Luis and the headless
corpse of John Patrick Kelso, the fortune hunter come to ruin.
The stone fort. Cold rain. The death of Sheriff Reese and then the
creature he glimpsed perched on the crumbling wall—a vision of
darkness and depravity, half bat, part insect, somehow vaguely
human as well. And then, of course, the figures who'd been waiting for him in their silent circle on Enchanted Rock and all their
splintered pinwheel mysteries and the visionless penitence of
cold, hard stone holding him like a little boy holds an unlucky
bug in his fist before nonchalantly, perhaps even unknowingly,
crushing the life from its fragile form. Maybe it was the weight of
these mysteries that brought him to a stop. Or maybe it was the
crowd at the station. The people around him seemed so normal,
so unperturbed. None of them knew the things he did. Nobody
understood what was happening out west, what was *out there*,
despite every standard of rationality, alive and unfettered and
possibly incomprehensible. Save perhaps for Al Woodard, there
wasn't a soul in the city who could grasp how illusory the sense
of reality shared by those around him really was.

When he glanced up, Freda was standing in front of him in a neatly tailored green skirt and a pressed white blouse, accented with three white bows and a button from which descended a guidon of red, white, and blue. She wore a sensible green hat as well. Her black shoes were shined, and her gloves were as white as snow. In the moment after they'd embraced, her face fell the several stories from joyous to dismayed. And then, perhaps because it had become customary, she started to scold.

"Lord Almighty," she exclaimed. "Look what you've done to yourself. Your neck all bandaged up. Limping. Your eyes. You're exhausted. Jewel Lightfoot, you need to be in bed."

The ranger didn't care who saw. He wrapped Freda in his arms and buried his face in the flesh of her neck. She smelled like freshly laundered sheets and cut grass in the sunshine. Like a little piece of heaven. He surprised himself with his own affection. Somewhere nearby, an onlooker whistled. Lightfoot bristled, but Freda just smiled.

"By God," said the ranger. "Look at you. A regular society matron. You're gonna be picketing in front of your own establishment before the end of the year."

She shook her head as she resumed her fleshly inventory. "Your whole face is bruised. I didn't even know that was possible. Your hand's all— What will it take? Do you not understand that I worry about you? And that this is why?"

Lightfoot worked up a wan smile. "Don't get carried away, now. And don't you try to tote that bag. I ain't dead yet. You're gonna get me thrown off the force, folks see me lettin' a woman carry my kit."

"Here, then. You take it. But I'd be happy if they would throw you off. You are coming to Zenger's, yes? I will look after you."

"Of course I'm coming, sweetheart. Tonight. I got one thing to do, and then—"

She stopped in her tracks. "I thought you might say that."

"Freda. Listen."

"Very well. I am fine with this. Go and vote. I think you should. Poor Mr. Bryan needs all the help he can get."

"Vote," said Lightfoot. "Right. And then I might just . . ."

"Ah. Here's where I am saying no. We have plans. That one thing you say you have to do always turns into ten more. And then the next thing I know you're riding back out of town again to sleep with the snakes and eat your horrible biscuits."

"It's routine police work. I've just got a few questions I need to ask a friend, right here at the university. Let me chuck my gear in the wagon and catch up with you later. What plans?"

"We're invited to dinner with Al and Ellen."

"Al Woodard?"

"Yes, Al Woodard," she said, shaking her head. "Who do you think? Ellen and I are hoping it will cheer him up."

"Al don't need no cheerin' up. He's— What?"

"You don't know."

"Jesus. Know what? Why all the mystery?"

Freda bent close. "Al," she whispered, "is very ill."

"No. I didn't know. He didn't tell me. Yes. I mean, let's go to dinner. My business won't take more than a few minutes."

"This I've heard before. Five o'clock?"

"Before five. Trust me."

She put a warm hand on the side of his face and gave him a crooked smile. "I know it's a crime," she said. "But I'm thinking I might have to kidnap you."

Lightfoot walked east to Congress, where he paid a nickel and boarded the streetcar headed north. He strode—hobbled, more like—onto campus twenty minutes later. Irma Shapiro greeted him as skeptically as she had the first time. Maybe more so, given the state of his face. She shook her head when the ranger asked to see the professor. He was out of luck, it seemed. Professor Kitzinger had just left town, bound for an important academic conference in Washington.

"D.C.," added the matron, as if the ranger couldn't be trusted to figure it out for himself.

"When?"

"Not half an hour ago. You can leave a note—"

"Heading east on the H&TC?" He knew it was a dumb question as soon as he said the words. The Houston & Texas Central was by far the fastest way to the nation's capital. He'd taken it as far as St. Louis once himself.

"Of course. You can write him a note if you'd like. I'll be forwarding his correspondence."

The ranger realized with a flash of anger that Kitzinger had probably been traveling south toward the station right around the time he was passing it in the opposite direction. He got down the stairs as fast as his injured knee could carry him, slamming into a gaggle of undergraduates in the process and sending their books cascading down the wooden staircase. The ranger was a courtly man, old-fashioned in certain respects. Ordinarily he would have stopped to make things right. Apologize to the ladies. Hold a door or two.

Not now.

He hauled himself down to Magnolia Street, piled onto another streetcar, and made it a total of two blocks before he found his route blocked by a parade. Election Day, he realized. Lord Almighty. BRYAN OR BUST, said the signs. FACING THE FUTURE. And WASHINGTON'S BLOATED: SO IS TAFT. There were women riding bicycles. A fire truck pulled by a team of eight horses. Kids and dogs. The Stars and Stripes. Someone throwing candy while perched on a camel. Cursing aloud, Lightfoot leapt from the streetcar onto the hard-packed dirt of Congress Avenue. Bad idea. He winced. He dodged through the procession and the ragged crowd of onlookers and onto the pine-board sidewalk. On 9th Street: a baby stroller barricade. On 7th: a Taft supporter, explaining himself. A brass band at Pecan Street. The ranger made it to the station, at the corner of 3rd and Congress, just as the train was leaving. Scarlet streaks of pain shot up from his knee as he willed himself down the platform in pursuit.

The H&TC was the first line in Texas to run oil-powered locomotives, and the smell of burning fuel hung heavy in the air. Lightfoot hoisted himself up on the next-to-last car and stopped to catch his breath before he yanked open the rear door of the car and let himself in. He made a quick survey of the passengers, only a few of whom even looked up. His quarry wasn't here, and Lightfoot wondered if he'd made a mistake. It was going to be a while before the ranger could make it back to Austin, and who knew where the German might get off to in the meantime? The next car was almost empty. The third carried a church group of some sort, happily singing "Closer My God to Thee," but there was still no sign of the professor. Lightfoot felt himself getting angrier, though it was mostly at himself.

A minute later, he found Kitzinger in a compartment of one of the train's two sleeper cars, gazing contentedly out the window at the cotton and sorghum fields east of Austin. The professor glanced up at the sound of the door opening. His expression was the usual admixture of studied disdain and amused arrogance. But his face fell fast when he recognized his visitor. He lunged for his briefcase.

"Herr Fromm!" he yelped.

Lightfoot didn't immediately see the stout, balding man who was riding with the professor.

"Excuse me," said the thug, rising to confront him. The Teutonic accent made the words a wall. "You are not welcome here."

Lightfoot drew his jacket back to reveal the badge. "Jumbo," he said, "you walk out of here now and you won't get hurt. I've got a few things to discuss with your boss."

"Then first you will discuss with me. *Ja?*"

"I ain't got the time, friend. And I sure as hell ain't in the mood."

The ranger reached for his revolver. He'd never been much for small talk. He planned to shoot the man somewhere south of the hip and exchange civilities later. But his hand touched nothing but his trousers, and Lightfoot remembered he was weaponless.

The thug grinned. Lightfoot tried to work up a smile in return. He hadn't quite got there when the big man put a fist in his solar plexus. It felt like he'd been kicked by a horse. A second blow connected with the back of his head, and the ranger fell to the floor of the little compartment.

Next time bring a gun, he told himself.

He felt himself being lifted off the floor. He was face to face with his attacker now. The man's breath smelled of sauerkraut and cigarette smoke. The ranger suddenly remembered the features in front of him. They belonged to the man who'd followed him to Llano on the train a lifetime ago. A lifetime or two weeks. He couldn't clearly recall.

"I told you," said the thug, "you are not *welcome* here."

Lightfoot glanced sideways. Ernst-Michael Kitzinger was clearly enjoying the festivities. Something about the academic's smirk bothered the ranger. He found his badge with one hand and freed it from his waistcoat. He bent the needlelike pin away from the frame with his thumb.

"Herr Fromm," said Kitzinger. "Perhaps you could take our visitor to the observation platform."

"*Jawohl*, Professor. I'll—"

The ranger jammed the pin of his badge into the big man's left eye. He winced at the scream that followed. But he was free. He grabbed the ornate walking stick that stood in the corner of the compartment and broke it over the German's skull.

Kitzinger was no longer smirking. The professor stood and tugged open the window of the little compartment. He tried to toss a sheaf of papers outside, but the wind blew most of the documents back into the train, along with a fair amount of oily smoke. The moans of the wounded bodyguard, now slumped in a sitting position and holding his hands to the bloody mess that had been his left eye, added to the general chaos of the scene.

"Going somewhere, Professor?" said Lightfoot. He stepped over the wounded man and picked up one of the pages scattered around the tiny chamber. It was a map of Texas, with the border regions shaded blue. Another page was a charcoal drawing of the macahuitl, surrounded by a swarm of small notes. Yet another was a telegram, in German, apparently meant for Kitzinger himself.

Lightfoot tossed the papers back on the floor. He grabbed the professor by the collar of his tweed jacket and the seat of his britches, then picked him up and forced him out the window of the train, holding him by his knees as the scholar kicked.

"You're gonna tell me what's going on, Professor! Or you're gonna get *ground up* like Hamburg steak on that track!"

"Let me up!" the academic screamed. "*Hilf mir!* Murder! Let me up!"

"What? The wind! It's too loud!"

"Let me up!"

"Up?"

"Please!"

Getting the panicky scholar—arms flailing, still screaming—back inside the train was more difficult than the ranger had anticipated. He had some help from a porter, a wiry colored man who grabbed one of the German's ankles and assisted in yanking him into the compartment. Lightfoot found his bent-up badge on the floor. He re-pinned it to his waistcoat and the porter, a judicious individual, held up his palms. When the wounded thug made a move to get up, the ranger pivoted and gave him a kick in the head. Then he shoved the professor into his seat.

"Are you ready to talk," he asked, "or do you want a little more air?"

Kitzinger was breathing heavily. A portion of one of his teeth was stuck in a corner of his mouth. "There will be repercussions for you, Sergeant. This affair will not be forgotten."

"You can be sure of that," said Lightfoot. "I found an Irishman in two pieces in a cave up in Coulter County, and I left a good man lying dead in the hills north of Fredericksburg with his guts pulled clean out of his body. Your hired band of gravediggers is out there somewhere with whatever broken branch on the tree of life they brought out of that cave, and they're probably ready to kill again, 'cause that's about all they seem to be able to do. And I ain't even got to the Petersons yet, you jumped-up, prissy-lipped partridge. You can be damned sure I ain't gonna forget a minute of it."

"No!" Kitzinger shrieked as Lightfoot jerked him to his feet and aimed him at the window.

"Talk," said the ranger. "Who are you working for?"

Ernst-Michael Kitzinger's eyes darted wildly around the compartment. They took in the porter, who stood at the door, watching impassively. They considered his bleeding bodyguard, who lay on one side, hands to his injured eye, and the scattered papers that lay beside the man. They came to rest, finally, on the broken walking stick.

The professor emitted an exhausted sigh as he adjusted his collar.

"Very well. You have me at a disadvantage. I work for the Fatherland, Sergeant. As I have always done. And I am entitled to the protection and counsel of my country's embassy, which I now formally demand."

Lightfoot and the porter exchanged glances.

"I'll leave y'all to it," said the porter. He closed the door behind him.

24. Duty Report

Date: November 4, 1908
Colonel Alfred P. Woodard, Texas Rangers

Sir: Yesterday, November 3, I availed myself of the opportunity to discuss certain details of my investigation of the Coulter County murders with Professor Ernst-Michael Kitzinger, a faculty member of the University of Texas. While I understand that I am not acting under your direction in this investigation, allegations were made during the course of my interview with the professor which may come to your attention. Thus, I felt it incumbent on me to lay these hasty words out for you beforehand, so as you can get the jump on them, so to speak.

Specifically, I asked Dr. Kitzinger how it came to be that he was in communication with Mr. John Patrick Kelso, a mining speculator and confidence man who was apparently killed in October, likely by a person or persons associated with the Peterson murders that are the subject of my investigation which you assigned to me.

My interview was not without incident. Dr. Kitzinger was not initially inclined to cooperate with my questioning, which he said put him in mind of a blind pig rooting for acorns. However, after some preliminary negotiations involving fisticuffs and a minor eye injury to one of the learned man's associates, the professor gave me to understand that he, acting as an agent of the government of Kaiser Wilhelm of the Empire of Germany, employed Mr. Kelso to locate antiquities associated with religious practices of one or more ancient Mesoamerican peoples (Indians of former days, now long deceased). According to Dr. Kitzinger, it is the Kaiser's intention to provide these relics as evidence to the government of Mexico that lands ceded by Mexico to its northern neighbor belong by right to the Mexican people, are of historical significance, and should never have been surrendered to the United States.

Certain individuals associated with his Royal Excellence, etc. the Kaiser evidently believe that the United States, an ally of Great Britain, is becoming too powerful, and that German interests can best be served by inciting unrest between America and its southern neighbor. A war between Mexico and the U.S. would leave Great Britain almost alone to oppose Germany's territorial ambitions in Europe and Africa. Professor Kitzinger also indicated that in the event Mexico could win back its former territories, Germany would be prepared to purchase cinnabar, which is mined in the Big Bend region and used for production of quicksilver, and as much helium gas as Mexico could produce. This gas is thought to exist in large quantities in underground fields in West Texas. Germany wants it to fill its dirigibles— giant airships built like bullets around steel frames and filled with gas to make them float. Since no helium is to be found in Europe, the Germans must rely on hydrogen, which is a poor substitute, on account of its tendency to conflagrate (which means to catch fire).

It is unclear how far Germany is willing to go in trying to cause such troubles, but Professor Kitzinger at least seems eager to see war between America and Mexico. As you know, such a war is always close—and indeed sometimes seems already to have broke out in certain parts of the state. I am enclosing with this report a copy of a telegram sent by the professor to the German embassy in Washington, D.C., some time before his departure from Austin. I have enlisted the help of my friend Mr. Otto Zenger, a local grocer, to translate. As you will see, the professor tells the German embassy that an important item he had previously located has been taken by thieves, who are traveling southwest from Central Texas toward the border. He says he sent a man to try to intercept them, but he was waylaid and unsuccessful in retrieving the treasure. He asks for certain information regarding this treasure to be transmitted to the appropriate officials in Mexico for their consideration, with a request that the governments of Germany and Mexico redouble their efforts to recover the stolen item, as it is of immeasurable value.

There is a reference in the message as well to compass coordinates. These coordinates were furnished to the thieves as a promise of safety. Evidently the thieves tried to get Kitzinger to meet them in San Antonio to pay them for recovery of the contents of the lost mine. He figured it for a set-up, and he was probably right. He wired our fugitives that they were now being hunted by the Rangers, but that they could obtain payment and the protection of the Mexican federal government from any Texas police or military force that might be trailing them if they could just make it across the Rio Grande. The coordinates provided are as follows: 29° 25' N; 102° 58' W. I have run the traps, and they lie plumb in the middle of the Sierra del Carmen range, which, as you know, is in the Big Bend region in the far west of the state.

Most if not all of these mountains are situated in the territory of Mexico.

Kitzinger professes innocence of any murder—either of the Petersons or of his agent, Kelso. I have no way of knowing if this is true. What I do know is that the men who killed Kelso now have the ancient "object" that Kitzinger wanted and that indeed he retained the renegade Sam Millicent to try to recover. The murderers were last seen in the vicinity of Enchanted Rock and remain at large. It is my intention—and please consider it my request—to return to the hunt for these men, who have demonstrated utter disregard for human life in their devotion to bloody rituals, which belong not in the pages of twentieth-century government records but rather in the campfire stories of a pagan race. I believe they have killed at least six people. Indeed, I saw one of these individuals, Sheriff Hawley Reese, killed in front of me, in a manner which does not bear repeating.

Sir, it is my recommendation that every resource be dedicated to apprehension of the three Mexican nationals I have previously described. Once sighted, they must be hunted down and either captured or killed with all deliberate haste. I have confirmed that they now travel with another individual, who may indeed be more dangerous than his three companions. I can give no accurate description of the individual in these pages but will brief you in person upon your return from illness to your official duties. Nevertheless, it is my recommendation that this fourth individual should be killed on sight. I plan to do it myself, if given the chance. I will emphasize that the renegades we seek are desperate and exceedingly dangerous. Any lawman in pursuit should go armed and prepared for a scrap. There will be fire and blood and no time for questions to be either asked or answered.

Authorities at the Breckenridge Hospital in Austin believe that Professor Kitzinger will recover from his injuries, some of which they have accused me of inflicting. The professor is a clever bird, and somewhat gristly. He was resistant to questioning. In consequence, I did in fact give him a ration, but I have not behaved in any respect that would cast discredit on the service. It is my understanding, and much to my regret, that authorities from the federal government have prohibited any further questioning of the professor, on account of he is an official consular agent of the Empire of Germany. I count this a shame, as I was enjoying our discussions and am eager to continue them, should the opportunity present itself.

Your humble svt, etc. Sgt. Jewel Lightfoot

25. The Message

November 6

ightfoot was later to look back on his conversation with Freda and wonder why he couldn't say more. But as hard as he sometimes was on himself—regarding Freda in particular—he had to admit he was distracted that morning.

Ernesto Zavala showed up at his bachelor's quarters on Pecan Street. Lightfoot was relieved to see the old man, embarrassed by the long hug Ernesto gave him, and apologetic that he hadn't anything stronger to offer his guest than well water. Ernesto didn't seem to mind. He needed to clear his head, he said. He sat on the ranger's narrow bed and gazed at his hands as Lightfoot finished shaving. But he didn't stay quiet for long.

He was still confused, he admitted, about what had happened at the stone fort the night Lightfoot was captured. Once Antonio's targets retreated into the darkness, the kid had gone back to find his grandfather, who had stayed with the animals, as he'd been told. Together Ernesto and Antonio laid up for the night, though neither man slept. Antonio was too anxious to close his eyes. He whispered strange stories about the men at the fort and the death of the sheriff. Ernesto found himself praying with a fervor he hadn't felt for a very long time. At dawn they ventured out again. The fort was empty save for the corpses, including that of Sheriff Reese.

"I've seen what the Comanches did," said Ernesto. "But it was not like this. Only something unknown to God could do these things. *Madre de Dios*. The bodies . . . pulled apart."

Ernesto had said a prayer for the sheriff and buried what they could find. It was ignoble of them to flee, he admitted. But Texas was no place for a brown-skinned man to be found near the scene of such carnage, so he and Antonio had made their way back to San Luis.

Ernesto had other things to say as well, and items to deliver. Among them were the Winchester and the ranger's revolver. "They must have forgotten to take the weapons when they fled. Antonio found them for you."

Lightfoot nodded his thanks. "He was the one fired them shots. I figured as much."

"Sí. It was he who fired. He does not listen."

"I would caution him against that sort of behavior, as it's a habit that wears on people. I know firsthand. But I'm straight up certain he saved my life. So . . . there's that."

Ernesto handed the ranger a green felt bag. Lightfoot opened it and dumped the contents on the table in front of him.

"What are these?"

"You know what they are. *Balas*. Bullets. And shells for the shotgun."

"Hell, I know what they are. But—"

"They're made of silver, Capitán. Silver is the only thing that can kill the . . . the thing you are looking for."

"Lead won't do it?"

"You would need a lot of lead."

"What about a bomb?"

"You have a bomb?"

The ranger shrugged. "I have dynamite. You remember. Two sticks, from Kelso's satchel. And I can always get more."

"Trust me," said Ernesto.

"Now why should I do that? You obviously ain't been telling me everything you know, right from the minute we started."

"What you say is true, and I am sorry for it. But I have obligations."

"Yeah? Obligations to who?"

"To God. Just as you do, my friend."

"God, huh? Well, I've got the commissioner of insurance to answer to, but I reckon you've got me beat. Go on."

"I was not a miner, Capitán. You know this now. I was a sentinel. *Un centinela.* The holes in that land were not dug originally to find silver, though that is what was said, and there was some small amount of the metal there. The holes were dug to find the Mayan god. The Church had an idea of where the god was hidden, but its information was not precise. The holy fathers placed me in the dry country near San Luis almost fifty years ago. My job was to watch for signs that someone knew more than the Church. To watch and warn if the god of darkness were ever to be awakened from his long confinement. I was full of fire in those days—*el fuego de la fe.* The fire of my faith. And so I took the mission and made my way into the hills.

"At first I too lived in the caves, for there was no one else there but the Comanche. I ate snakes when I could find them. I drank the rain that pooled in the rocks. Some among the Indians knew me and allowed me to live as I chose, as I was no harm to them. Others were not so kind. I have been left for dead on more than one occasion. And perhaps I *was* dead, because belief slowly drained from my heart. My devotion went out, like a candle in a storm. The horse lords, Buffalo Hump and Peta Noconah and the one they called Quanah, the Serpent Eagle, all died or drifted away. The Anglos took the country, and the land was surveyed and mapped, and fences and farmhouses went up. The Church bought some acres for me, though by this time only a few among the fathers even remembered who I was and what I was doing in that wild place. And they too are all dead. But still I stayed, and I watched. In a moment of weakness, I let my heart speak louder than my promise to God. I took a wife. And wives want more. So prospecting went from a pastime to my profession, though there was little silver to be found. I had a daughter. A precious girl who grew up too fast. My daughter married—unwisely, I think—and so I have a grandson. The angry one."

"We've met."

"*Claro*. Forgive me. My grandson came to me two years ago. He was made excited by talk he heard in his school in Bexar, where many from Mexico go to plan rebellion and unrest. They read unsound books. They reject the ways of the Church. My grandson had fights with students and teachers alike, and so he was made to leave his school. My daughter sent him, so now he resents both of us. I am just an old man, and I have little to tell him, and even this he does not care to listen to. And now my duty is done. But yours is just beginning. You must kill this thing that was buried in the cave. You know this, *sí*?"

Lightfoot looked around the room for someplace to spit. He finally just aimed at the corner. "I don't even know what it is, Ernesto. How can I kill it?"

"You know what it is. *Un demonio*. An evil thing that climbed up from the dark places of hell in an age long past and has devoured the flesh of men ever since. He came to the Maya out of the jungles, and they took him in and worshiped him like a god. But he poisoned them. He wore a necklace strung with human eyes. He built a throne of children's skulls, and he planted hatred in the hearts of all he touched. What I have given you will help. But it will take the power of God to deliver us."

Lightfoot listened to himself breathe. He ran a hand back through his hair. "I ain't a church-going man, Ernesto."

"I have never been to hell." The old man crossed himself. "But I know its creatures have visited this world. And I know this thing is one of them. The men who found it think it will help them restore the glories of our ancestors, but they are wrong. The dead have no love for the living. This unholy beast cares nothing for them, or for any man—white or black or brown. It will bring the world only darkness and death."

The two men went silent. Children talked excitedly as they passed near the house, but Lightfoot was unable to make out the topic of their conversation. There was a fire nearby, perhaps. Or someone had found a snake. Blue jays scolded each other in the live oaks out back. Everything seemed so normal here. No dreams walked the streets. No monsters haunted the alleys. And yet here he was, just like in the old days, the days with Al Woodard, thinking dark thoughts on a bright, cool morning.

"I saw something back at that fort, Ernesto. I saw it or maybe dreamt it, one. Just beyond the point where I could understand. It was . . . I can't describe it. Like a wolf or a bat, but hollowed out, somehow. Crazy-eyed, like a mad dog. When it looked at me, I felt like I'd run into a wall. I ain't no schoolgirl. I've seen things. I've done things I hope God can find His way to overlook. But I've never seen anything as ugly and angry as this. Whatever it is, you're right. It's no friend to anyone living."

"Yes. So you see. And—"

"These slugs," said the ranger, reaching for one of the bullets. "You dip 'em in holy water, or some such?"

"You don't believe in the mysteries. I understand. But trust me. Silver has always been poison to the enemies of the Almighty. The demon is still weak. It has been asleep for centuries, and it needs sustenance to grow strong. You must kill it. Soon. While you still can."

Lightfoot stood and walked, painfully, to the window. He propped himself against the wall as he watched the winter wind in the trees. He held one of the bullets up against the morning light. "I guess it can't hurt. As long as they shoot like any other round."

"Antonio tested the work. Those are for *la pistola*. The shells hold lead pellets with shavings of silver mixed in. Antonio has bullets for his rifle also."

"You goin' back to San Luis?"

"I'm too old to live out there anymore." Ernesto scratched the back of his neck. "I'm going to El Paso, where I have family. Distant family."

"What about the boy? You taking him with you?"

"No, Capitán."

The ranger knew what was coming, but he wasn't going to make it easy. "No?"

"I came to ask you to take him with you. He is too strong for me. Too wild. I fear that if he does not find something to do, he will ruin himself."

"Chomping at the bit, huh?"

"Sí. All the time chomping. Some men need soft chairs and meals on the table. Others need to sleep on the ground and feel *la escarcha*—the frost, yes?—in their teeth. He is one of such men. The passion runs strong in this one. Perhaps he is something like you."

The ranger frowned. This was a deeper subject than he cared to explore at the moment. "Well, he can ride. I'll give him that. And he can handle a rifle, though he could work on his accuracy."

"You will take him?"

"The State barely stands me enough for my own grub, Ernesto. They ain't gonna shell out for a seventeen-year-old Mexican with revolution on his mind."

Ernesto dug a handful of coins out of his bag and laid them on the table. They were twenty-peso gold pieces, the metal bright against the miner's arthritic hands. The ranger sighed. So there had been some silver in those hills after all. He pushed half the coins back toward the old man and counted the remainder.

"This ought to do it. The kid can have what's left when we're done. You know this is going to be dangerous, right?"

"*Concuerdo.*"

"I ain't no nursemaid."

"He doesn't need a nursemaid. He needs a purpose. But his fate is not in my hands, nor in yours. It is in God's alone." With this, the old man turned and headed for the door.

He stopped before he got there. "I meant to tell you," he said.

"What?"

"After you escaped from the fort, the men who wanted to kill you followed. The Mayans. They chased you. You know that. The one who thinks himself a priest must have left later, with his cart and the monstrous thing he serves. But you were not the only one to escape with your life."

"What do you mean?"

"The big white man. The *güero.*"

"Millicent?"

"I don't know the name. But my grandson saw him stand and leave that place. Pale as a ghost. Looking neither ahead nor behind."

Lightfoot shook his head in disgust. "Stabbed in the neck, and he still walks away. That is one slippery sonofabitch. I imagine he's gotten himself as far away from that thing as he can get by now. Hell, Ernesto. I'm sorry I doubted you."

"There is no reason to apologize. I have doubted too. What was brought out of that hole in the ground attracts bad men and bad luck. It lives now because it is so hard for us to think that it can. It is the work of the demon, not a fault of ours."

The ranger ran a hand over the silver slugs. "Maybe so. You tell Antonio to be ready when I send for him."

"There is no need for that, Capitán. He's outside."

The ranger chuckled for the first time in a week. He walked over to the window. "Well, I'll be damned. So he is. I'll tell you what. Take one of them coins and find him a bed at the Hotel Republic for a night or two. Tell the desk clerk Lightfoot sent you, and make sure he gives you change, 'cause that crooked sonofabitch would steal from Jesus if he had the chance. And tell Antonio we'll be setting out as soon as I get word from Al Woodard. They keep telling me he's sick, but . . . hell. Al ain't been sick a day in his life. And anyhow he's got men watching all over the state. Thank you, Ernesto. And *vaya con Dios.*"

"*Seguro,* Capitán. *Vaya con Dios.* I think you will need Him."

The ranger was still musing on his conversation with Ernesto when he called on Freda. She was in no mood for contemplation. She sat him down at the little table just inside her front door and took her place across from him.

"We can't keep doing this to each other, Jewel."

The ranger realized it was going to be a long afternoon. Freda spoke before he could ask the question. "You know what. You keep leaving. You keep riding off. And I can tell by the way you're scratching under your collar, you're about to do it again."

"It ain't by choice, darling. I follow orders."

Her eyes widened, as if she'd heard a youngster tell a particularly unwieldy fib. "It *is* by choice. You don't have to follow orders. You're a grown man."

Lightfoot looked down at the hat he held in his hands. "I'm a grown man with no prospects, and you know it. Hell, I'm a man with negative prospects. You've seen how I am around a bottle. And when I can't get that, it's worse. You know what they say. Be careful what you wish for. I'm pretty sure you shouldn't be wishing for me."

If she was impressed with his attempt at candor, she didn't show it. "I'm your prospect. Why can't you see that? Otto is opening another store. I'm not supposed to tell anyone yet, but this one is going to be across the river, on South Congress. I'm going to be keeping the books for both. And he's getting out of the brothel business altogether."

"The hell he is. That's his favorite part."

"Otto's favorite part of anything is Otto. He wants to be mayor someday. And running a bordello doesn't sit too well with the female population of Austin."

The ranger sat back in his chair. "Well, that's fine for Otto. Fine for you too. But we've been through this before. I'm not taking money from a woman, and I ain't owning property through a woman neither. And I thought Little Otto was coming home this summer to learn the business. You sure he's not gonna be keeping the books?"

"Little Otto's not coming back for a while. The Navy went ahead and commissioned all the midshipmen at the Naval Academy and sent them out to sea. Otto says he's on a battleship. People are talking about war, Jewel. War with Germany. Anyhow, you're changing the subject. Bobby LeVan married money. Nobody makes sport of him."

True enough. Bobby LeVan had surprised everyone when he turned in his notice and announced his intentions. He married a wealthy widow up in Georgetown and quit Company B to run Angus cattle on the widow's six-hundred-acre ranch. Jewel hadn't heard a word about him—or from him—in almost a year, though the ranger had considered Bobby one of his few friends. He didn't have a good answer to this line of argument, and Freda knew it.

"Well, that's Bobby's lookout. He was always a little different."

Freda sat back too, as if to echo her man's passivity. "Are you holding out for something bigger?"

He let his gaze drop to her chest. "Honey, I don't think I'm ever gonna be able to put my hands on anything bigger."

She gave him a look that could have frozen a teardrop. "If you think you're entitled to trifle with me at a time like this, I'll break this vase over your head. You know what I mean. Are you looking for someone more refined?"

Lightfoot shook his head.

"Younger?" she said, her eyes searching his.

"Not hardly."

She straightened in her chair and delivered her words like a prosecutor summing up a murder case. "Then goddammit, Jewel, what the hell are you waiting for?"

In ordinary conversation, this might have been taken as an insult. But the ranger knew his woman's voice. The question was sincere. Freda was genuinely puzzled by his failure to take some action, or even to make a decision, that would set them on a permanent path together. Lightfoot kneaded his forehead. He examined his boots. And he tried to pay attention to Freda, but it didn't work very well. Though he couldn't say it, she'd already won the argument. There was nothing better in his life than her, and sooner or later, unless the whiskey got him, he was going to have to admit it.

Having conceded this point internally, the ranger felt compelled to focus on the more immediate problem. Ramon and his crew were out there, far to the west, with a walking curse of a creature he couldn't even name, much less comprehend, and the group of them—men and beast—were receding with each moment he sat here trying to explain himself and his own inability to be something other than an appetite and a set of reflexes. It made him so anxious he could hardly keep his heart in his chest. It wasn't that he didn't care for Freda. He knew he did. He thought about her. He missed her when they were apart. He worried when she was sick and he smiled when she was well and she was making plans and her mind was moving faster than his ever could. Everything was going to be fine. He'd tell her. He just couldn't talk about it now.

Freda came to him across the long bridge of their silence. He didn't deserve it. He never had.

"I love you, Jewel," she said, kneeling in front of him. She placed her hands on his knees and he laid his on top. The skin of her hands was dry, and her face was lined around the eyes and the corners of her mouth, and yet she seemed precious and new to him in this moment, and he almost told her. "I know we've been shy about saying it. Maybe for too long. And I don't know exactly what it means at our age, but I know it means something, at any age. I'll wait for you if you tell me you want me to. But I can't keep waiting if you aren't coming."

The ranger leaned his face into her hair. "I can't blame you for that."

"No," she said. "You can't. So give me an answer. Do something. Say something."

He nodded. "That's fair. It's been long enough."

"I'll see you tonight?"

"Tonight," he said. "We'll figure it out. I promise."

Lightfoot tried for several minutes to apply himself to profound and systematic thoughts about his future with the woman he loved, but he was no more successful at the task this time than he ever was. He wondered if a change of scenery would help. He considered wandering over to the livery stable, saddling up Loki, and heading out for a ride. He could cross the Colorado and wander up into the hills west of the city, where Comanches once camped and it was still possible to find old arrowheads and buffalo skulls and the like. An Italian named Dellana owned the land these days. He farmed it, ran some cattle on the side, and leased out the caves to gatherers of bat guano, who collected the stuff and sent it down the river to Montopolis to be sold as fertilizer. Freda always said there were two kinds of men she wouldn't let into her establishment: undertakers and guano harvesters, both of whom she claimed smelled of things she didn't want to be reminded of.

Freda again.

Try as he might to keep her out, she kept slipping into his thoughts. Finally he relented. He took dead aim at the target. Freda Mikulska. Freda and Jewel. Married, maybe? And that little homestead up on Shoal Creek she kept talking about. He hiked south, but he only got as far as Maple Street, where he stood for several minutes looking out over the bustling city toward the river. It was no use. He kept checking the horizon. He wasn't a thinker. He realized once again that he'd never been able to plan much beyond the following day. That the only thing that got him out of bed or a bottle was something or someone out there in front of him, coming at him or running away. He had trouble dealing with abstractions. He did better with fear and anger and hunger and the cold creeping into his bones. Damn. What was keeping Al Woodard, anyhow? The trail wasn't going to get any fresher. And as long as the Mayans traveled with the thing they'd taken from the cave near San Luis, they were going to keep killing. They seemed to be good at it. Hell. Who was he kidding, trying to imagine a future with Freda? He wasn't even sure he *had* a future, much less some kind of an orderly plan he could share with a woman. His belly was rumbling, and he needed a drink. He loved Freda. He was starting to believe in her. In the words. In whatever they were supposed to mean. But making them consequential—using them as the spur to an organized course of action—seemed too daunting and steep a slope. So, in the end, Lightfoot found himself back at Zenger's, sitting in the cool of that underground saloon, eating cold chicken and cabbage, drinking a pilsner, and conversating with John Nemo. And that meant, as usual, questioning the man.

"Not right?" said the ranger. "What's that supposed to mean?"

"I mean just what I said. There's somethin' not quite right with you," said John. "I ain't stupid. I can hear it in your voice. I can hear it in your breath."

Lightfoot sniffed and took another sip. "John, tell me something."

"I got ten minutes before I gotta start playing, Cap'n. I'll tell you whatever I can squeeze in."

"Tell me how you got here again."

The blind man made a sort of humming sound. "Avoiding the subject, huh? All right. You mean about Galveston, and the hurricane and all?"

"I do."

"You know that story. Eight years ago. Worst storm known to man. Six thousand people dead and rotting in the sand, or out floating in the Gulf. They say they found me when the tide went out, curled up on the beach underneath a church door. Head stove in and my eyes all full of blood."

"And you couldn't recollect who you were."

"No, sir. Never have."

"Or where you come from?"

Nemo shook his head.

A note of skepticism crept into the ranger's voice here, as it always did. "But you could play the piano. You remembered that much."

"I didn't really remember how to play. I just did it. Your turn."

The ranger examined the backs of his hands. "I want to tell you something, but I don't exactly know how."

"Aw, Cap'n. Everyone strays from the straight and narrow every once in a while. You tell Freda?"

"That ain't it."

"Well, if it ain't that, what are you worried about? Tell her. A woman likes to know things. Even the bad things."

"Not likely she'd want to know this. She'd think I was crazy."

"She already thinks you're crazy. And we're down to seven minutes."

"I was out on this . . . mountain. Or hill. Enchanted Rock. You heard of it?"

"Heard of it. Sure. Never been out that way."

"Granite thing. It ain't a mountain, exactly, but it does a good job trying. Shaped like a giant tit."

"No wonder you was on it."

"John, you ain't makin' this any easier. I was being chased."

Nemo let out a soft snort of amusement. "Well, that ain't supposed to be the way it goes. A ranger gettin' chased, I mean. That happen often?"

"Often enough. I was being chased, and just when I thought I couldn't run anymore, I happened on these men."

"What kind of men?"

"Or maybe not exactly men. They were there one minute, and then they weren't. It was like I couldn't see 'em unless I wasn't looking."

John fingered a single note on the piano.

"They took me somewhere. I fell into some hole in the rock and I was trapped there, in my body at least, but my mind—my *head*—was . . . traveling. They told me who I was. Not who I was *pretending* to be, but who I am. These were men or the spirits of men who had no love for me or everwhat I'd done, and yet they seemed not to want vengeance. And they told me there was a use for me. As a soldier, like."

Again with the note. John Nemo listened as if the sound carried with it a whole library of information. "A soldier. Like, in the army? They say why? 'Cause you don't seem like the soldierin' type to me."

"There ain't an army in the world would have me. But this ain't an army of the world, John. It's a . . . brotherhood. That's what they called us. And there's a war going on."

The piano player tilted his head back, as if to keep as much distance as possible from the man who was talking. "All right, Cap'n. You're starting to give me the heebie-jeebies. Who all's in this brotherhood? This ain't like them Klan boys, is it? Where's there a war going on?"

"It ain't nothing like that. The war is all around us. A war between the light and the dark. Good and evil. And they want me in it."

"On which side?" John Nemo waited to hear the ranger chuckle. Nothing came. "Hey. You still with me?"

"I'm serious. They said I had a gift. They were as bright as the sun, John. It hurt to look at them. Their faces were like anyone's and no one's. I don't know how long I was with them, but even after all that time I wasn't hungry or thirsty. Not the least bit. I didn't even worry that there was bad men after me that wanted me dead. They all had these markings—tattoos, I guess—on the insides of their left arms. Like, a cross, but inside a box, and in between the bars of the cross were four leaves, or petals, like petals of a flower." The ranger took his pencil out of his waist-coat and opened his notebook. He sketched the image as best he could remember it, which was imperfectly, though of course it didn't matter to John Nemo.

"They said I had this gift that I needed to be using for something more important than chasing whores and horse thieves. And drinking my pay. And—"

"And what?"

"And leaving Freda here the way I do."

John Nemo's chuckles shaded into a wholehearted laugh.

"What's so funny?"

"I'm sorry, Cap'n. It ain't about Freda. You just sounded so puzzled when you said that word. *Gift*. Did they have to set about convincin' you?"

"They weren't the arguing type. But I reckon I could have used a little more convincing. 'Cause I never felt like I had no gift."

"Well?"

"Well what?"

"What was the gift?"

Just then a boy burst into the saloon. He looked to be about ten years old, but he was wearing man-size shoes and breathing hard.

"Lightfoot?" he called. "Sergeant Jewel Lightfoot?"

"Captain Jewel Lightfoot!" Jess shouted.

The ranger raised his hand. "Over here."

"Message for you."

Lightfoot gave the kid a nickel and took the note. He read it and crumpled the paper in one fist. The beer went down in a single draught. "John," he said. "Listen. Tell Freda I said so long, will you?"

"Of course I will. But what was the gift?"

"Another time, friend."

"Let's hope," said the piano player. He listened as the sound of Jewel Lightfoot's boots moved quickly across the floor and up the steps. There was a gust of cool air from outside. Then the door slammed shut again and Lightfoot was gone.

"Jess!" the piano player called.

"Yeah?" The big man stuck his head out the kitchen door.

"Read me something, would you?"

Jess slung a towel over his shoulder and wandered over to the table. "As long as it ain't music."

"Piece of paper. Seems like maybe he slapped it down on the table."

"Sure. It's right here. Wrote out by hand."

"What's it say?"

"Hold on." The big man reached into a pocket of his apron and brought out a pair of spectacles. "Says here, 'Suspects spotted. Come quick.' Signed, 'AW.'"

John Nemo slumped on his bench. "Lord Almighty," he sighed.

"Gone again?" said Jess.

"Tell the girls to tread easy tonight, brother. Freda ain't gonna like it."

26. The Land of Dead Horses

West Texas

Al Woodard had done him right, and he wouldn't forget it. Even though Lightfoot was technically working for the commissioner of insurance rather than the state police, the colonel had pulled two of his best men up from Alice to assist in the hunt. Floyd Farrell and White Dave McCluskey were veteran rangers who could ride and track. They knew how to keep themselves warm in the winter and how to find water in the summer and, most importantly, how to keep their mouths shut.

Farrell was a thick-set individual of thirty-four years, red-headed, with bulky thighs and forearms and a reputation for physical violence. He wore a loden tweed overcoat and bowler, a black waistcoat, and a blue cravat. A one-time dental student in Rochester, New York, he'd come west, he sometimes said, for no reason at all. This generally meant trouble with a woman or the law, or maybe both, but in Texas it was still possible to outdistance such difficulties and start a new life, and it was thought rude to pursue too intently the particulars of a man's former years.

Floyd Farrell was not forthcoming about his past, but he seemed quite comfortable in the present. Instantly recognizable by virtue of his ginger hair and handlebar moustache, he was a popular man with the brass. Most folks thought him an up-and-comer, a future officer. It helped that he could drink like a fish and tell a joke about any group of people a man could name. But what cemented his status among the rank and file was that he was the rangers' middleweight boxing champ—their only boxing champ, now that the force had dwindled so—and regularly pounded into submission whatever bare-knuckles man the San Antonio constabulary could dig up to face him.

Dave McCluskey, by contrast, was pale and spidery and rarely spoke. He was called White Dave to distinguish him from Dave O'Malley, a dark-complected Irishman serving in Company D, and Big Dave Diefenbach, who'd left the rangers a few months previous to take a job with the Pinkerton Agency. White Dave had thinning brown hair and a long, mournful face with almost no eyebrows. Dressed in an oversize black suit and festooned with two bandoliers that crisscrossed his narrow chest, he ate little, drank less, and mostly kept to himself. Someone who met White Dave on the street might have mistaken him—minus the bandoliers, of course—for an overworked shop clerk or an undertaker's apprentice who'd just had a close call with a runaway ice wagon.

A word of greeting would go unreturned. Instead White Dave would offer the slightest nod of acknowledgment and then duck into a nearby alley, as if determined to avoid human interaction of even the most desultory kind. Despite his social shortcomings, McCluskey was a valuable hand. He was an obsessive type who could stay on a trail while other men fell exhausted from their saddles. He was also deadly at up to a quarter of a mile with his thirty-inch Sharps rifle, a prehistoric beast of a weapon that he kept in a deer-hide scabbard lashed to his saddle. Some said he belonged in a Wild West show for his uncanny marksmanship.

Others thought he would be a better fit for a wax museum, given his strange, sallow countenance and wholesale indifference to the conventions of human intercourse.

The three men met at the train station near the river, where they shook hands and performed an even briefer version of the customarily curt ranger introductions, which consisted primarily of an exchange of nods. Lightfoot introduced his comrades to Antonio Ramos as well. Antonio's dark hair spilled out from under a battered straw hat, and he chewed on a stalk of spear grass as he looked on impassively, as if he were the one reviewing these veterans for their suitability to ride with him.

The rangers traded glances, and though their eyes held questions, the inquiries never made it to their mouths. Jewel Lightfoot was a name to conjure with. In this land, Mexicans were the enemy more often than not, but if the kid was good enough for the sergeant, they weren't going to kick. McCluskey spat. Farrell grinned, as if he were in on whatever joke the storied veteran was playing, and the matter was settled. The four men boarded the train for the two-day trip to Junction, where they hired horses and a pack mule, bought supplies, and set out. Antonio pitched in to pay for the flour and bacon. Lightfoot strongly advised him to invest in a pair of gloves.

"Rough country," he said.

The kid was unresponsive. But when he mounted his horse a few minutes later, his hands were no longer bare.

They picked up the fugitives' trail just west of Ozona, a scab of a settlement in the rugged caldera country that contained, as its name suggested, mostly air. There, the county sheriff showed them a bullet-ridden body that he'd set out to rot in the bed of a wheel-shot milk wagon. The sheriff had posted the bulletin sent out by Austin containing descriptions of the suspects headed west. The dead man had been taken by two of the county's deputies, surprised as he watered a mule in Honey Creek, northeast of town. The deputies had killed the mule, too, but they'd been unable to locate the other members of the party.

Farrell sniffed. "I've seen catfish prettier than this."

In truth, it was an ugly corpse. Norberto had been unprepossessing in life, and death had not improved his features. He'd grown emaciated, notably so even in a land of want, and though he was young, two of his teeth were missing. His fingernails were long and cracked and ill-tended. One of his eyes had been shot out, possibly at close range, since the socket was scorched by what looked to be a powder burn, and he'd been hit at least six other times in the head and neck. Nevertheless, Lightfoot recognized the dead man as the slender Mexican who'd come close to killing him at the stone fort near Fredericksburg. At Norberto's feet lay a single dust-stained huarache and a battered straw hat. The ranger picked up the hat. Inside it were letters written in green ink on the greasy band. He mouthed the name: *Kelso*.

The sheriff was an older man, not given to idle talk, and yet he felt prolix and foolish in the presence of the rangers, who considered him with eyes half-shut, like lizards, reflecting neither disdain nor approval. Lightfoot thanked the lawman for his time and the diligence of his deputies but allowed as how delay was the enemy of his posse now. They were nearing the border, with nothing to slow the men they hunted but the terrain and their own fatigue. It was time to move. The sheriff was asked to bury the body and instructed to wire details of the killing to Al Woodard in Austin.

By the time he'd agreed, Lightfoot was mounted. "How's the water to the west?" he asked.

"You're good for a day or two. Live Oak Creek is up. That's about fifteen miles. The Pecos is another ten after that. Then it's a mite dry till Fort Stockton."

The ranger put a finger to the brim of his hat, then reined his horse to the right. His companions followed. "Oso Creek might be running," offered the sheriff. But his advice went unacknowledged.

The earth they entered now was desolate and starved of life, a scroll of perdition unfurled by the Almighty as promise or warning of some brand of punishment eternal and unremitting. The vegetation was creosote and mesquite, parched and thorny, and it tore at them as they passed, catching their hats and the sleeves of their shirts, raking the flanks and fetlocks of the horses. Vocal in his contempt for their discomforts, Antonio cursed at first, but his imprecations died out in the arid land as he realized words were no currency with the men he rode with, who took in all around them with little outward show of judgment or even acknowledgment. They were men who watched the ground and sky and the shimmering horizon and among whom, for long hours at a time, no speech would pass.

They traveled all day through the broken country, the low caprock mesas of the Chihuahuan Desert studded with sotol and shin-stabbers standing stark on the slopes of the bluffs, the flowering stalks of the vegetation brown and dead. There was little comfort to be found in this grim region, but these were souls accustomed to dry places and they moved silent and uncomplaining down through the rimpled canyons with their shadows thick and dark as underground lakes and then back up again into the meager consolations of the late-autumn sun. The wind blew always across the khaki-colored grasses and the poisonous yellow blooms of the snakeweed, and the rocky soil crunched beneath the hooves of the animals. As the day warmed, insects could be heard chuffing and buzzing in the brush as they passed, but there was no game to be seen, nor even birds, and water was their chief concern.

The land opened up in front of them and they could see from every promontory a wrinkled scape that stood empty and uncompromising. The hills passed from sunlight into shadow as the clouds traveled over them, and sometimes rainstorms glimmered in the middle distance but moved away, and farther still the dim gray rumors of mountains formed distant barriers as if the world itself were some fortified redoubt and beyond it horrors too massive and indistinct to be named. The trail they followed was faint but consistent and it told a story plain to men who could read it.

The fugitives they hunted were of a race as ancient and tenacious as the roots of some vast tree dug deep into the black and unforgetting earth, and they too were born to hardship and acquainted with its rough embrace. Still, they were people of the jungle lowlands, a country of gorges and riotous, rainbow-colored birds, where the air was heavy, freighted with moisture, and mist crept through the valleys like serpents released from an underworld kingdom. The desert was no friend to such as these. Its assaults were starting to tell. The fugitives were hampered too by the god they served, which was also the cargo they hauled, and by their knowledge that the land held no welcome or refuge and that discovery would mean their death. They butchered the old mare for sustenance. They hid in the daylight hours and traveled by night like revenants from a realm of shadows, following the ravines and washes and what faint paths they could, taking turns whipping the one gaunt mule that dragged the cart through the dust. So they struggled on, haunted and quick-eyed, and they grew hungry in this empty place. Their progress slowed.

Ramon fretted over the thing that pounded and shrieked

within its wooden box during the hours of waning daylight. He prayed to it and offered it whatever animal blood could be obtained, but human life was scarce here and moved warily through the land, and so provisions ran low. With Norberto missing and presumably dead, only Ramon and Paco remained to join the mule, like beasts themselves, in dragging the battered wagon. Always the restless god moved in their minds, his presence like a sullen stranger, seeding their thoughts with hopeless visions and violent urges. At times Ramon found himself crawling on the earth, his head splitting in pain, the deity seemingly intent on breaking him from within, its voice a litany of threats and incantations repeated incessantly like the cries of an idiot railing at the summer sun.

"Yes!" Ramon would scream. "I will find it for you. I will bring it." And then, so softly he could barely hear himself: "I will bring you blood."

Ramon had imagined the god would have other ideas in mind. That he would communicate with his followers in something other than a shriek. That there was rationality or even wisdom in the creature's head. None was forthcoming. And yet the earth provided little, and the border stayed just out of reach. The Anglos were closing in. He could feel them coming, and at this pace Ramon and his god were still a week away from the compass coordinates the German had provided. He was starting to wonder if they would make it in time. And what awaited them at the designated spot? He didn't want to expose himself to further danger, and he didn't want to lose what he'd found. But the money would be useful, if he could take it from the German's emissaries. He could use Paco for that—and the god himself.

It seemed to grow bigger every day. And more demanding. They'd taken two sheep in the low country north of Sanderson. This helped, but the dark lord had consumed them himself, and when he was done, there was little left for the men to eat. Just when Ramon thought he could travel no more—that he would have to sink down by the side of the wagon and sleep, regardless of the risk—just then, he saw the thin column of smoke ahead. The god must have smelled it. Ramon heard it stirring in its pine-board box—the rasp of claws raking the lid, the creak of the wooden planks as the creature shifted its weight.

"People," he said to himself. And then, as he realized the implications of his announcement: "Food."

A little girl stood watching them from twenty yards ahead, her angular figure silhouetted against a purple sunset. She wore a simple cotton shift and eyed them through the tangled locks of her dark hair.

Every instinct in Ramon wanted to tell her to run, to warn whomever she could find, to leave this place until he and his unholy cargo were well clear of it.

And then the god spoke in the gaunt priest's mind. Ramon shuddered with the pain. He slumped to his knees and tried to blink the sting of the sweat and grit out of his eyes. His hands were torn and bloody. His feet were worse. He hadn't eaten in two days, and he wasn't hungry now. He lived only to push the wagon forward, to scout for sustenance for the thing he served, to do as it commanded. His jaguar headdress was long gone. He wasn't even sure when it had disappeared. He wasn't a priest any longer anyway. He was only a slave.

He knew what he had to do. He had to kill this thing that controlled him.

The girl still stood there, watching. Ramon shut his eyes tight, fighting the sudden association his mind was making for him. She looked like his little sister, Itzel. Now buried beneath some forlorn patch of Yucatan jungle. She seemed to call to him. He thought for a moment he heard his real name ringing in his ears.

But he shook it off. It wasn't Itzel. Itzel was dead, and nothing mattered anyway. The pain again. Tearing his head in two. His life was no longer his own.

He stood up beside the battered wagon. He tried to smile. He waved.

"*Mija*," he called. "Help me. *Ayúdame, por favor.*"

A tear snaked down Ramon's dirty cheek. He heard the cover of the wooden box slide to one side as the girl started forward. She stopped when she saw the thing rise up from the bed of the cart. She screamed, and a stream of urine wet her legs and the dust between them. The god was on her before she could scream again.

"You enjoyin' yourself, son?" asked the ranger. He tossed the kid another piece of biscuit.

Antonio dipped his head almost imperceptibly. "You get six shells in that shotgun?" he asked. His eyes shifted to take in the ranger's Winchester, which lay in its scabbard next to the rest of his kit.

"Pardon?"

"Your shotgun. Six shells?"

"Five. But I've never needed more."

"Barrel's short, I think."

"Good eye. Thing ain't much good for target shooting, but it'll clear a room. Trust me."

Lightfoot had to credit the kid's behavior. The straw hat he wore now had a two-inch hole on one side, thanks to a mesquite thorn, but he didn't complain. The kid endured the cold at night with the aid of a scarlet serape. He was quick with a knife, knew what would burn and what wouldn't, stayed awake when assigned to watchdog the camp. They'd brought a pack mule on the trip to carry their supplies, and Antonio was tasked with tending it. He fed and watered the mule, as well as his own mount. He carried its lead rope as they rode and made sure the mule's *aparejo* was properly blanketed each morning. He also took it upon himself to wrap all the animals' fetlocks in cloth to shield them from the worst of the thorny vegetation they rode through, and he rubbed them down with whatever grass he could find at the end of the day. And yet the boy refrained from complaint and indeed seemed to grow stronger as they rode.

This was more than the ranger could say for himself. The dart wound in his neck was only a minor irritant now, but the shotgun punctures were a misery, and his knee still hurt. His back ached with all the miles in the saddle, and he found himself lying awake in the early-morning hours with his stomach burning from their meager campfire fare—principally beans and hot water cornbread with a few chunks of fatty beef mixed in. At such times his thoughts turned to Austin, which meant they turned to Freda. Her bed, in particular, and the soft expanse of her hips and rump, the warmth of her sleeping beside him when the room grew chilly and the stars creaked past overhead, bent on their mysterious errands. When he felt the need to piss burning between his legs, he tried to ignore it, to burrow deeper in his blankets, to find her again at the far end of his dreams. Which was dangerous. So he dragged himself up out of sleep into the dark, cold world and searched the rocks around him for signs of his enemies.

The thing he'd seen was out there. He couldn't name it, but he could feel it. And though he couldn't say what the creature was— god or demon or something in between—he knew well enough what it wanted. It wanted him dead. Not him, personally. It wanted him dead for the simple fact that he lived. It wanted all

of them dead, whether they served it or not, hunted it or worshiped it, whether they were brown or white or yellow or black.
And sometimes, in the half-light of dawn, the ranger thought
he could see it, slipping into and out of the shadowy clefts in
the cliffs around them, waiting for an opportunity, an accident,
a moment of disregard. Waiting to strike. Waiting to kill them
all. He was wide awake now. His knee told him that, and his
sore hips, and the holes in his shoulder. And still he stood. His
piss steamed in the early-morning chill as, with the thumb of
his right hand, he felt for the hammer of his shotgun. He wasn't
ready to admit it, but he knew it was true. He was afraid.

27. A Difficult Confession

November 11

FREDA:

I am not a top hand for writing, as you must know by now. Still, I have had considerable time for reflection on this expedition, along with cause for such. I therefore propose to express my sentiments to you once and for all. It is my belief, and now my intention, that we should grow old together. You have showed me great patience in many matters, large and small. I regret that it has taken me so long to see what has been as "plain as the nose" on my face. You have wondered if it is my reluctance to wed a woman who out-earns me and is clearly a quick study of things I have no patience for. It is not that. I will just have to figure out how to make an honest dollar! You have also asked me oftentimes to share with you some portion of my work and the cold visions it has planted in me, in the hopes I think that you could shoulder part of the burden. I know you mean every word of it, however I am afraid I may not ever be able to do as you ask. For one thing, I am not sure you would believe me. For another, I am not sure I want you to. This is a queer thing to say, I know.

But the fact is, I have been employed at various times at Al Woodard's command, or as he calls it "request," in the investigation of strange and brutal mysteries.

My current assignment is no different. Today in our tracking of a group of bandits—for that is all I can say by way of description at present—we came upon the scene of their most recent visitation, an encampment of candelilla gatherers. These poor people are of Indian heritage and live very humbly in this desolate land. They survive by harvesting the candelilla plant and boiling it to make a sort of wax that water-proofs garments and seafaring gear. It is a hard life, with little to recommend it. And yet it is a living, or was, until snuffed out in summary and monstrous fashion by the outlaws we seek. The butcher's bill stands at seven: two men, two women, two boys, and what appears to have been a little girl. Killed—and worse, though I will spare you the details of this savage holocaust. You may ask if it is hard to fathom the degree of depravity that must be required to commit such acts of violence. The truth is no, it is not hard for me to understand. I have seen it too often. My greatest fear is that such depravity is not only something that a man can become accustomed to, but that it might actually be catching, like a disease of the lungs or blood, and that indeed I carry it within me already. This is what wakes me in the middle of the night. Not the nightmares, but the desire to keep them from you. And if you will have me, I caution you: You will have them too. It is a troublesome parcel. So consider well, my darling. I love you. But I know I am not the golden goose, and I would not blame you one minute for choosing to spend your life with one of the thousand or so more eligible and deserving men I know are out there.

If you still want me, I see now that we have no time to waste. I am tired, as you know, and ready to retire this badge—but only if there is some reason to do so. I have come to believe that you are that reason. I hope you still feel the same way about me, and that you will wear my ring when I return.

Your devoted servant, Jewel

28. Encounter

Brewster County

Six days out of Ozona, White Dave killed Paco from two hundred yards away, sending a .45-caliber slug from the Sharps rifle straight through the back of the big man's neck and out his broad forehead. McCluskey stopped to take the scalp, and his companions said no word either of congratulation or condemnation but watched as the tall man sawed a circle around the crown of the fallen fugitive's skull and then yanked the flesh and coarse hair from the bone with an audible pop. No burial was effected, Christian or otherwise, and no psalter consulted. They left the big man where he lay. Beside him were the head and feet of a rat. He'd eaten the rest. A piece of the tail was still stuck in his gold-capped teeth.

They trailed the creature and his lone remaining caretaker another three days, as the sky grew parched and color drained from the land. Now they could track it from portions of the bodies it left behind—ruined fragments, skin and bone and clothing, of the candelilla harvesters it had killed and kept. The scent of the butchered carcasses brought vultures, and so the fugitives were easily followed. In the failing light of mid-November, the posse crossed into Brewster County and neared the broken knees of the Sierra del Caballo Muerto—the Dead Horse Mountains—a long, spiny spur of the Sierra Madre Occidental that points into Texas from Mexico like a witch's finger. There the trail doubled back, headed southeast.

That night the lawmen slept beneath an overhang at the foot of a rock ridge where a seep bled water over the cool stone and into a broad, shallow pool. There were open hands painted on the granite and faded pictographs from a time beyond telling of antelope running from men with spears. Lightfoot searched the soil for arrowheads to bring back to Freda but found none. The tracks of coyotes, deer, and pigs led to and from the water, but the tracks were old, a week at least, and the night was quiet. He slept very little and poorly at that, prodded by his sense of responsibility for those he traveled with and by visions, twenty years old and more, of faces he'd seen smeared with crowns of their own blood, black faces and shattered skulls and the twisted limbs of the servant girls in the very first case he'd ever worked with Al Woodard. The ranger took the dog watch, hunched for warmth near a fitful fire of cedar and mesquite that popped and sent showers of cinders up into the darkness. Sometime past midnight he looked up and saw, or thought he saw, an animal gazing down at him from the sheer wall fifty feet above. The eyes glowed red in the guttering firelight. Lightfoot's heart froze. He reached for his sidearm. It lay just beyond his grasp, and he stole a glance sideward to retrieve it. When he looked up again, the face that had seemed so near was lost in the shadows, and when dawn came, so strange was the occurrence that he did not mention it to his companions lest they think him daunted by this harsh territory and the things that moved within it.

Ramon was injured. It was obvious from his footprints, the left imprinting deeper than the right, as they led toward the Sierra del Carmen. Lightfoot gathered from the sudden shift in direction that the priest was still lucid. He had seemed to be headed west toward the Ghost Mountains before he veered off in the direction of the compass coordinates he'd been given. Whatever the reason for the delayed turn, the ranger was grateful. There were homesteads in the slightly more hospitable Ghosts to the west, and in the valley just beyond those peaks a thriving mining town, Terlingua, where men, mostly Indians, scratched the blood-colored ore called cinnabar from beneath the desert floor and slowly went mad from the poisons that seeped into their skin.

Lightfoot knew Ernst-Michael Kitzinger had sent Ramon the coordinates, to allow him to find someone or something that would allow him to complete his mission. But Kitzinger was no altruist. Why would a German academic want to help Mexican nationals transport a nightmare like the creature they were hunting? Unless the Germans wanted to take possession of the creature for themselves. Again, though, why? What possible use could anyone have for such a thing? Lightfoot shook his head. None of it made sense.

The ranger had heard of the Dead Horse region, though he'd not traversed it, and only Floyd Farrell was familiar with its skeletal contours. He said the name came from the slaughter of Apache ponies by Captain Charlie Neville four decades earlier. Neville had captured the ponies and didn't want to run the risk of their being lost or stolen back by the Indians, so he shot the animals where they stood. Such a measure was not unheard of. Ranald Mackenzie and the U.S. Cavalry had done the same with hundreds of Comanche horses in Palo Duro Canyon in 1876. But a horse was esteemed in Texas not only as property but also as companion, and so the killings had a heightened import. Indeed, Charlie Neville was widely despised for this and similar acts that seemed questionable even to men who sought out the badlands as if to find some analog for the emptiness that stretched out bitter and disconsolate inside them.

But White Dave, in one of his rare experiments with conversation, said he'd heard it different. "The Spanish," he said. His voice was pinched and reedy, betraying a possible motive for his general silence. "They come through here three hundred years ago, looking for gold. Apaches didn't much like it, from what I've heard. Followed them Spaniards clean down from New Mexico through this here desert. The horses gave out for lack of water. The Spaniards left the bodies where they fell. Said you coulda followed the trail down to the Rio Grande just by walking from carcass to carcass. Indians finally hit 'em just over the river. Three men survived by hiding under the horses. Three men. Out of over a hundred. The rest was hauled off by the Apaches, who burned 'em alive and then ate their hearts. That's their way."

There was no dissent. It was indeed the Apache way, and the brutality of their methods seemed to hang over these environs like the last lingering notes of a discordant symphony. But the story did nothing to lighten the men's mood. This was ghost country now—what the old hands called *los Despoblados*, or the empty regions. Bristling with yucca and lechuguilla, the land lay desolate and vengeful, riven by ruts, and none among them rode at ease among its folds. They crossed the Rio Grande, shallow and sandy here, and barely fifty feet wide, two miles east of Boquillas Canyon and entered Mexican territory. Then they started climbing, following game trails and what scattered clues they could find as they inched up into the highlands.

The massive central ridge of the Sierra del Carmen is forty-five miles long and stands thousands of feet above the desert floor, higher at its jut-jawed peaks in the south. The lands below it are rimpled by weather-sculpted washes and in these scars the spindly willows and catclaw bushes stand desperate in the dust, but the walls of the Sierra rise high enough from the surrounding barrens to create their own world, an island atop the limestone bluffs where stands of pine and spruce trees grow and the woods are home to bears and wild pigs and the most elusive and lethal of the desert's hunters, the cougar. It is difficult to overstate the beauty of this land, for it seems to rise like a frozen wave of rock, a fortress of dreams, unyielding and tremendous, wreathed by storm clouds in the afternoon and glowing with stripes of pink and orange in the dying light of dusk. Its summits remain bright long after darkness has settled over the ruined territories beneath them.

The posse moved tiny and powerless through this abject kingdom. At night the moon glided through a sky flecked with stars as thick and hard as snow, and the world was so still Lightfoot could almost hear the eternal creaking of God's cold machinery at work. This was coyote country, and this the time of year of their mating, but none were to be heard—a curious and unsettling circumstance. In the morning the men woke with frost on their blankets, the moisture wrung from the air and deposited like some rime or crust of age on their saddles and bedrolls and in their hair, and they could see the small geometry created by mice and shrews in the dirt, but these creatures passed as if frightened by some shadow in the heavens and the rangers never saw them. So too with the quail and hawk and white-tailed deer, the small variety of deer often seen in this region, which were absent in the chill of fall as if startled from the land by a force silent but undeniable and intrusive in some register of existence too low to be detected by the men but unmistakable to those who spent their lives in communion with the earth.

The next day at dusk they found Ramon waiting for them on a ledge high above the rocky trail they were walking. Antonio was the first to spot him. The priest was apparently dozing, with a brown felt hat pulled low over his forehead and a shotgun cradled in his arms. He'd positioned himself between the canyon wall and a boulder, with only a foot of space between them for firing. But rather than planting himself on the far side of this little parapet, he'd settled down in front of it—in plain sight from the trail below.

Lightfoot breathed a sigh of relief that they'd seen him first. The Mexican had a perfect view of the trail they were following. If only they could reach him before he woke. Taken alive, he might be the key to finding the monstrous thing he served. Lightfoot raised a palm for silence and ordered the posse forward by gesture alone. It took an hour of tedious inching up the wall to determine that Ramon wasn't sleeping at all. By the time they reached him, it was almost dark. McCluskey pushed the inert figure over with the butt of his rifle. Floyd Farrell crouched and struck a match. By the meager light they could see that most of the Mayan's face was gone. Though the eyes were intact and open wide, the skin and lips and even portions of the skull had been peeled and removed like the rind of an orange to expose the teeth and gums and what looked like the lower portion of the brain. They rolled the body over. The legs and hips had been savaged as well, but Lightfoot could see through the blood the long scars that cut the Mexican's back. Like snakes, Lyssa Peterson had said. Now it seemed the snakes would crawl no more.

"Conscience has been eating away at him," said Farrell. But no one laughed.

Lightfoot pointed out that Ramon had given his life for his god. He had been a priest of some sort, the celebrant of whatever blood ritual the creature demanded before it ate the flesh of its victims, and priests devote their lives to their deities. So maybe the priest had died happily in service to his dark lord. But it sure didn't look that way. At any rate, the posse's quarry now numbered one only. The most dangerous one.

White Dave exhaled as he unfolded his long frame to its full height. He'd rolled the corpse faceup again and pulled his knife to take what was left of Ramon's scalp when the dead man awoke. The priest's eyes focused as if in obedience to some whispered command. He sat upright, grabbed the shotgun beside him, and fired, blowing the hat off Dave McCluskey's head and sending the tall man reeling backward, stunned by the blast. The ranger struggled to understand what he was seeing: a mutilated corpse pulling itself up off the rock and turning to find another target. Its breath was a rattling horror, its eyes emotionless and empty.

Lightfoot fumbled with his sidearm as the priest fired the second barrel of his gun, which was aimed directly at him. There was a dull click in the chamber—a dud. It was all the ranger needed. He emptied his six-shooter into the corpse, which shuddered as the slugs entered its body but continued to advance. Nothing could be standing after that. Nothing human. But the lifeless thing lurched forward again.

Forward—toward him.

The ranger threw the empty revolver and struck the corpse in the face. Still it moved closer, its bloody hands reaching for him. Lightfoot edged backward, feeling down and to one side for the Winchester he'd left standing beside a rock. He touched it at just the same moment the walking horror lunged. It flung its cold arms around his neck, pressed its broken teeth against the skin of the ranger's throat, and carried him off the ledge. The two men, alive and dead, tumbled down the loose rock and dirt of the canyon wall, still grappling with each other. When they stopped sliding, the ranger slammed an elbow into what was left of the dead priest's jaw. He twisted loose of the corpse's grasp and dove for his rifle, which lay just a few feet farther down the slope.

The creature grabbed his boot and pulled him back. Now, though, Antonio threw himself down the slope in pursuit. He hit Ramon just as his teeth were sinking into the leather of the ranger's boot. Antonio and the priest wound up farther down the slope, coming to rest at the lip of a long, steep drop to the canyon floor. The ranger grabbed his Winchester. He half leapt, half fell down the rock face.

"Move, kid!"

Ramon turned to face the ranger again. The dead thing's face was a mask of blood and dust, its eyes dark and emotionless. Antonio dove to one side, and before the priest could react, Lightfoot fired at point-blank range, splitting the corpse's head in two. Now, finally, the body collapsed.

The ranger stepped forward and fired again, straight into the thing's one remaining eye. Then he kicked it—once, twice, a third time, shaking with shock and anger. It was only then that he became aware of the cries of panic coming from the mouth of the canyon.

"The horses!" Lightfoot shouted.

Floyd Farrell and White Dave were already moving, threading their way back down the difficult route they'd climbed to get to Ramon just a few minutes earlier. Lightfoot and Antonio had to clamber back up the slope ten yards, then make their way laterally to a spot where they could descend, using hands and feet both, to the canyon floor. They heard rifle shots, then the thinner reports of pistol fire. Two men shouted. One of them screamed. A moment later, the ranger ducked as a dark figure glided past him, maybe fifteen feet off the ground. The figure might have been a vulture, but it was huge, much bigger than any bird. The ranger turned and fired his Winchester. As far as he could tell, he missed his target completely. At any rate, the thing showed no sign of injury. Lightfoot watched two membranes of skin unfurl around its form like wings as the creature glided down the narrow canyon into the darkness.

White Dave was lying faceup in the dirt with his rifle in his hand. Farrell knelt over him. The big man was panting, and his face had gone a bright red. McCluskey's horse was close to death. The pack mule's head had been ripped from its body, and a portion of the animal's intestines lay beside it on the rock. The three remaining horses had fled. Lightfoot could hear them calling to one another in the middle distance. Farrell contemplated the mare that lay dying just a few feet away, a deep gash carved into its left side, its hind legs still moving as if it could run.

"Sweet Jesus," he said, when he'd caught his breath. He shook his head as he turned and surveyed the dark peaks around them. "It flew."

White Dave had been just a few steps faster than Farrell in getting back to check on the animals, and he paid for it. He arrived at the spot where the horses were hobbled just in time to find a creature—at first he'd thought it was a bear—ripping the throat out of the mule. He'd fired twice, hitting it once, he'd thought, before he was knocked off his feet and found himself face to face with something that definitely wasn't a bear. "A bat," he said. "It was almost like a bat. Only—"

"Hey," said Lightfoot. "Simmer down. Stop talking. Floyd, take care of that mare."

"Shoot it?"

"Knife or pistol one. She ain't enjoying this." McCluskey's face and neck were slashed in a dozen places. His left ankle was broken, and he could barely stand for the pain in his back, but he claimed to be fit to ride. The men heard Antonio heaving in the mesquite brush for several minutes, but no one mentioned it. Like the ranger, the kid was scraped and sore from his fight with the dead priest but otherwise unhurt. The posse set up camp twenty-five yards back down the trail, just to be away from the mutilated animals. Farrell and Antonio tracked down the stray horses and brought them back, still skittish and panicky, while the ranger painted White Dave's wounds with carbolic acid and wrapped them in cotton strips. McCluskey was lucky. One of the scratches on his neck had come dangerously close to severing the carotid artery. He'd have been dead in minutes. As it was, his face and scalp were a mess, and he was still bleeding from a deeper wound just below the left side of his rib cage.

"Lie still," said Lightfoot.

"How bad?" asked the wounded man.

"Hell, I've had worse on my lip and kept whistling."

The ranger offered him a sip of whiskey from the flask he kept in his saddle bag, and White Dave drank gratefully. A minute later, he was asleep. The ranger watched over him until the moon appeared in the east. He couldn't help it. He took a long pull at the bottle. He was poised to take another when he looked through the firelight and saw his companions staring back at him, silent but questioning, relying on him for direction, for leadership—hell, for a simple answer or two. He'd gotten them into this fix, after all. He owed it to them to get them back out.

Lightfoot put the bottle back in his saddle bag. Save McCluskey, none of the men slept that night. There was no sense tempting bad dreams when the real thing was to be found so close at hand. In the early morning hours, they could hear the creature just around the outcropping of rock up the trail, devouring the cold juices of the dead animals the posse hadn't bothered to move. The sounds of its feast—snapping bones and the wet rasp of intestines being pulled from the carcasses—were oppressive enough. Worse for Lightfoot was the sense he had that the creature was cannier than he'd realized. The dead priest had been a distraction—a ploy to lure the men away from the animals. It had worked to perfection. Goddamned *perfection*. He should have known better. Could have. Should have. What was it his mother said, all those years ago? *If could and should were firewood, we'd all be warm on*

Christmas Eve. The ranger spat. He couldn't let them be outfoxed again. It wasn't just a matter of pride. He wasn't worried about his pride at the moment. As weak and under-provisioned as they were, he knew the next trick they fell for might well be their last. Lightfoot glanced at his companions, who were still trying to rest. He leaned over to where his saddle bags lay in the sand, fished in one of the compartments, and brought out the felt bag that held Ernesto's ammunition. He pulled out one of the silver bullets and held it up to the gray light spreading across the desert. The ranger still couldn't quite bring himself to believe what the old man had told him. But hell, he'd seen what he'd seen. Demon or not, lead slugs didn't seem to have much stopping power with the thing he'd fired on the previous evening. He snapped open the cylinder of his revolver and began replacing the rounds.

If Floyd Farrell and Dave McCluskey had thoughts of quitting, they kept such thoughts to themselves.

"Sergeant?" asked the redheaded man, hoisting himself into the saddle the next morning. His horse edged sideways, as if the animal was anticipating his question and not sure it wanted to hear the answer. "You're gonna have to tell me what we're tracking. I don't guess nobody wanted to talk about it last night, but I know I hit that thing with my .45 and it didn't seem to notice. You know what I mean. You emptied your Colt into that faceless sack of shit we thought was dead, and he just kept comin'."

Lightfoot nodded at the rising sun as if it was a helpful neighbor.

Farrell was a bluff, plainspoken man. He pointed out the obvious: "That ain't normal."

The sergeant struggled with his answer, though he'd known the question would come. "I don't know what to think," he admitted, kicking sand over the embers of their campfire. "It ain't natural, that's for sure. I have a friend in San Luis—Antonio's grandfather, as a matter of fact—says it's some kind of a demon. A fellow from a tribe of Indians down in southern Mexico didn't get the message exactly right and decided it was a god. The god of darkness that the Mayans worshiped a thousand years ago. But that don't look like any god I ever heard of. And hell. You've seen it. This bunch that dug it up had a map. They partnered with a con man name of Kelso, who rustled up the funds for an expedition. They found the thing we're tracking buried in a tomb up in the hills near San Luis, and somehow they brought it back to life. Now it's big, and it's getting bigger. It might have been worshiped. Maybe it still is. But I'm thinking it's something older and angrier than anyone counted on, and I also think this speculating ain't going to do us a hell of a lot of good, because whatever it is, god or devil, it's hungry, and it's dangerous, and it's gonna kill us if it gets half a chance, just like it killed our animals and them candelilla gatherers and its own high priest—that poor sonofabitch who was missing his face back there and still managed to get up and start wandering around like a drunk at a church picnic. I know that ain't much of an answer, but it's all I got."

"I believe that's more words than you've ever spoke at one time, Sergeant."

"Well, I'm glad you're amused."

"And you still didn't make a lick of sense."

"Hell," said White Dave, "we seen them tracks west of Sanderson. We knew somethin' wasn't right."

The men watched as Antonio tightened the girth strap on his horse. He was getting good at it. Something about the silence called for further explanation. The ranger tried again. "A woman took me to a play once. Freda. You know who Freda is, right?"

"You might have mentioned her," said Farrell.

"About a hundred times," added White Dave. He winced when he spoke.

"All right. Well, she took me to see a play once. A Shakespeare play, at the theatre. And one of the fellows in that play said something I've been thinking about ever since. He said there are more things in heaven and earth than we could ever figure on in our philosophy."

"We ain't at college," said Farrell. "We're in Mexico. What are you trying to say?"

Lightfoot ran his tongue over his lips. "I reckon," he concluded, "this is one of them things."

Farrell leaned down to check the length of one of his stirrups. "But why here? This trail ain't making a lot of sense. Where's this thing going?"

"It makes a little sense. We're in Mexico now, so we're outside our jurisdiction. We ought not to be here. This goddamned gargoyle we're tracking may not know it, but Ramon was trying to get him somewhere in particular. A set of compass coordinates, which according to the folks back in Austin, ought to be right about where we're standing. If I'm right, he was hoping to meet up with some friends of a German history professor back in Austin. The man who backed the expedition in the first place. German friends, I reckon. Or maybe Mexicans. Maybe both. I guess what I'm saying is, we may have more than just this bat thing to worry about if a bunch of *federales* are out here looking for it as well. All right. That's enough jawing. Antonio, I want you and Dave to double up on the buckskin. He's hurt. Don't let him fall off, son. You hear me?"

"I hear you."

"I ain't gonna fall off," McCluskey snarled.

"Germans?" said Farrell, still ruminating. "What the hell do Germans have to do with any of this?"

"Search me. Some say the German Empire wants to get bigger. They figure maybe if they get Mexico riled up against us, maybe we won't be as apt to get involved in stopping Germany elsewhere. Or maybe they figure they could use this thing we're following as a weapon."

The ranger's companions exchanged glances.

"That's about as clear as mud, Sergeant," said Farrell.

"You can leave if you've a mind to," said Lightfoot. "Dave? You in particular. You look like hell, son. I won't hold it against you."

White Dave pulled himself to his feet. "I can ride. I just can't walk."

"I ain't leaving," said Antonio, stuffing his long hair up under his hat. They'd almost forgotten he had a voice.

Floyd Farrell chuckled. "That's because you're too young to know any better," he said, and he flicked his reins.

The ranger suspected the creature was getting weaker. True, it had eaten its fill of the dead horse and mule. He wished they'd had a way to conceal the animals before that could happen, but the land wasn't much good for burial. Still, food here was scarce, and the weather was turning, and they had to have hit it with gunfire. Regardless of its monstrous form, it was flesh and blood, and flesh and blood could be torn and twisted. So Lightfoot did the only thing he knew to do. He tried as best he could to keep the demon moving up into the high country. He suspected the thing would be desperate and unpredictable without its human familiar—and reckoned also that it might think of the posse trailing it not only as a threat but also as prey. Were they hunters, or the hunted? Lightfoot was certain they were being watched, and he told his companions as much, though they could all feel its presence and such warnings were in fact unnecessary.

Willing as they were, they too were hungry, and their provisions were running low. They had enough cornmeal for another couple of days, but no beans or meat and only a little salt. The

oats were long gone, and the remaining horses were surviving on forage alone. Traveling with four men on three animals
was a hindrance as well. The men seldom spoke as they rode.
McCluskey was tight-lipped at the best of times, but now he
rode hunched and haggard, feverish from the seeping wounds in
his neck and side. Though he swore he was fine, he was uncon-
vincing. Lightfoot knew he couldn't keep him much longer, and
the plan he formulated was as much a recognition of necessity as
anything else. The notion met with disagreement from his companions, even Antonio, and eventually to outright protest. But
the senior ranger persisted in his stubbornness and—the others
let him know—stupidity.

"Just supposin'," said Farrell as they rode. "Supposin' we were
to go along with your plan. Tell me how it goes."

"First," said Lightfoot, "you're going to have to cut me."

The arguments intensified. The men grew visibly angry and
shouted at each other. And one cold autumn afternoon, shots rang
out loud and plain as the last band of red light gradually flattened
itself to nothing on the western horizon. From a distance—from
a niche in the cold rock high above the tallest tree—the con-
flict was clear. The posse had camped on a clearing hard by the
western edge of the sky island, a series of flat and stony plateaus
that stair-stepped down to a sheer cliff. Beyond the cliff lay the
tip of Texas and, south of the silver ribbon of the Rio Bravo,
the great brown deserts of Chihuahua. The men laid up all afternoon, squatting near a fire that guttered in the wind, sharing a
bottle and occasionally cursing each other. One of the men in the
group was wounded and rarely moved. Near the end of the day,
the arguments grew heated. Two of the men fired at a third, their
companion, the smallest of the group, who fell to the ground. A
moment later, he rolled to one side. One of the killers advanced
toward the body. Now he stood over it. The killer sighted down

along the barrel of his pistol and pumped another round into the fallen body. Then he and his comrades—the long-haired boy rode with them as well—gathered their belongings and mounted their horses. They looked around the scene, obviously nervous, and departed at a canter. The body lay unmoving on the rock. For an hour, nothing stirred on the high bluff.

And then, finally, the creature emerged.

It moved like mist in the feeble moonlight, advancing like a suspicion across the face of the luminous rock. It progressed in a crouch, long arms extended beside it, almost as if crawling, thin membranes of translucent flesh suspended between its limbs and torso. Larger than a man, it had features that were nevertheless vaguely human. Its dark eyes were set close beside a short snout with wide, upturned nostrils. Its long lower jaw shelved a mouth with two rows of sharply pointed teeth. It glanced around cautiously as it came, surveying the terrain, checking for threats. Twice the creature raised its head to filter the air for hints of danger. Nothing. All it could smell was rock and dust and blood—the dead man's blood, cooling on the granite. The scent made it frantic with hunger and anticipation. It must not be hurried, it remembered. It must stay safe. And yet here was sustenance. The creature had outlasted the little man and his companions, as it had outlasted and evaded and eventually destroyed so many others who had meant it harm before. The killers would be miles away by this time. Only the ranger remained. It would be a pleasant conversation, this: a colloquy of flesh and gristle and all that sweet internal soup, with nothing to disturb their discussions. The creature shifted its weight back on its haunches. It gripped the dead man's shoulder and turned the corpse to expose the throat and belly. It was not surprised to see the corpse's eyes were open. Many of the dead still tried to see. But then the eyes blinked. The big six-shooter was in the creature's rib cage and the blast came as the demon god twisted away. The impact broke bones, tore into its flesh. It started to burn.

It knew this sensation.

Silver.

Poison.

It screamed.

The pistol barked again and again, tearing holes in its side. Even in its pain, even as the silver exploded in the creature's bloodstream, polluting its senses, still it was aware of its enemy. The thing could see Lightfoot approach, knife in hand. It knew when the blade touched its skin and felt it start to bite. The creature struck the ranger and knocked him to the ground, but the little man rose and moved forward. The creature sprang at the man and he went down again. It could dispatch this puny thing with hardly a thought, but . . . it couldn't. It was burning. The metallic poison was spreading, and its blood was turning to fire. It had to concentrate. It had to kill this pathetic flea of an attacker if it did nothing else. The creature moved forward and the little man gave ground— back a step, and another, until he had backed to the edge of the cliff. Good. The fight would end here. It would take the head of this impudent slave and drink till it dropped the body to the desert below. But what it saw next made no sense.

The little man cowered as he held something out toward it. A torch. A candle, perhaps, burning on a long wick, spitting sparks into the air. The man tossed the fiery object toward the creature as if it were an offering, a tribute. And then he did something even stranger. The human gave up. He turned and hurled himself off the cliff.

The creature looked down just as the little wick burned out. The air turned to fire. White, then yellow.

No sound.

All sounds.

The sky bent and trembled over the creature's head. The demon-god fought to understand what had happened. It pulled itself up off the rock. At almost the same moment, the little man's face reappeared above the edge of the cliff. The man hadn't fallen at all. He had to be standing on some lower ledge or shelf of rock. He hauled himself up onto the mesa, then staggered off at an angle from where the creature was trying to move again in some organized fashion. It knew it had been tricked. Injured. There was no time to fight now. It knew it had to escape. It reeled toward the cliff. The moon stood low on the horizon, bright and too impossibly far to reach, but there was something else in the sky as well. A smaller object, but closer, and glowing with the possibility of refuge. It looked like a bullet—an airship of some sort, strange in aspect but clearly human-made. The creature knew what it had to do. It could not be taken. It couldn't go down, to be imprisoned in another cell of dirt and stone. The world was going black, but the demon-god realized its means of escape was at hand. The airship was waiting. It could fly to safety. It could grow strong again. Feed. Rule. Reign. It stood at the edge of the cliff and looked out over the freezing waste toward the craft that moved like a cloud across the sky.

Salvation.

The creature spread its wings, stepped off the rock, and flew. It climbed higher in the sky and allowed itself an impulse of relief. It was going to survive. It never even heard the report of the ranger's Winchester, but silver pellets fired from the slide-action shotgun tore into its spine, and this was enough. The creature shrieked with frustration as its ascent slowed and stalled. Then the dream began, and it found itself journeying into the shadow lands, even as its dark and failing physical form plummeted toward the desert floor. It was going home. Back into the darkness. Back into the realm of dreams, where those of its kind would be waiting, angry and envious, to tear it apart.

Lightfoot was on his knees when he saw the creature fall. For several moments after the creature sank from his field of vision, he waited to see what would happen with the Zeppelin. It was a strange and somehow beautiful apparition, a giant torpedo, silver and gray where it floated in the moonlight high in the sky. It had started turning away from the mountains when the ranger fired the blast that brought the creature down. Lightfoot mouthed a silent prayer that no one had spotted the demon-god as it swam up through the atmosphere toward the aircraft, seeking refuge. He willed the craft to keep moving. Now, though, it was turning back. Were there men on horseback down there in the desert shadowing the aircraft, waiting to seize what the eyes above them saw? Possibly they were headed toward his position even now. The fears raced through his brain like unruly children, without any conscious answer or even acknowledgment. But there was little the ranger could do about it. He scrambled across the rock to pick up his pistol, and then he hid himself as best he could as the airship approached. He watched the sky for half an hour without making a sound save his own ragged breathing. At one point the giant craft passed fifty feet overhead, its piston engines assaulting the autumn air. Finally the Zeppelin, a considerable distance farther away at this point, heeled off and headed west, its operators ignorant of the drama that had played itself out on the mountaintop not far below. And only then did the ranger succumb to the weight of his own exhaustion and fear. He slept then, long and deep, and for the first time in many weeks his mind was untroubled by dreams.

29. The Homestead

Freda was pleased with herself. This didn't happen often. She was too busy for it to be a regular occurrence, but when it came, the pleasure was visible on her face. Her stride lengthened, and she had a tendency to hum—polkas, typically, but occasionally a bar or two of "Won't You Come Home, Bill Bailey?"

The tract she'd bought for herself and Jewel was situated on the west side of Shoal Creek, on a bluff dominated by a giant oak. The creek was running strong today, giggling in the rocks due to a combination of some timely rainfall farther north and the constant, if sluggish, spring a few hundred feet upstream. Freda had finally settled on a carpenter and was hoping to get started in April. If everything went according to plan, she'd be in her new house by next Thanksgiving. And so would her ranger.

This particular element of the plan was a little less clear than the rest of it, but Freda had reason to hope. For one thing, she could tell Jewel was getting tired of the job. Or, not tired of the job, exactly. Just tired. He still loved the idea of rangering as much as any man alive. It was the physical part that was getting to him. The demands were difficult even for a young man to handle. And he—no matter what he sometimes pretended—was no longer young. Sooner or later, he was going to have to let himself, or make himself, rest. So this would be the bedroom, and here, between the bedroom and the kitchen, she envisioned a parlor of sorts, though small. Out back, facing the creek, they'd have a garden for growing tomatoes and squash and pumpkins, and close by they would build a hen house, not only for the eggs but also because chickens would keep bugs off the plants. It would be fine. And if Jewel Lightfoot wasn't inclined to come to her in her present circumstances, maybe the house would persuade him. She wasn't proud. If that's what it took, so be it.

Ah, but the sun. It was late in the year, and the sun was sinking early in the hills out west. The sky was tinged with that peculiar purple that a local writer once called the violet crown. A nice sound, that. The City of the Violet Crown. *And where do you live?* a well-dressed matron might ask her in an unlikely but possible future. On a train pulling into Philadelphia, for example. *I have a little place in Austin*, she'd respond. *The City of the Violet Crown. It's not much. A rose garden. A pretty view. But we get by. Yes. In fact, we do quite well, my husband and I.* But enough daydreaming. It was time for her to get back to Zenger's. She had budgets to prepare, girls to scold and counsel, accounts to reconcile. She didn't see the man until she was almost across the creek. He stood there at the crest of the far bank in the center of the trail, watching her with his curiously cold green eyes.

"Hello, Freda," he said. It was Sam Millicent. She knew enough to run.

30. Austin

November 29

ightfoot strode into Al Woodard's office without bothering to knock and tossed a burlap bag on the big desk.

"Just thought you'd want to know," he announced. "We caught up with the killers in them Coulter County murders."

Deak Ross glanced up at the ranger from his paperwork. A pipe sat smoking in a glass ashtray, and the office was a little too warm for Lightfoot's taste. For a moment Lightfoot had the impression that the little bureaucrat didn't remember who he was. Then the man's eyes narrowed. It was clear Deak Ross *did* remember—and that he wasn't pleased by what he saw.

"Sergeant Lightfoot," he said. "Is this a joke?"

"I heard Al was at home with his people. Thought I'd check in with you first." The ranger pointed with his chin. "Take a look."

Deak Ross's disgust was evident. Maybe it was the smell. It was as if Lightfoot had hauled a steaming sack of the underworld into the gleaming marble confines of the capitol. The major cautiously opened the bag and dumped its contents out on his desk. A misshapen gray head—at first, the major took it for a large stone, or possibly a coconut—rolled to a stop against a stack of files. One side of the hairless skull was stove in, and dried streaks of dark blood showed black in the lamplight. The long canine teeth of the creature were clearly visible where the skin of the mouth was torn away on one side. The thing's small eyes were closed, though

Lightfoot had tried to force them open for theatrical effect when he'd figured out how he wanted to display his prize. It hadn't been easy to collect, this trophy. He'd had to work his way down to the broad *bajada* at the base of the Sierra del Carmen. This had taken two days. He spent most of another afternoon searching in the talus for the body, which he'd finally found crumpled in the center of a heap of broken granite, the carcass torn almost in two by the force of the creature's impact with earth. The ranger hacked the head from the torso with his Bowie knife and tied it tightly in a bag. Then he attached a long fuse to the remaining stick of dynamite he'd recovered from the cave in San Luis. He shoved it as far down the gullet of the monster as he could, lit the fuse, and hustled away. The explosion ripped the corpse into a hundred shreds of oily dark flesh and deposited the fragments in a rough circle a hundred yards around. Still not satisfied, Lightfoot dug five holes and buried portions of the body in each. He kept the head, though he hadn't much liked to handle it, even through the burlap.

"God damn you, Lightfoot. This is an outrage. Explain yourself."

"It's in my report, Major. Hard to believe, but it's true."

"Farrell told me to expect your return. But what is this filthy thing, and why have you brought it to Austin? And it had better be good."

"Looks like a bat, don't it? Some kind of a walking nightmare. Gave us a hell of a time. Had to put on a little pantomime show, in fact. You'll be surprised to learn Floyd and a kid named Antonio cut me on the neck and the calf to get some blood flowing, then shot me up out in the Big Bend Country and left me for dead." The ranger walked around the desk and spat into Al Woodard's spittoon. "Only they was shootin' blanks, and I hadn't died quite yet."

"This is nonsense. You're drunk again. And I'm going to

want an accounting of any and all state funds you spent on your Mexican deputy."

"Antonio ain't Mexican. He's just as Texan as you or me."

"Where is he now?"

"Mexico, last I heard. Went to fight Porfirio Díaz. And I'm as sober as a judge. Haven't touched a bottle in over a week."

"Jesus. Just give me your report, Sergeant."

"I'm afraid I can't do that."

"And why not?"

"On account of my report is highly confidential and has been delivered under seal for review by the commissioner of insurance. Some of my findings are considered too, um, speculative for release to the public. The ones about a group of Mexican Indians unearthing an ancient Mayan god in the hopes it could spark up some kind of uprising to turn back the last four hundred years or so of history. I'm not supposed to talk about that. However, I can tell you it is my official determination and conclusion that Mr. and Mrs. Nils Peterson were murdered, that no suicide occurred, and that the death benefits attendant on their life insurance policies should be paid out forthwith, henceforth, and any other legal term you can think of to their only surviving heir, Lyssa Peterson, age five. Or to her guardian ad litem, as the case may be. And that's a mouthful."

Deak Ross nodded. His features showed the mixture of anger and frustration feuding in the tidy man's head.

"Now," said the ranger, placing his hat back on his head, "if you'll excuse me."

"No, I will not excuse you. Where are you going?"

Lightfoot grabbed the severed head by the coarse hair and stuffed it back in its bag. "Gotta turn this nasty thing in to the commissioner. It's evidence. And after that, I got an engagement to get to."

The silence that followed was louder than anything Deak Ross could have said.

"What?" asked Lightfoot.

"Good Lord," said Ross. "Miss Mikulska. You haven't heard?"

"I haven't heard anything. I just got back."

"Your lady friend, Sergeant." Deak Ross sat back in his chair. He reached for his pipe, thought better of it, and rested his hand on the desk. "I'm afraid she's dead."

"What? What are you talking about?"

"Five days ago. She was found on some property she'd bought, just north of town. Colonel Woodard has a few—"

"What happened, goddammit?"

"Nobody knows. The coroner says she was beaten. There was a man spotted near there on the day she died. Tall man. Blond. Looked pretty rough, is what the neighbor said."

"Millicent," said Lightfoot.

"The ranger gone bad? That name did come up. But before you go casting aspersions on a former member of the force . . . Sergeant? Sergeant Lightfoot!"

But Lightfoot was halfway down the hall.

31. Farewell

They'd gotten it wrong. He didn't blame them. They didn't know, or maybe they didn't care, but nevertheless: all wrong. Otto Zenger had arranged to have Freda buried in a narrow plot in the Crestwood Cemetery, northeast of town. It wasn't a bad spot. Crestwood was Austin's largest graveyard and home to many of its most prominent deceased. In fact, Freda's marker was just a few yards away from where Otto had buried his mother-in-law two years earlier. But Lightfoot knew Freda would have wanted someplace less crowded. She'd have wanted to rest on that little piece of property she'd bought, on a section of high ground not far from the big live oak just west of Shoal Creek.

The stone was a simple one, in accordance with what Otto Zenger supposed Freda would have composed for herself:

FREDA ANNE MIKULSKA
1875–1908
FAITHFUL AND DILIGENT

Lightfoot shook his head. Faithful and Diligent. Leave it to a German, he thought. Why not, *Warmhearted and funny and kinder to strangers than they could possibly have deserved*? Why not,

The woman who kept my books and made sure no one was stealing from me and kept my whores from fighting each other so I could run around looking like God's gift to Central Texas? And why no mention of Jewel Lightfoot?

Hell, that was an easy one. There was no mention of him because he hadn't stepped up. Because he wasn't there when he needed to be.

Because he'd never been there when he needed to be.

A north wind rattled the branches of the elms that shaded this portion of the cemetery, but the sun stood high in the sky, and the grass was warm where he sat. The ranger tied a long stem of spear grass around the little bouquet of Blackfoot daisies and frostweed he'd brought, and he laid the flowers in the dirt beside a wilted stand of white lilies. He stayed for three hours, trying to remember it all. All the opportunities. All her plans, and his host of excuses. At one point he lay back and napped. Maybe he'd just stay here, he thought. Maybe he'd let the grass grow over his legs and arms and lie here forever beside his friend and last best chance. He only sat up when a lumber wagon came to a halt just beyond the cemetery's wrought iron fence. Loud sonofabitch, though not quite loud enough to wake those slumbering around him. The ranger rubbed a hand through his hair. It took him a moment to figure out why the wagon might have stopped. *Probably think I keeled over myself.* He waved absentmindedly at the driver and passenger and then reclined again as the clatter of the wheels receded. It was no use. He was no closer to forgiving himself at the end of his vigil than he'd been when he started. He wasn't the forgiving kind, and that extended to his own failings first and foremost. So he touched the cool surface of Freda's headstone—Faithful and Diligent—a last time and said a wordless goodbye. Then he did what he always did. He found his horse and climbed into the saddle.

Riding back into town on 16th Street, headed for his boarding house digs, he saw John Nemo tapping his way along the wooden sidewalk that bordered Guadalupe. The man's hat was askew and his shirttail was untucked, but his brogans were polished to a high gloss. The ranger reined up. John almost passed him, but at the last moment he paused and cocked his head. How did he know? Lightfoot pondered the question anew. Perhaps the man could smell a passerby and know immediately who it was. Perhaps he had some sense that others simply didn't possess.

"All right," said Nemo. "Cap'n Lightfoot."

"It is."

"Leavin' us again?"

"Looks like it."

"Got your orders, huh?"

Lightfoot ran a hand over Loki's left shoulder. "No. No more orders. I won't be rangering anymore."

Nemo pursed his lips as he nodded. Maybe he believed it, but most likely he didn't. "I'm sorry you missed the funeral. I know you would have wanted to see her."

"I would have been there. That's so."

The two men waited as a beer wagon passed, the bells on the draft animals' traces tinkling as they pulled.

"Heard she left you that land she bought."

"I don't want land," said the ranger.

"I guess you got it anyway. She loved you something fierce, Cap'n. I know you all weren't so good at saying such like. But we all knew. And so did you. That's all that matters."

Lightfoot winced. He looked down at his saddle horn as if someone might have left a message there for him. But no one had. No one ever did.

"You take care of yourself, John." The ranger started to say something else that wouldn't quite form itself on his lips. "You—"

"Don't worry about me, Cap'n. I'll manage."

The ranger raised his eyes to focus on the green ribbon of the Colorado River in the distance. Wagons, horses, men on foot. Austin was an up-and-comer. She buried her dead and kept building. She didn't have time for reflection. Hell, neither did he. If he kept on thinking about it, he was going to end up down in that cellar at Zenger's, swimming in pilsner. Lightfoot touched Loki with one heel, and the big gelding started forward. He'd only gone a few strides when John Nemo called out again.

"By the way," said the blind man, following along on the wooden sidewalk. "What did they say? The men on that mountaintop. Enchanted Rock."

Lightfoot reined up a second time. He thought about the question.

Nemo caught up with him. A grin tugged at the corners of his mouth.

"About why they picked you to join the Brotherhood and all. Good and evil. Angels and devils. You know what I'm talking about."

"I remember."

"What did they say about your gift?"

The ranger sniffed. "They said I was hard to kill."

"That's it? That's your gift?"

The ranger was aware of the sound before he could classify it. The rasp of metal on metal. That lumber cart—the one he'd seen at the cemetery. Back again. Here in town. And close. He'd drawn his pistol and turned before John Nemo could ask his next question. Sure enough, the passenger on the lumber wagon's seat was bringing a double-barreled shotgun to bear. Blond hair. Green eyes. Sam Millicent had the beginnings of a grin on his face, but it faded quickly. Lightfoot fired three times. Two of the slugs caught Millicent in the chest. Another one tore into his neck. For several moments the blood surged from the dying man's throat like a spring, drenching the left side of his body.

The driver held up one hand as he tried to steady his wagon team with the other. "Please," he said. There was a quaver in his voice. "I don't even know this fella."

"Lord have mercy," said Nemo, head cocked to one side. "I don't know what's happening, but it don't sound productive."

The ranger holstered his sidearm. "Old friend of mine. Not big on hellos."

Lightfoot watched Sam Millicent die. He glanced at the driver again. Vehicular and pedestrian traffic had ceased around them.

"You saw what happened?" said Lightfoot.

"I did. He was laying for you, mister. I didn't know. He paid me to drive him around like this. Talking crazy the whole time."

"Crazy how?"

"Said you left him to the devil. Or such like."

"I didn't leave him nowhere he wasn't trying to get to himself. You tell that to whoever asks. And take him to a doctor."

The driver edged away from the corpse, which only leaned farther toward him. "What for?"

"'Cause I told you to, that's what for."

"Down two blocks on the right," Nemo offered. "Just past the hotel."

The driver shook his reins and made a hissing sound, and the wagon went rattling off down the street, Sam Millicent's lifeless body leaning against the driver as if they were lovers out for a Sunday picnic. Lightfoot and his interrogator were silent until the rattling of the lumber wagon's wheels faded away. Pedestrians started moving again, but they gave the two men a wide berth.

"So if it's a gift," Nemo continued, "who gave it to you?"

"I don't know," Lightfoot answered, and now he was talking more to himself than to anyone else. He glanced to the north.

Clouds up that way. The sky a mottled blue that promised unrest. He touched his spurs to Loki's flanks. "Hard to kill. Hell. I'm not even sure that *is* a gift. But at least I know one thing."

"Yeah? What's that?"

"Knowing what you lost. It don't make it any easier."

"No. I can see where it wouldn't."

"Ah, hell. So long, my friend."

"Whoa. Hold up a minute. What if some of those men was to come looking for you? The ones on the mountain, I mean. Where could they find you, if they were to have work for you?"

"Work?"

"You know what I mean."

"I'll be damned," said Lightfoot, surveying John Nemo from head to toe. "If you and I ever meet up again, we're gonna have to have us a long talk. Anybody's looking for me, tell 'em to check the saloons. And look down."

Nemo chuckled. "I'll do that," he called. "I'll tell 'em." The blind man raised his left arm to wave goodbye. His sleeve slid down when he did so and revealed on his brown skin an indistinct design. A cross, outlined by a square. And in between the bars of the cross, four petals, or possibly leaves, as of an ancient and undying tree.

32. The Cable

Washington, D.C., December 24

"Well, sir, it's official."

First Secretary Fellowes glanced up from the serious business of lighting his pipe. "Bloody hell, March. You're going to have to cease with these cryptic introductions. I'm not Sherlock Holmes, you know."

"Oh, dear. I've done it again, haven't I? Do forgive me."

"I'll consider it. Now please, pray tell, what is official, and where do I send the cable?"

"The Mexicans, sir. And the Germans. That joint expedition I mentioned."

"Ah, yes. Sent to recover a mysterious treasure."

"That they were. In the wastelands along the Rio Grande. Some of the most inhospitable land in the world, I'm told. The three men they were looking for were revolutionaries working on behalf of the Yucatan Free State, a successor to Chan Santa Cruz. They had initially tried to make it to San Antonio. A known subversive hotbed."

"Well, all the beds are hot down there, if I'm remembering my geography correctly. Desert, isn't it?"

"Indeed. Much of Texas is inhospitable in the extreme."

"Yes. And the rest is desert."

The two men shared a chuckle.

250 BRUCE McCANDLESS III

"Ah. Apologies for the frivolity, March, but the holidays are upon us, you know, like a great shambling beast. So what's the news?"

"The news is that it's officially over. The joint expedition failed to find the grail and has returned to the capital, airship and all."

"The Zeppelin made it out and back?"

"Apparently so. No problems reported."

"Gadzooks. Just what the kaiser needs. Another war toy."

"Just so, sir. But for now the border remains intact, and Mexico is quiet. Shall I discontinue the intercepts?"

"Hmm? The intercepts?" Roger Fellowes gazed out the window at the busy street. Christmas shoppers were out in full force this evening. A few flakes of snow swirled in the air, and he could hear the faint strains of carolers singing "Silent Night" in the distance. "No, I think not. Let's keep the line open. I'm not sure why anyone would want that part of the world, but if the Germans are determined to make mischief down south, we'd better pay attention."

"Understood. Oh, and there was one queer bit of information we managed to tease out of the cables. It appears the Germans very badly wanted whatever the Mexican fugitives had with them. Indeed, the plan was to take possession of the item and bring it back to Berlin."

"So the Mexicans were to be double-crossed, eh? I don't suppose I'm surprised by *that*. The vaunted German high-mindedness seems remarkably flexible when attempting to advance the interests of its empire. But nothing was found?"

The younger man shrugged. "Not a thing, as far as we can tell."

"Then we needn't worry about it. All's well that ends well, and all that?"

"Apparently," said March, "the kaiser's scheme has come to naught."

"That's exactly what His Majesty's government likes to hear. I know you're of a gloomy disposition, March, and sometimes that's exactly what's needed in this line of work. But then again, sometimes things are exactly as they seem to be. Let's not make up shadows where they don't exist."

"Agreed. I'll put this Texas business out of my mind."

"We have enough to worry about with the Irish. And having thus concluded, I will now take the opportunity to chase you out of my office. It's Christmas Eve, my boy. No one should have to think about Texas at the Yuletide. Let's see about locking up and venturing out into the flickering firelight of ancient custom and reassuring superstition. It seems to get dark so early these days."

"Indeed. Very dark. And very early. Happy Christmas, sir," said George March, and he turned off the lights.

The End

Ride with Jewel Lightfoot on his
next adventure in *Sour Lake*, available on Amazon.